Where the Sun Lights the Shadows

JENNA ROGERS

ISBN: 979-8-9899425-2-7

❀ Created with Vellum

To all those who have struggled to find the light.

Content Warning

This novel is a friends to lovers romance story of overcoming obstacles like grief and fear. While the story is uplifting, it also contains topics and scenes that may be sensitive to some readers, including death of a loved one, discussions of grief and trauma, and witnessing death.

CHAPTER 1

Summer 18

"Are you trying to get me killed? Last time we had this conversation, I almost died."

"He has a point," I chime in.

"That was a brilliant idea! It's not my fault Andrew's head is no match for my elbow," Rebecca grumbles, rolling her eyes at her twin.

"Maybe we should just keep things low-key tonight."

I look to Andrew for backup, but Rebecca won't have it. "Emma, you're supposed to be on my side! We are leaving *tomorrow*. I know you tend to overthink in that head of yours, but I won't let you tonight. We are going to make our last night at the lake memorable!" Rebecca's blue eyes sparkle with mischief and excitement, and she practically bounces up and down in her seat. I wince as the truth of her words settle on me. I know she just wants me to have a good time tonight, but hearing my best friend put into words the part of myself that I'm most self-conscious about is hard.

Despite Rebecca's buzzing excitement, I stay strong, silently hoping a low-key night can gain me some alone time with Andrew to finish what we started earlier today. "Just because we are leaving for college tomorrow doesn't mean we have to do anything crazy."

"Yeah, maybe we just stay up all night hanging out here tonight," Andrew offers, exchanging a sly look with me.

"You two are so boring!" Rebecca crosses her arms and glowers at Andrew and me as we sit closely on the Martin family's back deck. The fire blazes fiercely, emulating the blazing heat between our two bodies. With the lake gracefully looming in the background, it's a picture-perfect moment.

Before anyone can argue, Rebecca completely switches gears. "I think we should take the UTV out into the woods tonight!" Ignoring my nervous energy, Rebecca hops to her feet and pulls me by the elbow right off my chair. "This is a night to be celebrated! After all we've been through, I'm going to miss you extra this summer." I could be mistaken, but I swear her eyes flit between Andrew and me as she says it, smirking the slightest bit so that only I can see.

Her excitement pours into me, and something about the turn today has taken makes me want to take some chances. I need to stop overthinking. I nod and allow her to lead the way to the massive shop next to Rebecca and Andrew's house. When the lights are flipped on, the sixteen-hundred-square-foot shop is illuminated. The UTV sits up front. The riding lawn mower sits behind it. The boat's trailer sits empty, missing its other half to its mistress, the lake. You imagine it, the Martins certainly have it.

It would be easy for me to be jealous of the Martin family's fortune if it weren't for how down-to-earth the Martin twins were raised to be.

Turning the key in the UTV, Rebecca squeals. "Now *this* is going to be a night to remember! Trust me, this is going to be so much better than just sitting around the fire on our last night!"

Andrew just smiles and shakes his head as he gestures for me to slide into the center seat before him. As he scoots in next to me, I can feel the warmth of his entire left side pressed against me. My stomach does a small flutter at the comfort of his close presence. After I snap the half buckle across my lap, Andrew follows suit.

We begin to pick up speed as we cross the pavement and fling out onto the dirt road. The trees quickly swallow us up into the shadows, and all of the light from the lake houses across the street rapidly dims to black. My stomach sinks to my toes. As we bump along the road, the headlights bounce between the ground and the trees ahead of us.

A large bump lurches me forward, and I instantly reach out to Andrew's thigh for support. With the contact, he coolly smiles at me and grabs hold of my hand. "Why don't you slow down? I think you're scaring Emma."

"Oh, come on! We aren't out here to go slow. We are here to go fast and make memories! Besides, Emma is always scared," Rebecca chuckles. "I've never steered you wrong."

"Uh, I beg to differ."

"I wasn't talking to you, Andy." Rebecca presses her foot down on the gas pedal even further.

The path quickly splits into two, and Rebecca throws the wheel to the right at the last minute, trying too late to take the path with a sharper curve. There's a sudden lurch as the UTV snags on a tree stump. At that moment, I realize our night of fun is over. The UTV will certainly be destroyed. The Martin twins are going to be in a world of trouble for taking it out in the dark and being so irresponsible, and I will be sent home on our last night together.

The trunk proves to be bigger and sturdier than I expected, and the UTV comes to an abrupt stop. I see Andrew fly forward before I feel my own body lurching with the momentum. Rebecca shrieks, and there's a thud as Andrew's head smashes into the dashboard. My seatbelt locks and I already feel the ache in my neck from the whiplash.

As I orient myself and begin to ask if everyone is okay, Andrew leaps over me and out of the UTV. He runs to the front of the vehicle, and it's only then that I see Rebecca lying on the ground amidst the tree stumps. Yes, there are multiple. No wonder we had such an impact.

As the shock of the situation wears off, I hear Andrew desperately saying, "You're okay. You're okay. You're going to be okay." Then I see the blood.

Oh no. Oh no. *Was Rebecca even wearing her seat belt?* I don't remember. She must've launched straight over the dash and out into the trees. *Where's the blood coming from? Did she scratch her shoulder? Is it a bloody nose?* I already know what it is, but I can't accept it.

"Emma! Do you have your phone on you?" Andrew's voice brings me back to the scene in front of me.

"Yeah," I say, fumbling to get my phone out of my back pocket.

"Call 9-1-1," Andrew urges with a shaky voice as he pulls his shirt off and begins to wrap it around Rebecca's head. *Is he crying?*

We were supposed to have a fun night, filled with memories. We made memories that night. I absolutely will not forget that night, no matter how hard I try, but it's not because of the silly fun we had. It will forever leave a scar on my heart as the night I lost my best friend.

CHAPTER 2

Summer 9

Three weeks ago, my parents broke the news they bought a lake house where our family will start spending our summers. My dad grew up going to his family's lake cabin in Minnesota every summer, and he thought our family needed to start that tradition now that he and my mom have reached a point in their careers where they can work from nearly anywhere. I'm still not sure how to feel about it. On the one hand, I must admit, the drive in has been beautiful. The light reflects off the lake in such a way that makes it sparkle, and there are humungous evergreens and pine trees surrounding the road. On the other hand, I'm going to miss spending my summers with my friends from school. My sister, Dani, is great and all, but sometimes our two-year age gap feels like ten, and she tends to keep to herself.

As our car pulls into the driveway of our new home for the next several months, my dad cheerily asks, "Well, what do you think, kids?"

My mom eagerly turns in her seat with a beaming smile across her face. "You guys are going to love the cabin! We have our own dock and a nice view of the water from the back deck."

Dani and I trade excited looks as we take in the cabin. It's wonderful!

I step out of the car and dutifully start unloading the trunk. My dad leads us to the front door, keys in hand. He opens the door, and I catch my first glimpse of the cabin. It's nothing like I imagined. It doesn't have the rustic, woodsy vibe I expected a lake cabin to have. Instead, it's modern and spacious. It's the kind of place I wouldn't mind living in all year round. Large windows cover the back side of the house, just off the living room. Through the windows, I see a large deck and the lake, glistening in the late morning sun, begging for me to take a dip. Several boats off in the distance pull people on skis and inner tubes. The sight makes me practically vibrate with excitement. It's just now hitting me this is how I get to spend my summers!

To the left of us, I see a dock that is twice the size of our own. There are two kids who look to be about my age squealing and pushing each other off the dock. Hope fills me. I might have friends to spend my summers with after all. A woman lies on a towel across the dock, with large sunglasses covering her face and a book in her hand. Her wardrobe alone screams the word "rich," and it's flat-out intimidating.

"Oh, look, the Martin family is already out on the water!" My mom interrupts my daze.

I turn and look at her with a questioning look. "The Martins are the family next door. They live here year-round. I spoke to Mrs. Martin when we were checking out the house. I believe they have twins your age. Maybe you will have some friends to play with during the summers? They invited us over for their annual barbecue, which just so happens to be tonight." I don't think I've ever seen my mom so giddy. It must be all the fresh air talking.

I gaze at the two children on the dock with longing. It sure would be nice to have some friends, but I'm not looking forward to going to a barbecue with a bunch of strangers. Isn't moving into a new place for the summer adventure enough for one day?

The woman from earlier with the big sunglasses opens the door. Her sunglasses are no longer on her face, but on top of her head, revealing stunning blue eyes that immediately catch my attention. She welcomes us into the Martin's mansion. That's not an exaggeration. That's simply what it is, a mansion. There are massive windows in the front and double doors. The house sprawls across the landscape, covering twice the length our cabin does. As we step inside, we find ourselves in a grand entryway with staircases on either side of us that go to the same level. An open room at the top of the stairs overlooks the large entry. I've only seen a house like this in movies. *Who are these people?*

My mom and dad hold out a plate of fresh-cut fruit and a bowl of our family's famous baked beans. "Where should I put these, Lynelle?"

"Oh yes, I will take those from you," the sunglasses woman, Lynelle I guess, gestures for my mom and dad to follow her as she looks at Dani and me and says over her shoulder, "The children are in the backyard if you two want to go say hi!"

Dani and I mosey toward the back of the house, taking in the rest of its magnificence. We find a clean white kitchen with marble countertops, two ovens, and the largest fridge I've ever seen. To the right, the living room contains a massive leather couch and a TV I swear is twice as wide as my dad is tall. Hint, he's 6'4. The dining room extends off from the kitchen to more open windows with a stunning view of the lake. I can't even imagine living like this. This house makes our cabin look like a tool shed.

As we open the slider, and step out onto the back deck, I see a three-year-old little girl throwing a ball back and forth with an older boy, probably her brother. I watch the two of them as he lightly tosses the ball to her, and she fumbles with it. When she barely catches it, he throws his arms up in celebration and begins whooping. I can't see his face, but hers is one of pure delight. It's sweet.

Suddenly a girl about my age comes bounding up the stairs. She immediately wraps her arms around me and then Dani. "I'm Rebecca! I'm the oldest Martin kid. I'm so excited you guys moved in. The couple who owned the cabin before you was old and grumpy. They always got mad when Andy and I swam races between our dock and theirs. They said they came here for quiet time." She scowls. "Anyway, I can already tell you will be an upgrade because you are at the barbecue. All the cool people around the lake come to our barbecue." She winks. She has the same striking blue eyes as her mom, paired with dark brown waves pulled back into a messy ponytail.

I don't know what to make of this girl. She's supposed to be my age, but she exudes confidence I definitely do not have. I like her spirit though. I've always been drawn to people who are more outgoing than me. I appreciate it when someone else can hold the conversation. If she keeps talking, that's less talking for me. Plus, there's just something about her that immediately feels warm and welcoming.

"I'm Dani. I'm eleven. This is my little sister, Emma. You guys should be about the same age."

"I thought my mom said you were a twin?" I ask, surprising myself by speaking up at all.

"Oh yeah. Andy and I are twins, but I was born two minutes before him, so I'm the oldest," Rebecca explains easily with a teasing smirk.

I can't help but laugh. I like her. "Your brother's name is Andy? What about your little sister?" I gesture to the little girl throwing the ball.

"His name is Andrew, but I call him Andy. He hates it, which means I love it." She laughs again with a light-hearted ease that shows me she clearly adores her twin. "The little girl is Adi Weller. My parents have known her parents for ages."

I look at Dani as if to say *she's pretty fun, isn't she?* Dani smiles back but quickly excuses herself. "I'm going to go see if they need any help in the kitchen." She waves and turns to walk back into the house.

"Sorry about Dani. She kind of keeps to herself, but she's not so bad once you get to know her." I chuckle sheepishly, slightly embarrassed Dani wasn't more polite to our kind host.

Rebecca shrugs and grabs my hand, pulling me down the stairs to the grass lawn. "Andy! Andy, come meet my new friend Emma." A swell of pride rises in my chest at her words. *She already thinks of me as her friend?* I press my lips together to try to hide the smile quickly curling across my lips.

Andrew takes his eyes off the little girl he's playing with. As our eyes meet, the little girl pulls her arm back and launches the ball. It smacks him right across the face, and I can't help but flinch. He just blinks and laughs. He bends down to pick it up, squeezes it, and says with a chuckle, light like his sister's, "It's a softball."

As I step closer, I see his eyes match his mom's and his sister's. Except I swear his are somehow brighter. If we were to compete in a staring contest, I know I'd win easily looking at those eyes. He has dark, messy hair that looks like it hasn't been so much as combed today, but it works for him. He's tall for his age and rail thin.

He seems to be taking me in too, and I can't help but blush as his eyes move from my strawberry-blonde curls to my green eyes, the smattering of freckles across my nose and cheeks, and down to my new summer dress I wore specifically to impress the new neighbors.

"So, you moved into the house next door? Thank goodness!

Those old farts before you needed to move," he scoffs, handing the ball back to the little girl. "Adi, why don't you go find your mom? Rebecca and I are going to show Emma around."

Adi gives a slight nod and runs her little legs across the yard.

Rebecca, still holding me by the hand, asks, "Do you have your swimsuit, Emma? We can get a game of colors going. I bet the Hernandez kids will join. Maybe Dani will want to play too?"

I hesitate before admitting, "I didn't wear my swimsuit over. I can go home and get it. I just thought we were here for a barbecue."

"Well yes, you're here for a barbecue, but what would a barbecue at the lake be without enjoying the lake? This is our family's way of kicking off the summer!" Rebecca replies light-heartedly. "We can walk back with you to get your suit."

Rebecca begins marching toward my backyard, and Andrew follows quickly behind. I open our back slider and let myself in. I try to tamp down the embarrassment that rises inside me as I imagine what they must be seeing as they walk into our cabin. There are still boxes and bags lying around, needing to be unpacked. The kitchen is half the size of theirs, and we don't even have a TV in our living room. I quickly head down the hallway toward my room, but Rebecca pauses and says, "I love your house! It looks so cozy."

I could take offense to her remark, assuming it's a back-handed comment, but somehow, I already know she genuinely means it. I push open my bedroom door and begin rifling through my dresser drawer. My wardrobe is simple enough that I was able to unpack my clothes into the dresser this afternoon before we had to leave for the barbecue.

Rebecca hovers overhead, and Andrew lingers in the door-way, taking everything in. His eyes land on my pile of books resting on the bench seat in front of the bay window. "You like to read?"

I nod. "I love to read."

His smile grows wide. "Me too. It looks like you have good taste! I love fantasy books," he remarks, gesturing to my book pile.

Rebecca leans down and plucks a yellow ruffled one piece from my drawer. "This one is so cute! Definitely wear this one!"

I take it and go to the bathroom down the hall to change. As soon as I come out, Rebecca squeals in excitement and drags me back out of the house to their dock so we can start our game.

I sit between the twins on the deck to enjoy our dinner. Since our game earlier, I've felt quickly accepted by both of them. I'd even go so far as to say I'm excited to be spending my summer here. These two could easily top my two best friends from school.

It's just after 8 pm as we are sitting down to begin our barbecue feast, but the sun is only just beginning to set. The sky is becoming a reddish-orange that reflects across the water. I could get used to this.

I nudge Andrew and nod toward the bratwursts sitting in front of him. "Can you pass the brats?"

A smirk spreads across his face. "You've had a burger, a brat, and you want a second? Dang girl!"

Rebecca interjects, "What's the matter with that, Andy? The food is good, and she's hungry!"

Andrew drops his head down a little and mumbles, "I'm just saying… it's impressive. I like people who can eat as much as me." He hands me the bratwursts and remains quiet.

I turn to him and smile. "I'll compete with you any time."

His look of dismay changes back into a smile, and a playful glint appears in his eyes. He places another burger on his plate, grinning. "Challenge accepted!"

CHAPTER 3

Summer 19

The four of us stand on the Martin's porch, listening to the doorbell chime. We've done this plenty of times before. It feels normal and comforting, and yet, it doesn't. Everything is different. It may have been nine months since the accident, but this is our first night back at the lake since then. Rebecca isn't going to welcome me with her usual squeal and embrace. We aren't going to catch each other up on everything that has happened in our lives for the past nine months.

After all this time, I thought the wound had begun to heal. I thought I was okay, but as I stand on the doorstep where all my summers have begun for the past ten years, I realize I'm not okay. Every feeling that had begun to hide in the shadows while I was away is now coming right to the surface. My throat constricts. My hands begin to shake, and tears threaten my eyes.

Dani reaches out to me and grabs my hand, just as my mom grabs my other hand, and Andrew opens the door. My heart melts at the sight of him. He looks good. He looks okay. Despite losing his best friend, his twin sister, he looks okay. The thought somehow eases some of my emotions. I finally release the breath I'd been holding and subtly wipe at the corner of my eye before a tear falls.

I always stayed in touch with Rebecca and Andrew over the summer. I had different ways of communicating with each of them. When we were younger, Rebecca would call me regularly, and Andrew and I would send each other hand-written letters with book recommendations. As we grew older, calls with Rebecca turned to Facetimes, and letters to Andrew turned to texts with the occasional Facetime call. This past year, Andrew and I did not stay in touch. I sent him a few texts, but he didn't respond. I'm not sure why, but I can only imagine the last time we saw each other changed a lot of things. I finally got the message.

Andrew smiles that easy smile of his. "Hey, guys!" He turns and shouts inside the house. "The O'Doughertys are here!"

My mom gives him a tight hug and asks how he's been doing. I step into the house and squeeze him too, on autopilot. The warm feeling of his muscles wrapped around me feels amazing. It's like his hug alone can piece me back together and alleviate all of my sorrow. I've been waiting nine months for his hug.

We walk silently through the house, all the way to outside. There's music playing throughout the house and off the back deck. I can't help but think how normal everything feels, even though it isn't.

Andrew tilts his head toward the dock, wordlessly telling me to follow him. We walk to the end of the dock, and he sits down, slipping his flip-flops off, and placing his feet into the water.

He doesn't even turn toward me. He just waits for me to follow suit. After ten years, we know each other well enough to communicate easily without words, even after not speaking for so long.

Once I'm seated next to him with my feet floating in the

shockingly chilly water, he finally speaks. "How has college been?"

I hesitate. *Are we just ignoring the elephant in the room?* I want to know how he really is. I want to know how his family is. I want to know why he didn't talk to me for the past nine months after everything we've been through. I guess we have a lot to catch up on after not talking for so long.

"It was good. I decided not to run this year, so I've been interning at a publishing company to make up for the scholarship money I'm losing out on. I overloaded my schedule a bit, but it helped keep me busy." I stare down at the water, swishing my feet back and forth.

"You're not running?" He frowns. "You love to run! What happened?"

It almost feels like old times. *Almost.* Except I have this feeling starting to simmer inside me because things shouldn't be normal between us, and after a whole nine months of not even speaking to me when we should've been able to help each other through the aching pain of our loss, it's not fair for him to act like things are normal. *Is this anger? I've never been mad at Andrew before.*

"Running just reminded me of Rebecca." I pause. "Can we go to the beach and skip rocks?"

He looks at me with confusion. "Yeah, I guess. Why?"

"It was a thing Rebecca and I used to do." I walk to the beach and pick up a stone to skip. "You know, we started running together as conditioning for soccer. Then I grew to like it, and she hated it." I chuckle as I remember. "One morning I came and woke her up for our run, and she got so mad she threw her pillow at my face. She fell back asleep before I could even give her the pillow back."

My smile slowly smooths out as I'm reminded of reality. My chin trembles as I hold back tears for the second time in about ten minutes. I knew it'd be hard to come back here, but I wasn't expecting it to be this hard. All the memories are just flooding back.

"You should've still done it." That's all he says. He has a glazed-over look in his eye like maybe more thoughts and emotions are going on inside him than he's willing to share with me right now.

"Why? It just would've hurt more. At least this way I'm working toward my future. I've always wanted to be an editor. You know that. To get my foot in the door as a freshman is amazing, unheard of."

"Come on. This isn't what she would've wanted. I know she's my twin, but you knew her just as well as I did. She would be angry at you right now for giving up running because of her. Rebecca was like the poster child of living your life to the fullest. Do you really think you're doing that?"

"I am living my life, Andrew! I'm working toward my future, setting myself up for success. I'd say I'm living my life pretty damn well."

The frustration is turning from a simmer to a boil, and it's a weird feeling, but I'd prefer this anger over the sadness or betrayal I feel. I can't believe Andrew's complete ignorance of me the last nine months after everything we had begun to build before the accident.

"Em, no."

My heart swells like a balloon at the sound of his nickname for me. No one else calls me Em, and I've always loved it. Gosh, I've missed him almost as much as I've missed Rebecca. I want him to reach out and hold me right now. I want nothing more than to just sit in silence in his warm embrace. That would fix everything. Except it won't. I don't reach out to him. Instead, I whisper, "No what?"

A frown washes over his face, and he takes a deep sigh. "I mean you can't just bury yourself in work. That's not living. There's so much more to life. Rebecca died trying to show us that. It was a stupid way of doing it, but don't let that go to waste."

I narrow my eyes at him. "Is that what you've been busy doing the last nine months? Living your life? Is that why you completely ignored me when I tried to reach out to you? You were too busy living as if Rebecca never existed, as if *I* never existed?!" I see the hurt coming across his face, but I continue. "Aren't you sad at all that your sister is gone? How can you just move on so quickly and ignore the life you used to have?"

I regret those bitter words as soon as they're out of my mouth. I know the answer to that question. Of course he missed her, but I can't take the words back. I stutter, "Andrew, I'm sorry. I didn't mean it."

Anger sweeps over his face for a second, and then it turns into a look of sadness. "Maybe we need to have this conversation another time when you've had some time to sit with everything. But you need to know losing my sister was the hardest thing I've ever gone through. She's my twin. We shared a womb. She drove me absolutely nuts, but I still loved her. Not a day goes by that I don't think about her." He pauses and takes a step away. "I had my reasons for keeping my distance, and when you're ready to have an actual conversation, we can talk about them. I'm going to go see if my dad needs help with the grill."

I want to stop him or follow him, do something to fix this moment. I just can't. I stand there with a rock in my hand, feet rooted to the ground, watching him walk away. This wasn't how this was supposed to go. Now, not only do I have my still-healing wound from Rebecca, but I have a fresh cut from Andrew. Except, I caused this cut. This is my fault, and I have to fix it.

CHAPTER 4

Summer 11

I can't wait until 4:30 this afternoon to head over for the annual barbecue. I have so much to tell Rebecca. As the last year progressed, our weekly phone calls became more like every other week due to our busy schedules and our reliance on using our parents' phones to call one another. I'm excited to see Andrew too, of course, but Rebecca is my best friend. I know I can tell her anything. We talk about boys, soccer, our dysfunctional families, and our hopes and dreams. I've never bonded with someone like I have with her, especially not as quickly as we did.

It's only 2 pm, but I've finished unpacking my things, done my arrival chores, and even finished reading my book while waiting to go over. Now, I just can't wait. I'm sure Mr. and Mrs. Martin won't mind if I show up early.

I flounce off my bed and perfectly place the book I just finished on my bookshelf. I rush down the hall and quietly open the back door. I'm sure if my parents hear me leaving, they will try to stop me or give me even more unnecessary chores. After quietly closing the door behind me, I race down the stairs, across my lawn, and to the Martin's house. I don't see Rebecca or Andrew outside, so I walk around to the far side of their house where Rebecca's bedroom window is and throw small pebbles from the planters at the window.

We've watched rom-coms together and talked about how silly it was to tap rocks on someone's window, but we both exchanged a look at the end of the conversation that suggested we both secretly thought it was cute, even if it's cheesy.

I quickly learn it isn't as easy as it looks to throw pebbles up to her second-floor window, but Andrew's bedroom is in the basement, much easier to access. I start peeking down the window well to see if his bedroom light is on. *Come on, please be home!* I see his light and hop down into the well. He's lying on his bed reading. It warms my heart to see him blissfully occupied with another world. He's reading one of the books on the list of recommendations I gave him this year.

As I tap twice on the window, he jumps out of his skin. I start laughing while he glares at me but comes over to open his window anyway. "Hey! What're you doing, scaring me like that?" He shakes his head at me and stifles a chuckle.

"I couldn't wait anymore to see you guys. I tried to get Rebecca first, but I couldn't reach her window."

"Rebecca is with my mom getting a few last-minute groceries for the barbecue. Is there a reason you couldn't come to the front door and ring the bell?"

"Part of it was an inside joke with Rebecca," I trail off. "I'm not supposed to be bothering your family before the barbecue, but I wanted to see you guys."

"Well come on in," he says excitedly.

I just look at him. "Which door should I go to then?"

"You said you didn't want to bug my parents, so you're probably better off crawling through the window." A devilish grin spreads across his face.

"Come on, Andrew. Don't be ridiculous. I'm not crawling

through the window. Besides, you have a screen. I can't just pass through it."

He easily pops the screen out and pushes it off to the side. Then he holds his hand out. "I'm still not understanding why you'd come to my window to avoid the front door and then ask me to let you in through the front door."

I roll my eyes. "Well, if *you* let me in through your front door, I'm not bothering your parents."

He shrugs. "Whatever." He picks up the book he left on his bed. "Check out the book I'm reading! You were right, this is going to be a good one. I'm so glad there's a series. It should keep me busy for at least a couple of weeks."

"A couple of weeks?! There are seven books in the series, and they're each five hundred pages minimum. You can't possibly read all of them in just two weeks."

"You underestimate me," he says with confidence. "Come sit down." He pats his bed. "There's something I want to show you." He reaches for a drawer in his nightstand and pulls out another book.

He hands it over so I can inspect its beautiful baby blue cover with a shimmery castle on the front. Then he sidles up next to me on the bed. I don't immediately recognize the title. Before I can say anything, Andrew launches into an explanation, "I haven't read this one, but all the girls in my class have been reading it. It's fantasy, and I heard something about there being a love story in it, which you know, bleh. It reminded me of you, though, and I thought you'd like it, so I used some of my allowance to buy it for you. It's yours." He smiles shyly.

Wrapping my arms around him, I exclaim, "Thank you! It's not my birthday, though," I trail off, a little confused.

Andrew shakes his head. "It's not a birthday gift. I got it for you just because I thought you'd like it."

My heart swells, and I cross my arms uncomfortably as my cheeks flush. The gesture is so kind and unexpected, I suddenly don't know what to do or say. I know we are good friends, but I didn't realize we had the sort of relationship where we get each other gifts when we see something that reminds us of each other. Rebecca hasn't even done that for me.

"Well gee, Andrew. Now you're making me look bad. I didn't get you anything," I deflect, pushing his shoulder with a smile.

He laughs too, and we spend the next thirty minutes just talking about books, school, and life. It's nice. I've never really had this kind of one-on-one time with Andrew. I didn't realize I could talk to him almost the same way I can with Rebecca.

"How long does it take to buy a few last-minute grocery items?" I ask after some time.

Shrugging, Andrew explains, "I think it was more than a few. For all I know, with those two, they stopped to go shoe shopping and buy smoothies while they were in town. Do you want to read for a bit? I can tell you're dying to open up that book."

I nod, a smile spreading across my face, light reaching my eyes. So we sit there, the two of us, on Andrew's bed, just reading our books. Every once in a while, he pauses to remark about how he was not expecting so much to happen so early, or if he were the main character, he would have been much smarter than that. It's cool to have a friend to talk about books with. Rebecca and I talk about a lot, but she is *not* a reader. None of my school friends enjoy reading the same types of books as me either. Isabella only reads biographies. Seriously, what kind of eleven-year-old likes biographies?

I hear the garage open overhead and then the door between the garage and the house opens and slams. I immediately hear Rebecca jabbering away, and we both sit up. "Should we head upstairs?"

Andrew hesitates, like he's not ready to part with his book or this moment just yet, and for a moment, I feel that too. Then he nods and gets up first to head upstairs and find his sister.

When we come up the stairs, we find Mr. and Mrs. Martin

talking with Rebecca. Mr. Martin sees Andrew and me first, and his eyes widen slightly for a second. Then he shifts his hands to his hips. "Hello there, Emma. When did you get here?"

I turn to Andrew. All sense of time is lost on me after our conversations and time spent reading. "She just got here a little bit ago. You didn't hear her knock?" Andrew interjects.

I keep my mouth shut. *Why would he lie to his dad?* I try to give Andrew a wide-eyed look, as if to ask him that exact question. He gives me a look right back. We haven't had many of these wordless conversations before, but I'm pretty sure that look means we will talk about it later. We most certainly will.

Rebecca interrupts our exchange as she rushes over and swallows me up in a big hug. I wrap my arms around her too, reveling in the reunion with my best friend.

"Emma! How are you? I have so much to tell you, dude! Come with me!" Rebecca practically squeals. Just like that, she pulls me upstairs to her room. I throw a glance back over my shoulder to Andrew. He just stands there, looking disappointed.

As we enter Rebecca's room, she yells, "Ta da!" She throws in a small twirl with her hands up to gesture to her surrounding room.

Her bright pink walls are replaced by a soft lavender color, and her flashy bedspread, which I always hated, is gone. It's replaced by a cream bedspread with small lavender and yellow flowers. It is more mature, but it still matches Rebecca's personality perfectly.

"Wow! When did you change it? Your bedding is so cute!"

Her smile is the biggest I've ever seen. "I had it done in April. I wanted it to be a surprise for you when you came this summer."

I take it all in. On the one hand, I am disappointed that I miss out on these things by only getting to see her for a few months a year, but on the other hand, I'm honored that she wanted to make it a surprise for me. "I can't believe you kept this from me for two months!"

She shrugs. "We had so many other things to talk about. It was pretty easy."

I know exactly what she's talking about. "What's the latest update on Sam?" I inquire, eager to live vicariously.

She blushes a little. "He told me he liked me on the last day of school. Can you believe it, Emma? I knew it! He teased me the whole school year."

"That's so exciting! Now what?" I'm genuinely curious.

"I don't know," she kind of chuckles. "I'm not allowed to date until I'm in high school, which is way far away. Maybe he will start sitting with me at lunch next year."

"You can't date until high school? I didn't expect your parents to be so strict." What I don't admit is that I didn't expect Rebecca to be the type to follow the rules her parents lay out for her.

"When can you date?"

I just shrug. I haven't had that discussion with my parents, but it's not like it's been necessary. "I'll be single my whole life anyway, so what's it matter? I'm way too shy around boys. They don't like me." I huff and fall onto her bed.

She rolls her eyes and teases, "Where'd you learn to be so dramatic?"

"I learned it from you!"

"Oh, that's right." She pretends as if she's just now remembering. "Don't worry, Emma, you'll find someone who's perfect for you. Maybe it could be Andrew!" She waggles her brows.

I scoff. "Yeah right!"

She joins me in my laughter. "So, what do you want to do first, play Littlest Pet Shop?"

I beam, and she knowingly grabs her tub of animals before I can even respond.

CHAPTER 5

Summer 19

Unable to shake the events at the barbecue last night, I opted to go for a run to clear my head. Despite being awake before the sun, I waited for it to rise before finally going out the door. It wouldn't be the same going for a sunrise run on the lake without Rebecca.

As I step out the door, I press a few buttons to set my watch. When it gives me the approving beep, indicating the GPS has connected to the satellites to track my mileage, I take off.

It feels weird to run again. Somehow, despite this being such a big part of my life for so many years, nine months off made me forget what it feels like to run. The movement feels foreign and wrong. *Is this the way my legs always moved? Am I heel planting or running on the balls of my feet? Are my hips supposed to feel this way?*

My music drifts into the background, my conscious mind completely unaware of it as I recount the events of last night. I left the barbecue early after not getting a single chance to talk with Andrew alone again. As I was helping Mrs. Martin set out the display for the s'mores, I noticed a family-size bag of Starburst, and memories from many summers ago flooded back to me. Rebecca was initially disgusted at the thought of roasting Starbursts over the fire, but she came around to them and even asked for them the following year. The memory only made me think about how she wasn't here, and Andrew was mad at me, and everything was all messed up. Once I was in the quiet safety of my bedroom, I burst into tears, unable to catch my breath. *How did things change so much in less than a year?*

I approach the end of our road, which diverges into two directions. The left is a shorter road, but the right takes me to the other side of the lake, and I'm not ready to go over there just yet. I make a left and find my thoughts going to Andrew. *How did I already screw things up so badly?* It seemed like we were in a really good place right before Rebecca's accident. Then we stopped talking for months, and the first time we talked again, I completely insulted him with things I didn't even mean. I'm *such* an idiot.

An idea pops into my head. I know how I'm going to fix things with us, besides apologizing profusely. I hit one and a half miles and turn around to head home. I'll need to grab my car and head into town once I get back.

I feel a little more at ease on the way home. The movement no longer feels so foreign. My legs are a little embarrassingly fatigued, and my breathing is a bit heavier than it used to be on a three-mile run, despite doing other forms of exercise throughout my time away from running. Even so, it feels good to be back. I didn't realize I missed running until now.

I step onto the porch, open the front door, and grab my keys off the ring to the right of the door. Without even stepping into the house all the way, I'm already headed back out.

The nearest bookstore is a thirty-minute drive from here. There are some closer shops near the lake, but they're more for groceries, necessities, and knick-knacks for the tourists. When I pull into the parking lot, I realize this is one of the few places at the lake that isn't tarnished by memories with Rebecca. It's refreshing. She would never be caught dead in this place. Books were one thing I couldn't really talk with her about. She'd listen if I was excited about a plot because she was a good friend, but she never really cared like Andrew did. *Great, now I'm thinking about Rebecca.*

I focus my mind instead on the task at hand. I need a book for Andrew. It has to be something he hasn't read, which normally wouldn't be too difficult to find, but considering we haven't spoken in nine months, I don't know what he's been reading this year. Knowing his taste, I can at least make some guesses. I head straight toward the middle left of the bookstore, where the fantasy books are. I smile as I remember the first time Andrew brought me in here. *Finally, a good memory!* That might be the first memory I've had since being back that hasn't made me want to burst into tears.

I begin browsing through the bookshelves, looking for something Andrew would like. It needs to be something adventurous and creative. A newer book might be my best bet because it'll be less likely he's already read it. I shuffle some books around, picking one up, reading the back, and placing it back on the shelf.

I move on to the next shelf and immediately know this is the one. It's a new release written by the same author of the book Andrew got me when we were eleven. The author has moved away from preteen novels over the years, and his new material is really good. This one is loosely based on Greek mythology, which I know Andrew is a total nerd for. Best of all, the main character's best friend is named M. It's not quite Em, but it's close enough. It's perfect.

I bring it to the register, check out, and drive back. When I pull into my driveway, I debate going inside to shower first. I probably smell awful after sitting in my sweat for the past hour and a half, but I want Andrew to know I ran. I want him to see it for himself.

I head inside the house and dig around in the storage closet for something to wrap the book. Once it is satisfactorily wrapped in delicate blue wrapping paper, I head over to the Martin's house. It's only 9:30 in the morning, but I'm almost certain Andrew is up.

I walk to the far side of the house and plop myself into his bedroom window well. I peer into the window, checking to see if he's in his room. Sure enough, he's lying on his bed with a book in hand. I knock on the window, and he looks up with very little surprise when he sees me.

He comes to the window, pops out his screen, and helps me crawl through. He smells clean. His wet, combed hair and lack of a shirt indicate he just showered. He must've just gotten back from weight training with Brendan. I'm lucky I caught him. The two of them can spend half a day at the gym together.

"I came to apologize and give you this," I say, handing him the wrapped book.

He takes it and inspects the wrapping paper. "Are you trying to buy me?"

I see a small twinge of a smile forming on his lips, giving me hope.

"Just open it."

I sit down on his bed as he does the same, beginning to tear into the wrapping paper. "Andrew, I—" He holds up a finger as he continues unwrapping.

When he finally gets the wrapping paper off, a grin spreads wide across his face. This has to be a good sign. "Thanks, Em. It's perfect! This one has been on my to-read list since I heard he was writing it like six months ago. You've always done a good job at picking out books."

Silence follows. I can tell he's still guarded. "I'm glad you like it." I shift nervously. "Listen, I'm sorry about yesterday. It was hard coming back here after all this time. I thought I was handling things better than I am, and it was sucky to have you point that out to me. I know you loved Rebecca more than anyone, and I shouldn't have questioned that no matter how much I'm hurting. I'm sorry." He puts his hand on my thigh, and with that little gesture, I can tell I'm forgiven. "I don't know what your reasoning is for not talking to me during the school year, and I won't pretend it didn't hurt me, but I'm willing to at least hear you out. I know you better than to believe you had bad intentions while doing so."

He leans his head on my shoulder for a moment, and I freeze. His touch charges me instantly. I'm almost certain the next thing I touch will receive an epic shock. I want to pause our conversation for another time and just stay like this. The world feels right again knowing I have his forgiveness.

"I may not have been the most eloquent with my words yesterday either," he admits, disrupting my tender thoughts. "I'm not saying I've been perfect, far from it. I've had moments when I've been so sad over losing her that I couldn't even get out of bed, but I have to try to move on because I can only imagine how disappointed she would be to see me like that. I have to be better."

"You were right. You *are* right. I *hate* that," I cross my arms and pout my lower lip, trying to hide the chuckle that's slipping out. "I need help being pushed. I always have." I pause for a moment, taking in his reaction. His deep blue eyes stay focused on me as he waits for me to continue, knowing I have more to say. "I went for a run today." I hold out my arms to show him all my sweaty glory.

"You've had a busy morning. How was it?"

"I couldn't bring myself to run to the other side of the lake because of all of the memories, but it felt good to get back out again. I didn't realize how much I missed it."

He wraps one arm around me. "Even so, I'm proud of you. It's a start. If you need me to, I'll run with you this summer. It'd be good for me to do some endurance training this summer for track."

"You'd do that?" I'm stunned.

"Em, you know I'd do anything for you." He rolls his eyes, oblivious to the fact that he's melting my heart right now with his words, sweeter than chocolate.

"So about not talking to me last year...?"

He shifts in unease before responding. "I thought I was doing the right thing. A lot of my best, and some of my worst, memories with Rebecca involve you too, and all I wanted to do was cut ties with all the memories that were bringing me pain. I thought the only way I could heal was alone." He gives me an apologetic smile. "I learned pretty quickly that I needed people, but I still didn't think those people should include you. I guess I just thought you'd make it too hard. I was already hurting so badly... I'm sorry. It kills me to say it, so I can only imagine what it must feel like for you to hear it."

He winces at me as he takes in my reaction. A whole world of emotions is filling me, sadness for Andrew's pain, hurt that he felt he needed to cut me out, and hope that we can move forward.

"I see I was wrong now. Seeing you yesterday made me feel like I was home again, until you were an absolute brat to me." He winks and leans his shoulder into mine teasingly. His touch once again makes me shiver. "I saw a counselor, and she's helped me start to lean on my family and friends again. I'm doing okay now. I just take it day by day, and I'm trying as hard as I can to live my life for both of us now. There are so many little things she didn't get a chance to do."

"I want to do that too. I always held us back. I don't want to live in fear anymore. I want to live boldly like Rebecca."

He pulls me in tight with one arm and presses his lips to my forehead. I know this is just a friendly gesture to show he cares, but I close my eyes and take a moment to feel his love.

He pulls my chin up so my eyes meet his. "I don't want to hear you talk about yourself like that. You never held us back." His eyes bore into mine, making sure I get the message. I nod ever so slightly. Satisfied, he continues, "We can help each other."

CHAPTER 6

Summer 12

The sun floats high in the sky, radiating its late July heat directly on us as we pound back down the dock after enjoying peanut butter and jelly sandwiches for lunch.

Mr. Martin and my dad trail behind Andrew, Rebecca, and I with less enthusiasm. I don't blame them. Us kids get to have all the fun, but we can't have it without the adults to drive us.

Andrew leaps from the dock onto the boat, already untangling the rope for the tube. Rebecca and I follow.

"Come on, Dad! We're burning daylight here," Rebecca urges with excitement.

"It's only 12:30. You have plenty of daylight left." Mr. Martin frowns and adds, "And I'm certainly not dragging you three around on the boat for all of it."

I swear all three of us deflate a little at his comment, but Andrew quickly recovers, bringing the excitement back. "I call middle!"

"What? No! You always get the middle, and you never get thrown off. I want the middle this time," I insist.

As much as I enjoy tubing, it's even more fun when I'm

safely flinging from side to side in the middle seat of the tube, where I know I won't be flung into the cruel water. Falling off is never too bad, but the anticipation of it still fills me with dread.

Andrew violently shakes his head. "I have to be in the middle. It just makes sense. You and Rebecca are much closer in weight than Rebecca and me."

Rebecca decides to chime in. I can always count on her for support. "Oh, please! Do you really think ten pounds is going to make that much of a difference? No. Be a gentleman and let Emma sit in the middle for once."

"It might make a difference when we are suspended six feet above the water. I'm just looking out for the safety of you two girls. I know how scared you can be on the tube."

Mr. Martin laughs a little at his son. I've noted over the past couple of years that he seems to relate to Andrew. I have a feeling young Mr. Martin was the same witty little daredevil Andrew is now.

"Okay, you three, let's go. If Emma wants the middle, let her have it this time. The difference in weight won't matter that much. Plus, it will give you a chance to show off your bravery," Mr. Martin raises his eyebrows at Andrew, clearly using his ego to convince him.

I watch Andrew's eyes light up at the prospect of showing us all how brave he is. "You can take the middle, Em."

The three of us gleefully toss the tube into the water and leap on as Mr. Martin starts up the boat and begins slowly pulling away from the dock. We watch the boat get further and further away until the rope is pulled taut and begins tugging us along at a snail's pace.

"Hit it, Dad!" Andrew shouts, indicating he's ready to get going.

Mr. Martin picks up speed, and we get whipped forward. As we zoom across the lake, I can't help but take a moment to enjoy the wind swirling in my face, sitting in the comfort and safety of the middle seat, with my two favorite people on either side of me.

Mr. Martin begins zig zagging, throwing us in and out of the wake. This is where it gets fun.

"Hey Andrew!" Rebecca shouts, leaning forward to peer past me and over to her brother. "I bet I can stay on longer than you."

I groan. *Oh no.* This is going to end in a blood bath. Any time one of the twins challenges the other, they always go way too far.

"You're *so* on!" Andrew grins. He holds his pointer finger up and begins circling it around, indicating to his dad we want him to do donuts.

"You guys are so stupid! Why does everything have to be a competition?" I holler over the wind whipping in our ears and the sound of the boat's motor barking loudly.

Andrew glares over at Rebecca accusingly. "She's the one who suggested a competition. I'm just trying to end it quickly for us."

When we are situated in the middle of the lake, Mr. Martin cranks the wheel hard, and we begin forming a circle. We shoot out of the wake on Rebecca's side, but other than that, the ride is still smooth. When the boat completes the loop, and we follow behind, massive waves threaten to throw us off into the merciless lake. We bounce up into the air and crash hard down on top of another wave.

I smile a little as I note Mr. Tough Guy white-knuckling his handles. Rebecca laughs and does the donut signal again to her dad. This time he turns the other way, causing us to fly out of the wake on Andrew's side. He leans in toward me, trying to keep from flinging over the little barrier on the edge of the tube that does very little to hold him in when we are catapulting to his side this quickly. Despite the cold water keeping us cool with its insistent mist, I can feel the warmth of Andrew's shoulder as it touches mine.

Then the waves hit, and we bounce from one wave to the next. I hold my breath as we shoot into the air in what feels like slow motion.

Rebecca is laughing with complete glee as we launch off the next bump and soar through the air.

We land and get a moment of peace, but then I see it. The mother of all waves. She's hurtling toward us with an evil smile. "Oh crap!" the twins shout together, making me burst into a fit of laughter.

We hit the wave, and the tube instantly goes vertical, tilting us so that our backs are to the water. We rocket into the air, and I'm certain we are at least five feet above the water now. Andrew's eyes go wide with horror, and Rebecca's calm demeanor from earlier is gone. Our butts lift completely off the tube, as we all try desperately to cling onto the handles below us. I watch Rebecca and Andrew both disappear with a splash before I return to the water, still on the tube.

Mr. Martin quickly slows the boat as my dad raises the orange flag indicating to other boaters that there are people in the water.

When we circle back to pick up the twins, the two are bickering over who let go first and whether it matters who came off the tube first or who hit the water first. They immediately whip their heads around to me, looking for me to make a judgment call on the matter.

"Who let go first? It was Rebecca, wasn't it?"

"No, it wasn't, and even if I did let go first, I heard you hit the water before I was in, so you fell first."

"Tell her she's wrong, and she lost."

I laugh in amusement. Dani and I are never like this with one another. I want to tell them it was a tie. I have no clue who came off first or who splashed into the water first, but I know my indifference will only spur them on to continue this ridiculous competition. While it has been fun to watch the two of them, this needs to end at some point. "Uh, sorry Andrew, but I think Rebecca beat you," I say.

The look of betrayal he gives me breaks my heart a little bit, but I have to side with Rebecca. We girls need to stick together. Andrew can hold his own.

"Rematch!" Andrew declares.

I guess I should've known my answer wouldn't end the battle.

The three of us buzz with adrenaline as we leap off the tube and dive into the water, swimming to the dock. The sun is setting, and Mr. Martin finally calls it a day.

I'm surprised we were able to go out for this long. We were forced to come in for dinner, but Andrew and Rebecca somehow convinced Mr. Martin to take us back out again. The twins gave up on their competition after our one-millionth run. I think after a while they both got tired of bickering and doing donuts until one of them was flung off the tube. *Thank goodness.*

"Can we swim for a while, Dad?" Rebecca asks as Mr. Martin secures the boat in its slip on the dock.

He glances at the sky. "You can stay out here for about fifteen more minutes, but then it's going to get too dark. Aren't you kids tired yet?"

"It takes a lot more than that to tire us out!" Andrew climbs up onto the dock and then takes a running start before doing a cannonball back into the water. He pops up and turns to Rebecca and me. "I bet I can make a bigger splash than you two with my cannonball."

"Dad, can you judge us?"

Mr. Martin just shakes his head as he turns toward the house. "I'm done for the day. You kids will have to judge each other," he laughs with a hint of amusement in his voice.

We alternate between leaping off the dock and racing each other between my dock and the Martin family's dock. Fifteen minutes go by way too quick, but it's a good thing when Mr. Martin calls us in for the evening because I'm exhausted. I don't think my little arms and legs could swim any longer to keep me from sinking.

"I'm starving!" I announce, turning to Andrew to back me up. I can always count on him to be hungry when I am.

"Me too! Let's go find snacks."

We enter the kitchen, and Andrew throws open the pantry door as he scans the shelves for food. I can't help but feel a small amount of adoration as I watch his bright eyes assess the food in the pantry with care.

"We have Oreos," he announces, snagging the package off the shelf and turning back toward the kitchen. He pulls the milk jug from the fridge and pours himself a glass. "Do you want a glass too, Em?" he asks, ignoring Rebecca entirely.

"Yes, please."

"Sure, I'll take a glass too. Thank you so much for asking," Rebecca frowns, her voice dripping with sarcasm.

We each grab paper towels to place our Oreos on. Rebecca grabs three, and Andrew and I begin grabbing ours. Andrew takes four, leaving three left for me. When he notices, he breaks his fourth Oreo in half and places it on my paper towel without even asking me if I want it.

I give him a soft smile. "Thank you! You didn't have to do that."

He shakes his head, brushing me off. "It was your idea to get food in the first place. Plus, you put up with Rebecca and I all day. You deserve it."

We go to sit on the barstools at the kitchen island, but when Mrs. Martin waltzes in, she stops us immediately. "What do you three think you're doing? You're not going to sit at those nice barstools soaked in lake water. Go dry off outside, please."

We rush back out onto the dock and plop ourselves down on our towels. It's a good thing we ended up out here because we get to watch the sun melt into the horizon, turning the sky into vibrant pink and orange hues. The last rays of sunlight bounce off the few clouds in the sky, reminding me of cotton candy. It's magic.

I dunk my first Oreo into my milk. "What do you guys want to do tomorrow?"

"The same thing," Andrew says simply.

"We can't just go tubing all day, every day. We need to find something else to do."

Andrew swallows his first bite of Oreo. "Fine, we can do something else, but we have to have Oreos and milk again after we swim because these are hitting the spot."

I take a bite of my soaked Oreo and quickly discover Andrew was right. I like Oreos. They're a great quick and easy dessert, but for some reason, these taste a million times better after a long day out on the water.

"Oh my gosh!" I gasp in delighted surprise as the chocolatey wafer mixes with the soft cream in a way that's better than any other Oreo experience I've had before. "Where did you get these Oreos? They taste so good."

"They're just from the market down the street," Rebecca says simply, taking a bite of hers now. "Wait, you're right! These are amazing!"

"It must be having them after being on the water all day."

"New tradition," Rebecca and Andrew chime together.

"We have to have these every day after swimming." Andrew decides.

Rebecca and I nod in agreement. And thus begins a new tradition, never to be broken.

CHAPTER 7

Summer 19

I was not expecting to be woken up at 5:30 this morning by the tapping of Andrew's knuckles on my window. I stayed up till 12:30 last night finishing my book. It was completely worth it until my sleep was interrupted prematurely.

Groaning, I roll out of bed, pulling the covers off the bed with me. I pick them up off the floor immediately, arranging them properly before I open my window to speak to Andrew. Watching me, he shakes his head with a knowing smile on his face.

Immediately upon opening the window, Andrew teases, "You just had to pick the covers off the floor?"

"Yes! I don't understand why everyone always gives me crap for it. It makes absolutely no sense to me that it's normal to live in a pigsty but laughable to like things clean and organized."

"Do you think I live in a pigsty?"

"Well, no, but sometimes Rebecca's room was like one." The lack of sleep and abrupt wakeup call is clearly leaving me flustered. "Why'd you wake me? I was up late reading, and the sun isn't even up yet."

Andrew opens his mouth to explain, but when I see he's dressed for a run, I cut him off. "It's too dark to run. Go back to bed and we can go later."

"I'm just following through on my promise to run with you." He bats his eyes innocently.

"Couldn't you have followed through yesterday or tomorrow... a day when I got more than five hours of sleep?"

"You can nap later. Just imagine how nice it'll feel to sleep in the sun on the dock this afternoon," he coaxes. "Get dressed. I promise it'll be worth it."

I give him a dramatic moan but head toward my dresser to grab shorts and a tank top anyway. That damn smile spreads across his face again as he takes a step away from the window to give me some privacy. "I'll meet you in five minutes at the end of your driveway."

Five minutes later, we are waiting for my watch to connect with the satellites. It emits a triumphant beep, and I hit start as we get going. Even without the sun beating down on us, the air still has a summer warmth.

Andrew, the track star he is, takes off from the start. "Hang on there, buddy." I tug on the back of his shirt, pulling him in line with me again. "No need to take off right out of the gate when we are running for distance."

He gives me a puppy dog look. "But I'm just so excited to be out running!" Quickly, his pout turns into a teasing smile.

"Well, you just woke me up five minutes ago, and I'm still shaking the sleep off. You're running with me to keep me accountable for going, not to whip my butt back into shape."

"That's what you think." He smirks. When I shoot him a glare, he quickly retracts his statement. "I'm just kidding, Em. Relax! This is supposed to be something you enjoy."

"I am enjoying it, minus being completely sleep-deprived."

"Not much of a morning person anymore, huh? Now you

know what Rebecca must've felt like." His laughter is tainted by a hint of sadness at the memory of his sister.

"I'm still a morning person. Years of waking up early for cross-country practice doesn't outweigh a few months of not training. You just caught me by surprise. Even when I woke up early for practices, I still regimented my sleep so that I was getting seven to eight hours of sleep every night."

"You always amazed me."

"Past tense?"

He gives me a soft smile, and I feel my cheeks heat. "You still do."

We shuffle on for a little while before I feel compelled to ask, "Why'd you drag me out here so early? I didn't think you were that much of a morning person yourself, let alone a morning runner."

He gives an exaggerated wheeze. "I'm not a runner. I'm dying already."

I nudge his side with my elbow. "Just imagine how you'd be doing if we were still going the pace you started at."

He holds up his hands in surrender. "You were right as always. What else can I say?"

"You can say that again." This time, the smug smile is on *my* face, and it feels good.

We reach the T in the road, and he turns right. I slow a bit in hesitation but follow him anyway. "You never explained why you dragged me out of bed for a run so early this morning." Realization hits me as we head toward the other side of the lake.

"It's a surprise!" Those words are the only clarification I need.

After another three-quarters of a mile, we reach the lookout point Rebecca and I would sit at weekly to watch the sunrise. Tears quickly well up in my eyes. "I don't know if I can do this. It's too soon. It's too weird doing it without Rebecca." I begin to step back, ready to turn around and head straight home.

Before I can, Andrew wraps me in his arms. "I know you think you can't, but you can. You're not going to do it alone. I'll be right here. You know Rebecca wouldn't want you to stop doing this on her behalf. Besides, this is going to be way different from when you and Rebecca would come here. I brought us snacks."

I look up at his smiling eyes with curiosity, laughter bubbling up inside of me at his nonchalant mention of food. He walks away from the lookout point back toward the road, and I notice his truck sitting there. I hear the chirp of the doors unlocking, and he opens one of the rear doors. He pulls out a cooler and two packages of muffins from Costco.

"Snacks, huh? Looks more like a meal to me," I muse.

The delight on his face is clear. "Yeah, I may have gotten a little excited when I went to Costco yesterday."

He sets the stuff down for a second while he grabs a thick blanket from his truck. He spreads it out on the grass and then begins setting up the food. There's double chocolate and apple crumb muffins, both of which I can gobble up any time, any day. He also pulls out orange juice, two plastic cups, a container of strawberries, and oranges. He pours us each some orange juice and begins peeling open an orange. I tear into the muffin packages.

"You're incredible, Andrew! How'd you pull this off?"

"It wasn't the easiest plan to execute. I packed everything up and left it here overnight. Then I rode my bike back home. I had to carefully pick the food I brought because I wanted to make sure it could sit in my truck for several hours overnight. The cooler only helps so much with the temperature warming up." He sips his orange juice. "Seems like everything stayed cold to me." He lifts his cup to show me.

"Will you split one of each muffin with me?"

He looks between the two packages. "There are twelve muffins here, and two of us. Do we need to share?"

A laugh slips out. "I know we just ran, but those muffins are huge."

He nods and begins cutting a chocolate muffin in half. He hands me the bigger half, and I take it without any complaints. I sink my teeth into it, and it's perfect, pillowy soft, and slightly melty from sitting in his warm truck. "Mmmm!" I can't contain my glee.

His entire face lights up at my sound of approval. In that moment, he reminds me of a puppy, eager to please. Between bites of muffin, I say, "Thank you for doing this. This was so sweet, and I have to admit, I'm enjoying myself."

He sets his muffin down gently. "It was my pleasure, Em." He pauses for a moment before continuing. The look on his face gets serious. "Besides, there's a part of me that feels responsible, as Rebecca's twin, for carrying on her legacy and making sure things are the way she would've wanted them."

Understanding, I nod. "I can see that. Just don't let it consume you. And don't forget to put yourself first! You know there's things she would want for you too, so don't let your efforts to help other people realize their potential keep you from meeting yours."

"I know. I know." He trails off.

"She always saw the best in people. She saw past my shyness, helped me to get out of my comfort zone, and pushed me to try new things when I never would've done it on my own."

He leans into me a little as if he can't carry the weight of this moment on his own. "Yeah, she was always good at that. I hope you know we don't *need* Rebecca to be good people. She made it a hell of a lot easier, but we can hold each other responsible now."

"You're already doing it for me." I lean back into him the slightest bit.

"You are for me, too," he insists. "I wouldn't be out here,

running or setting up this *amazing* breakfast if it weren't for you."

My insides warm. It doesn't feel like I'm doing anything for Andrew. I don't think anything I can do for him will ever be enough with how incredible he is, but it's nice to hear he feels like I'm helping him in some way.

We watch the sunrise in silence, beautiful golden rays peek over the mountain tops across the water and shoot through the bits of soft clouds in the sky overhead. A red line paints the edges of the mountains like a watercolor, indicating the day will be a hot one. I forgot how incredible these moments are. I'm sure the delicious bite of muffin in my mouth and this person whose existence I cherish in a more than platonic way adds to the experience.

"I can't believe I was going to completely give this up," I mutter.

Andrew pulls his eyes away from the stunning sky for a moment to look at me. "You're here now. You didn't give it up. Promise me you won't, even if I can't be with you every time."

I don't like the thought of being here alone with my thoughts, but I agree anyway. It's hard to say no to Andrew. He has this pure heart that makes me want to give him the world. He's just Andrew, the boy I've been in love with for as long as I can remember. "I promise."

CHAPTER 8

Summer 13

My stomach rumbles grumpily, matching my mood for the morning after waking up at the butt crack of dawn for no apparent reason. I reach into the fridge for eggs, only to discover we're out. *How did we run out of eggs?* My family always keep an extra package at the ready.

I sink into one of the barstools at the counter in defeat after putting a slice of bread in the toaster and peeling a banana. I guess this will have to do for now.

Upstairs, I hear a phone ring. It's pretty early for anyone to be calling, so I step off my stool to patter to the bottom of the stairs and listen. My mom's sleepy voice is mumbling. After a moment or two, her voice comes through clearer. "What?" There's a pause as whoever is on the other end answers her question. My mom sounds like she's crying as she responds. "I can't believe this. What happened?" There's a long, stunned pause. "I'll make plans to fly out as soon as possible."

I hear my dad's soft mumble and more movement as my mom's soft tears turn to loud sobs. I want to rush up to their room and figure out what's going on, but I don't want them to know I was eavesdropping, so I just sit at the bottom of the stairs as I wonder what could be going on.

After about half an hour, my mom and dad come out of their room. My mom's face is stained with tears. My dad has his arms wrapped around her as he holds a box of tissues in one hand. I stand from my spot on the stairs and meet my parents' gaze. At the sight of me, my mom's composure falters all over again, and my dad proceeds to console her.

"What's going on?" I whisper, unreasonably afraid of speaking too loudly.

My dad walks my mom to the couch in the living room and motions for me to follow. I sit down in the recliner. With a voice coated in sorrow, my dad explains, "Grandpa had a heart attack this morning. He didn't make it."

My stomach drops. Grandpa was in such good health. Just a month ago, I spent the night at his house, and we baked all day.

My throat closes up and tears build in the corners of my eyes. Dad opens his arms up as I walk over and sit between him and Mom. I cry so hard I begin hiccupping. This can't be happening. Grandpa was perfectly fine not that long ago. This doesn't make sense.

We sit in a group hug until my tears finally slow and my hiccups stop. When we separate, I look up at the clock. It's almost 9. Rebecca must be awake by now. I need to be with my best friend. I mutter some poor excuse for leaving as I run to my room and throw on denim shorts and a sweatshirt. I slip on a pair of flip-flops and walk out the back door without another word.

I head straight to the Martin's house. They should probably all be awake by now, so I just knock on the door. Luckily Rebecca answers it, and as soon as I see her smiling face, I burst into tears again. She pulls me in for a tight hug and closes the door behind her, walking us out to the front porch. She sits on the steps with me for a long while until I'm able to control the tears.

As I catch my breath and wipe my eyes, Rebecca suggests we walk down to the beach. "You'll feel better if we walk a little," she insists. Once we are down there, she picks up a pebble and skips it. I watch it graze the water five times before disappearing into the lake. She hands me a rock. "Let's do this for a little bit, and then, when you're ready, you can tell me what happened."

We stay out there skipping rocks for at least ten minutes before either of us says another word. I take my time before I speak up, knowing she's leaving everything up to me. I appreciate that. Rebecca's a good friend. Honestly, she's one of the best I could ever ask for.

"My mom just got a call from my aunt. My grandpa had a heart attack this morning, and they didn't get him treatment in time. He's gone." I sniffle. "He was *just* here doing normal things with me, and now he's gone."

"Oh, Emma, I'm so sorry." Rebecca hugs me and hands me another rock. "Don't stop skipping. We are going for a world record number of skips here." With a soft smile, she adds, "Based on your skipping, it's going to take some time." Despite the insult, I find myself laughing. I didn't even think I was capable of laughing at a time like this.

"I don't know what to do, Becs. My grandpa has been such a huge part of my life. It's only been a couple of hours since I knew he was gone, but it already hurts so badly. I want the aching to stop."

She kicks the rocks around a little, looking for another flat stone. When she finds one, she hands it to me. "It's okay for it to hurt. The hurting only means you care. Yes, it sucks that he won't be around anymore, but think about all the memories you have to be grateful for, all the lessons he probably taught you. When you think about it, you're lucky to be hurting right now."

She laughs lightly. "I know I sound like a lunatic for saying this, but it means you had someone great enough to be sad about losing. That's pretty special." There's a pause. I hate that she's right. It'd be so much easier to just spend the day curled up in bed, wallowing in my sorrow, but I know Rebecca isn't about to let that happen.

She hands me another rock and then skips one of her own. "Tell me more about your grandpa. I want to hear about what made him so special to you."

I skip mine, and it bounces the most I've seen so far today. It's almost as if Grandpa was looking down and saying *look what I can do now.* I sigh. "I don't even know where to begin. There were lots of things that made him special."

"I don't have any plans today. Start wherever you want." She shrugs. "I've got time."

"He was the one who got me into reading. It started as him telling me all kinds of stories about dragons, fairies, and goblins. They were pretty crazy stories. I can't believe he'd make them up on the spot like he did." I take a moment to reflect on the memory. "Then he bought me this book that he always kept at his house. Every time I came over, he'd read it with me. It was this giant book, unreasonably sized for being made for children." I gesture to show her its height and width. "It was filled with different fairytales like *The Princess and the Pea* and *Goldilocks and the Three Bears.* He helped me learn that reading can be an escape to another world with exciting adventures I'd never have on my own."

"I never knew your grandpa was the one who got you into reading."

"I guess that was something I had just taken for granted."

"What else did you guys do together?" She prods me to keep talking as she also hands me another rock to skip. I'll admit focusing on skipping rocks does help distract me from my emotions.

"We baked together a lot. He was a really good chef and baker, but I always preferred baking. He had this chocolate chip cookie recipe where he'd put cinnamon in the cookies. It seemed weird, so I refused to try for years, and then when I finally agreed to try them, I fell in love and regretted being so stubborn."

Rebecca laughs at that. "So you've always been this resistant to change?"

"Hey!" I laugh with her a little before turning serious again. "I guess so."

We skip rocks simultaneously, and I can't help but grin when mine skips once more than hers. I am getting good at this. "In the last year or two, he started teaching me other recipes he has like his sourdough bread and sugar cookies. I'm still partial to those chocolate chip cookies though. They're so soft, and the cinnamon brings out the chocolate. Maybe I can make them for you sometime."

"Would you want to make them together? Maybe we could bake them today to honor your grandpa."

"I think he'd like that. I know *I* would." I reach out to hug her and show her just how much I appreciate her.

A couple of hours later, I spoon cookie dough onto a baking sheet while Rebecca picks out chunks to pop into her mouth. Despite her lack of help now, she was rather involved in measuring out the ingredients and intermittently washing dishes as we made the dough.

"You know, you're supposed to wait to eat it until after it's cooked," I remark.

"Have you ever tried cookie dough? It's so much better than cookies!" She picks another glob out of the bowl and tosses it into her mouth before adding, "This stuff is especially delicious. It's like crack."

Mrs. Martin clears her throat from the dining room table where she is working on her laptop. She gives Rebecca a disapproving look, clearly not enthused about her thirteen-year-old daughter making drug references.

I try to hold in my laughter, but a small chuckle slips free. "You can't say the cookie dough is better if you haven't tried the cookies yet." I slide the first batch into the oven and set a timer. "Just imagine that cookie dough but with melty chocolate chips and an enhanced cinnamon flavor."

Her eyes roll in the back of her head as she imagines it. "Ugh, my mouth is watering now and there aren't any baked cookies to eat! I guess I'll have to eat more dough." She pinches her fingers together, picking up another chunk.

"Please wait to try the actual cookies. They're worth the wait." I look down at the ground, not able to meet her eyes for the next part of what I'm about to say. "Not to be dramatic, but every time you eat more cookie dough, a piece of my soul dies because it means there's that much less dough for the actual cookies. My grandpa and I never ate the cookie dough."

A small wave of sadness washes over me. It's hitting me now how weird it is to make these cookies without Grandpa. "I need to go wash the cookie dough off my hands," I mutter and beeline for the bathroom.

Rebecca watches me exit the kitchen. I can see the worried, knowing look on her face. I don't want to make her feel bad. I know this is just her goofy personality shining through and a failed attempt at trying to act like everything is normal for my sake. I wash my hands and hover over the sink, sucking in a deep breath and trying to hold back the tears. I'm so tired of crying. There have been so many tears today.

There's a knock on the door. "I'll be out in a sec to help

scoop the dough for the next sheet," I say to Rebecca, trying to hide the shakiness in my voice.

"Are you okay?" It's Andrew's soft whisper.

I crack the door open and peer up at him with watery eyes. "I'm fine. Did you need the bathroom?"

He shakes his head. "No, I just saw you walk by and thought you didn't look so good. I heard what happened. How are you doing?"

I shrug. "I'm sad, but Rebecca has helped a lot. I'm just having another moment. I'll be fine," I insist, stepping out of the bathroom. "Thanks for checking on me."

I start moving toward the kitchen, but he quickly pulls me into his embrace. He squeezes tight and holds on for a little longer than I expected. I let myself sink into the warming comfort of his touch and the dull smell of his cologne. *When did he start wearing cologne?*

We finally pull away, and I look up at him again, blushing a little. I swear he is too, as if he regrets holding me the extra two seconds. He abruptly takes a step back and throws an arm behind his head, playing with his hair. "I'm here if you need someone besides Rebecca to talk to."

"Thank you. I appreciate it."

We exchange one final lingering look before I step away and head back into the kitchen. Rebecca hops off the counter and rushes to me. "I'm sorry for eating the cookie dough. We can make another batch. We can bake all day if you want! Whatever helps you, we will do."

I grab her hand and squeeze it. "It's ok. I'm just a little emotional right now and need some time. I know you're trying hard to be here for me, and I appreciate it." I peer across the counter, looking for the bowl of cookie dough so we can start making another tray to go in the oven. "What'd you do with the dough?"

"I had to give it to my mom so she could guard it and make

sure I wouldn't eat any more." She gestures to the dining room table where the bowl sits.

I burst into laughter. "Just wait until the cookies come out of the oven. If you think the dough is that good, you have another thing coming." I think for a moment. "We better make a second batch."

Rebecca immediately rushes to pull more butter out of the fridge and goes into the pantry to find the sugars, flour, and baking soda. "On it!"

The timer goes off, and I pull the cookies out of the oven. They're perfectly fluffy and have slightly golden edges, the sign that they're done. I set them on the stove and look for my spoon to begin preparing another baking sheet with cookies. "Do you want to help me, Becs, or do I need to keep you away from the dough still?"

"I should be okay now that I can try a cookie fresh from the oven."

Holding my arm out to stop her, I explain, "The cookies need to sit on the tray for about five minutes to finish cooking through. Then you can try one."

"Then I take it back. Keep me away from that drug, please!" Mrs. Martin looks up again with narrowed eyes and Rebecca chooses to completely ignore her. "Why do we have to wait five more minutes? I'm so weak! I need help."

A smile crosses my face as I roll my eyes. "Trust me, they're worth the wait. You can start measuring the sugar again to keep busy." I scoop more dough onto the tray.

After five minutes, I pluck a cookie off the tray and hand it to Rebecca on a napkin. "Here."

She snatches the cookie up and takes a bite. "Oh my gosh!" She yells through a mouthful of cookie. "These are incredible! You were right. They *are* better than the dough!" With her mouth still full, she asks, "What are you waiting for? We need to get you one too before I eat the rest on the tray." She pushes past me and snags a warm cookie for me. She places it on a napkin and shoves it into my hands. "Cheers!"

We both take a bite, and I can't help the memory that comes flooding back with the swirl of cinnamon and chocolate on my tongue. I'm sitting at my grandpa's kitchen bar, having "life talks" while we eat two cookies each. For the first time today, the memory doesn't make me sad. I'm happy to have the memory. It's just like Rebecca said earlier. Now, because of Grandpa, I get to make new memories with these cookies. I'm going to remember today as a good day. Not only did Rebecca discover the magic of my Grandpa's cookies, but our friendship grew a lot stronger today too. I whisper a silent, "Thank you, Grandpa," and finish my cookie, happily grabbing a second.

CHAPTER 9

Summer 15

"He finally let go!" Rebecca yells to her dad. He slows to a stop as Rebecca throws up the orange flag, and I begin pulling Andrew back to the boat. "He's such a showoff. Why does he have to go for so long and do all those jumps?"

Mr. Martin chuckles. "He's a fifteen-year-old boy, honey. I'd expect nothing less." Brushing some of the fly aways along her hairline, he quickly adds, "Don't worry, you looked great out there too!" Watching Rebecca's facial expression, I can tell the compliment doesn't do much to soothe her.

Andrew reaches the back of the boat and climbs up the ladder, dripping all over the custom upholstery. As he unzips his life vest, I try not to stare at his broad shoulders, strong biceps, and traces of a six-pack. As a result of throwing javelin and doing the triple jump for his high school track team, Andrew started weight training this spring, and it has done miracles for his body.

Focusing on anything other than his taut muscles, I say, "You looked good out there. You're getting pretty good at jumping the wake."

He's been working on that since the beginning of the summer. At first, he would wipe out every time, but now, to Rebecca's dismay, he's basically perfected it. "Thanks! When are you going to try getting out on the wakeboard?"

"Ummm probably around never," I deadpan.

"Come on! The summer is almost over, and you still haven't tried it." Rebecca buts in. "You're great at water skiing. Why won't you try wake boarding?"

"I think you mean I'm mediocre at water skiing on a good day. I just don't want to go out there and follow that." I motion to Andrew.

He smiles. "Em, no one cares! It's just us."

I shake my head. "I can hardly water ski! What makes you think this will be any different? Let's just face the fact that I'm not good at water sports." I add, "It doesn't mean I'm not enjoying being out on the boat with you."

"You promised me you'd try something new this summer! You have to follow through on your promise." Rebecca gives me her best puppy dog look.

"I did say that. I'm not breaking my promise by not wake boarding. I'm just choosing to try something else."

"Do it for me!" Andrew begs. "Please. You'll love it! It's way more fun than water skiing."

He must still see the hesitation on my face because after a beat he adds, "If you go, I'll convince one of my parents to drive us to the bookstore I told you about. I'll buy you a book of your choice, and we can get ice cream from the place across the street. I hear it's homemade."

I *hate* that he knows me so well! How am I supposed to pass up an offer like that? A book *and* ice cream? Not to mention a day with Andrew all to myself.

"Fine. For the record, I'm not doing it for you. I'm doing it for the free book and ice cream."

Rebecca is already grabbing me a life jacket out of the

storage compartment underneath one of the seats. "That's what it takes? I'll keep that in mind." She hands me the life jacket. "I'm so proud of you!"

"What do I do?" My stomach churns as the nerves build. *What am I getting myself into?*

"You'll pretty much sit in the water with your knees bent, just like skiing only different," Rebecca begins.

My shoulders slouch. "This is why I didn't want to do it. You're awful at explaining things, Becs!"

She pretends to be hurt, but I know it takes a lot more than that to break through Rebecca's thick skin.

Andrew turns from shortening the rope hanging off the boat and asks his dad, "Why don't we get closer to our dock to start, and then I can get in the water with her?"

"Sure thing." Mr. Martin nods and turns the boat around to head back toward their cabin.

"Do you know what you're doing?" I ask uneasily.

"Did you not see me out there? I know what I'm doing."

"I mean do you know how to teach wake boarding." Exasperation begins to build. "Your ability to teach me can make or break this experience. I'm doing this once for a free book and dessert, but don't think I'll be bribed again."

He rolls his eyes. "I swear Rebecca is rubbing off on you." Turning to his sister with narrowed eyes, he adds, "Trust me, that's not a good thing." His words say one thing, but the smile on his face says another.

Rebecca frowns and smacks his arm.

He shoves her back hard enough for her to fall right into the seat behind her. Grabbing my hand, Andrew leads me toward the back of the boat to strap me into Rebecca's board.

"Are you ready?"

"No."

He laughs as if I'm joking. Then he helps ease me off the boat. He jumps in after me and grabs my waist, one hand on each hip. "What are you doing?" I jolt as if he just electrocuted me with his touch.

"Relax, I'm just trying to help you get seated in the water how you're supposed to."

I try to relax, but that's nearly impossible when Andrew is grabbing me like this. It's not like he's never touched me. We hug each other hello and goodbye, and we full-on wrestled my first summer at the lake. It's just different now.

For starters, I'm just in my bikini and a life jacket, and his hands are directly on the bare skin of my waist. Then there's the fact that Andrew has been treating me differently this summer. He's been a little extra sweet around me, complimenting me and looking out for me. Oh, and we can't forget the fact that every time he so much as grazes my pinky, I feel electricity through my whole body. Right now, it's a miracle I'm even conscious after this amount of skin-to-skin contact.

Andrew's words bring my attention away from his body and back to the task at hand. "I shortened the rope for you before we got off the boat. That will give you more upward pull and make it easier for you to stand up when my dad starts going. Bend your knees, like this." He hikes his knees up to his chest. "You'll sort of be crunched up like this." He motions again. "Stay crunched until you're over the top of the board then stand up slowly. Don't rush it."

My jaw drops. "That's all you're going to say? What if I get up? Then what?"

"If you do get up, you'd just shift your weight so your dominant foot is in the back. If you get up on your first try, I'll give you fifty bucks on top of the book and ice cream. That'd be incredibly impressive."

Determination fills my body. *I'll show him.* I could use fifty bucks. Think of all the books I could buy with that money! I bend my knees like he showed me. "Like this?"

He moves one of my knees a little bit. "More like this." He

motions for me to move my other leg to match. "Do you want me to tell my dad to hit it?"

Despite my determination a second ago, fear kicks in. "No, Andrew. I don't want to do this. I hate trying new things. I hate being bad at things."

"You don't know you'll be bad at this though because you've never done it before."

He's smart. I'll give him that. "I'm bad at water skiing though, and I don't want to fall. What if I face plant? That's going to hurt so bad!" Panic wells up inside of me. *Oh God! Am I on the verge of tears right now? Heck no! I'm not about to cry over this.*

He grabs my waist again, but this time his touch is firmer, a steadying hand to tell me he's here for me. "First of all, you're not bad a water skiing. Although you'd be much better if I had taught you instead of Rebecca. Just saying. Second of all, if you face-planted, you won't be going fast enough for it to hurt. Plus, it's not that far of a fall. You're kind of short."

I narrow my eyes at him, but the smile he gives me in return absolutely melts me, and I can't help but laugh and smile back as I mock offense. "Hey! I thought you're supposed to tell me there's no way I'll fall!"

"I'm just stating the facts. Come on. You'll be so proud of yourself for trying! You didn't get in the water *not* to try it. Plus, there's a reward waiting for you." He wiggles his eyebrows. I know he's talking about the bookstore and ice cream, but my pounding heart doesn't get the memo. Instead, it's picturing Andrew leaning in for a kiss. I bet he'd be a really good kisser with those full lips and the tenderness of his touch.

"So, you ready?"

I shake my head a little as I refocus again. "Yeah." I nod. "I can do this."

"That's my girl!" My heart flutters at his words. "I'll tell my dad to hit it. If you need to stop for anything, just use the same signal as tubing and skiing." He takes his hand and slices it across his neck to be sure I know it, as if I haven't been using it for the past six summers.

I nod as my hands feel a little shaky. *I've got this. I've got this. I've got this.* "She's ready, Dad! Hit it!"

"Woohoo, Emma!" Rebecca cheers me from the boat, waving her hands crazily in the air in her usual flamboyant manner.

Mr. Martin starts the boat's motor again and nods at me. "Starting now."

I feel the rope begin to pull, and I try to remember Andrew's instructions, but I panic. The rope tugs and I try to push with my legs to help me get up. As a result, I faceplant just like I said I would. The crash of the water fills my ears and I scramble back to the surface.

I see Rebecca hanging off the back of the boat, giving me an eager thumbs up. I turn to find Andrew swimming toward me. He's smiling. "Are you okay?"

"Yeah, I'm fine." At the sight of his face, I grow self-conscious. "Are you laughing at me?"

"What? No!" He looks genuinely offended that I'd think that. "I'm proud of you. You were right there! You just need to let the boat do more of the work for you. Don't fight it so much. Give it another try."

"Okay, I will. I was pretty close, huh?" I say, feeling comforted now.

His smile widens. "Yes, you were! We've got to give you another run."

He helps me set up once again. This time he hardly even needs to adjust my form for me. *I've so got this.* I give Mr. Martin the thumbs up, and the boat pulls forward again. This time, I let the boat get me most of the way there and then push up just a little with my legs. I get up, but I feel some resistance as I try to shift my weight to my dominant leg. Next thing I know, I'm swallowed by water again.

I come up gasping for air. Rebecca is cheering for me again. "I'm so proud of you, bestie!"

I laugh and swat my hand at her. She's being ridiculous. This is no amazing feat.

Andrew reaches out to pull me back closer to our starting point again and give me more pointers. "You're a natural! I told you Rebecca is just a bad teacher." He winks. "What happened this time?"

"I couldn't get the board turned."

"Okay, just try rotating your left foot back instead of shifting your full weight around. I have a good feeling about this next one." I don't think he's stopped smiling since my first run.

We start again. I let the boat pull me most of the way. Once I'm up, I lean on my heel a little to rotate my left foot back, and I'm doing it. *Oh my gosh! I'm doing it!* I look up at the boat in wide-eyed bewilderment as I skate across the water. Rebecca is whooping and hollering at me. I hear Andrew shouting from his spot in the water, "Go, Em!" I turn to see him, a goofy grin on my face, and I wipe out.

I went for two more runs. My first of the two being my longest. I have to admit, Andrew was right. I am proud of myself for doing this. Not only do my Oreos and milk taste sweeter today, but now Rebecca and Andrew are both super proud of me, and Andrew owes me a trip to the bookstore with some ice cream.

The sun hangs low, on the verge of setting but not quite to the point where the sky is changing colors. Rebecca, Andrew, and I sit on the dock wrapped in towels. Rebecca animatedly exclaims, "You should've seen yourself, Emma! You looked like a total badass out there!"

I humbly laugh. "Andrew was pretty helpful." My eyes meet

his for a moment. To Rebecca, I say, "I came through on my promise, so now you can stop bothering me about it."

"No no no no no!" she insists. "You just proved to me that I need to help bring you out of your shell so you can reach your full potential. The possibilities are endless now! I have to start brainstorming what else we can get you to try."

I shrink back. "Rebecca, I love you, but I think I need some time to recover from the new thing I *just* tried. My body is still stiff from the beating I took from the water."

"I love you too, which is why I'm pushing you to be your very best self." She grins big. Throwing her arms around me, she says, "I'm just so proud of you."

Behind her, Andrew calmly adds, "Me too."

I can't help but be slightly angry at myself for allowing his approval to hold so much weight, but it does. His words bring me to life.

I regain my composure. "Speaking of promises, when are we going to the bookstore? I have so many books on my wish list."

"Well, when do you want to go?"

"Right now."

Andrew looks up at the sky as the orangey hues begin to paint the horizon. "The store is definitely closed by now. How about tomorrow?"

"Done."

CHAPTER 10

Summer 15

As we pull up to the bookstore, Andrew and Mrs. Martin get out of the car, Mrs. Martin moving to the driver's seat. I unbuckle and slip out of the back seat, meeting Andrew in front of the store. "All right, kiddos, I'll be back in a couple of hours. Does that work?" Mrs. Martin chimes.

Andrew's face droops with a frown. "We aren't kiddos, Mom. I just drove us here."

She just chuckles at his frustration and drives off. I turn to take in the bookstore in all its glory. "This is it, huh?"

He nods, wearily watching me and waiting for my approval. I lead us in, practically shaking with excitement. For how much I love reading, I rarely get to go book shopping. There's a Barnes & Noble in the mall near my house that I'll occasionally poke around in while my mom makes a return, but twenty minutes in a bookstore is not even remotely enough time.

I take in the store with awe. It has a very cozy vibe with a fire crackling in one of the corners, even though it's eighty degrees outside. Each of the shelves are labeled clearly, and I can see the books are organized alphabetically by author, a huge plus for my organized self. There's a seating area in the center that looks like someone's living room, including coffee tables and comfy chairs. It is very inviting, inspiring people to just sit and read or chat about books.

"I love it."

Andrew's relieved smile grows quickly. "I'm so glad to hear that."

I start wandering around, reading the labels on the bookshelves. "Where's the science fiction?"

A woman who looks to be college-age approaches us. "Is this your first time in?"

Andrew immediately steps in to speak for us. "I've been in a few times before, but this is Emma's first time." He tilts his head in my direction.

She nods in excitement. "My dad owns the bookstore, so I know this place like the back of my hand. The nonfiction is toward the front. The fiction is in the middle, and the children's books are in the back. If you need anything at all, let me know," she says with a friendly smile.

"She seems nice," I note to Andrew as we walk toward the middle of the store.

"Her dad is amazing. I wish he was here. He gave me all kinds of book recommendations last time." He looks down at the ground, disappointed.

"It's okay. I don't like people bugging me at the bookstore anyway. I just like to browse and see what I find."

He perks up a bit. "Well, this is your reward, so you get to choose how this day goes."

"You don't have to buy me a book just because I went wakeboarding, you know. I had a good time doing it. It's not like it's something I regret trying."

He shakes his head adamantly. "I promised you I'd buy you a book. I'm not going to break a promise."

I give him a soft smile, but inside my heart is swelling as it hits me just how caring Andrew is. "Thank you."

He shrugs nonchalantly. "Of course!" He begins shuffling some books around on a shelf until he lifts one up to read the back.

We wander through the store in silence for a while, picking up books, reading the backs, and placing them back on the shelf. As I round the corner at the end of the bookshelf, I find the young adult section. Fantasy books have always been my go-to, but starting high school has exposed me to several new genres, so I decide to poke around.

I pick up a book with a beautiful green cover, its title written in delicate white cursive. I don't even know what it's about, but I already want to read it because the cover is so magnificent. I know what they say about not judging a book by its cover, but it doesn't mean a beautiful design won't catch my eye every once in a while.

I flip it over to read the back and discover it's a love story between a girl and the boy next door. It's the perfect book. It reminds me of Andrew and me. While I haven't read any romance books that aren't primarily categorized as fantasy, I know I'm a sucker for love because of all the rom-coms Rebecca and I have watched. We spent one rainy day earlier this summer binge-watching movies on Netflix for over twelve hours. We only left her room to grab pizza from the kitchen and ice cream from the freezer. It was the perfect day in my mind.

I open the book up to the first page, curious. I figure I'll just read a page or two and then keep looking for a book suitable for Andrew to buy for me.

Half an hour later, I'm several chapters deep. This book had me hooked from the beginning. There's a will they or won't they plot that leaves me wanting more with each page.

Andrew struts around the corner and catches me reading it. "Looks like you found a keeper."

I blush a little, hoping he can't tell what the book is and judge me for being a hopeless romantic.

"Is that the one you want?"

I close the book and hug it to my chest. I *do* want it, but I don't want to tell him that. I know it's completely nonsensical, but if he finds out what the book is about, I'm convinced he will know I picked it up because it made me think of him, and it will ruin the amazing friendship we have going right now.

I shrug my shoulders. "Maybe we can look around a little more."

"Are you sure? I saw you were already pretty deep in that book," he persists.

I glance at the clock on the wall behind him. We've already been in here for almost two hours, and we are still supposed to go for ice cream. *Stop being irrational and accept his offer!* "Okay, yes. This is the one."

He walks me up to the register, and we checkout with the nice store owner's daughter. She lifts the book to scan it. Peeking down at the cover she exclaims, "Oh, this is a great book! It's been very popular this summer. The story is *so* good. You know this author writes a lot of other good young adult romance books if you like this one. I personally think she has quite a few underrated gems." She smiles kindly as I die from the shame bearing down on me.

I can feel my cheeks growing tomato-red by the moment. Andrew doesn't seem too fazed, but I can see the slightest hint of shock at the mention of the word romance. If I pretend everything is normal, maybe he won't ask me about it, and I won't have to explain why I picked this book.

We walk out of the store, and he points out the ice cream shop that is right across the street. We cross over and enter with the musical ring of a bell overhead.

I find myself in awe for the second time today. This is no ordinary ice cream shop. There are two full freezers, each with at least a dozen flavors to pick from: fruity flavors with hand-picked fruit from local orchards, and sweet flavors with home-made fillings like cookie dough and brownies. There's even a dark chocolate ice cream with cocoa imported from Brazil.

"I don't know where to start," I whisper to Andrew as I gaze back and forth between the freezers. "Do they offer samples?"

"Oh yeah, they'll give you all the samples your heart desires," he boasts with an eager smile.

"What's your favorite?"

"I've only been here a couple of times, and I always try to get something different because they have so many flavors. They even rotate out their flavors sometimes for the seasons. They regularly have a chocolate and peanut butter ice cream I think you'll really like though."

I peer in at the tubs of heaven. I *do* love chocolate and peanut butter. "Ooh, that sounds great! Can I get more than one flavor?"

"You better! I might even get three!" He punctuates his laughter with a wink.

The man at the counter finishes up helping the couple before us and addresses us, "Welcome in! What can I get started for you today?"

Again, Andrew takes the lead on the conversation with the stranger, and I mentally thank him for knowing me so well. "She needs lots of samples. This is her first time in the store."

"Alrighty then! I think we can arrange that." He smiles. "What kind of ice cream do you normally like?"

"I love just about anything with chocolate in it."

Andrew peers over the counter to assess the flavors carefully. "Start her off with a sample of the chocolate and peanut butter flavor."

The man grabs a wooden spoon and loads it up with the perfect bite of ice cream, complete with a giant glob of brownie laced with peanut butter swirls.

"This is our peanut butter fudge brownie. It's one of the most popular flavors."

I take it eagerly and taste it in two bites, savoring it. It's extraordinary! The ice cream is perfectly creamy, not too rich. It has the perfect ratio of peanut butter to chocolate, and brownie to ice cream. I get a tease of peanut butter that doesn't outweigh the delicious chocolate, and I can get brownie in nearly every bite without being overwhelmed by it.

Right as I go to throw my spoon away, the man hands me another sample of ice cream. "This one is a dark chocolate ice cream with raspberry ribbons. It's mostly chocolate but with a hint of fruit."

I don't typically enjoy ice cream with fruity flavors, but I don't want to be rude, so I take the sample from the shop worker. Just as I finish my second sample, I'm handed another.

I turn to Andrew and find him already holding two more for me. The man behind the counter has apparently been scooping them as I tasted. He is more than following through on his promise to load me up with samples.

The next one is vanilla ice cream with brownie chunks and caramel. It's good but not quite my taste. He also throws in a cookie dough flavor with a chocolate base and insists I try their seasonal cherry flavor. I'm surprised to find it's really good, even though it isn't bursting with chocolate.

"It's going to be impossible to choose with all these options. I haven't tasted anything I don't like," I groan to Andrew.

The corner of his mouth quirks up, reaching an amused half-smile as he goes to place his order, mint cookie and cherry.

I crinkle my nose. "Aren't they going to mix and ruin the ice cream?"

"That's the best part! You'd be surprised how good mint and cherry is."

"You have horrible taste," I tease as I step up to order my ice cream, finally deciding on the chocolate raspberry and peanut butter fudge brownie.

We sit down at a bench outside that's a little way down the street. The second I sit, I'm greeted with a comforting stillness compared to the rest of the street, followed by the warmth of Andrew sliding in next to me. Even with the July heat attacking me, the feeling of his shoulder touching mine gives me goosebumps.

I take a bite of my ice cream and close my eyes as I enjoy the creamy, slightly melty goodness. I open my eyes to find Andrew watching me, looking pleased with himself for being the one to bring me here and bring me joy. I love that my happiness makes him happy.

"How's the ice cream?" he asks, knowing the answer.

"This is Heaven on earth, Andrew! I can't believe you didn't bring me here sooner!" I exclaim, shoving his shoulder.

He cracks a smile. "It's not my fault neither one of us can drive."

"We could bike here," I suggest. "I'd bike fifteen miles every day for books and ice cream."

His joy becomes evident as it radiates from the inside out, showing in his shining eyes and easy laugh. "Maybe you could do that, little miss runner, but I'm just a jumper and a thrower. I'd die on a fifteen-mile bike ride."

I giggle a little at the thought of Andrew attempting to bike that far. "I guess it's a good thing we will be able to drive next summer."

He nods in agreement. Then he nudges the plastic bag I have sitting at my feet, containing my new book. "So, a romance book, huh? Are you getting soft on me, moving on from fantasy to cheesy rom-coms?"

I know by his tone that he's teasing me, but I still can't help the fire that sets my cheeks ablaze as my embarrassment grows.

"This is the first romance book I've ever picked up, but it sounded like it had a good story. I like happy endings. What can I say?"

"Our fantasy books have happy endings too. Just usually it's the hero winning some battle or saving a whole civilization."

"Yeah, but every once in a while, a girl wants to be swept off her feet. No matter how tough we may act, we all want to love and be loved. If I can find a little piece of that feeling in a book, then so be it."

I'm a little shocked by the raw truth that just escaped me. I stuff another spoonful of ice cream into my mouth to distract myself from the thoughtful silence Andrew responds with.

"You're loved." Andrew finally says. "I mean your family loves you. Your friends love you. I don't know anyone who doesn't love you."

Does he love me? I push the thought aside. "Yes, that's true. I'm not saying I'm unhappy in my life, or I don't feel loved. I'm just saying I don't have the kind of love where you ache to spend every waking moment with that person because not only is he your favorite person, but you are your favorite version of yourself when you're with him. Eventually, I want someone who will take me out for a fancy dinner date or stay in to bake with me and build a blanket fort to watch movies in."

He raises his eyebrows. "For this being your first romance book and not having that kind of love in your life, you sure do know a lot about it."

I laugh. "I watch a lot of rom-coms with your sister."

He smiles and holds my gaze. "Well, I have no doubt you'll find that kind of love, Em. Any guy would be lucky to have you."

I break the eye contact, turning to spoon more ice cream. "Thank you." I stare intently at my bowl that's mostly melted now. Even as melty goo, it's still the best ice cream I've ever had.

He begins picking at one of his nails. "Is that your idea of a perfect date? A fancy dinner and movies under a blanket fort?" He glances back up at me with a teasing smile.

"Not quite," I answer seriously. "Dinner and a movie are overdone. I'd enjoy both of those things, but they'd have to be done separately."

He nods. "Okay, then what is your idea of a perfect date?"

I think about it. I guess I had never really planned it. It's not like I've had boys rushing to ask me out in school, or any place for that matter. I want to tell him *this is my perfect date.* Today was amazing, spending time with Andrew, looking at books, and eating ice cream. This right now is everything I could ever ask for, but I can't tell him that. I try to imagine myself on a date with another guy, my dream guy. *What would I want to do?* I can't picture any scenario where the guy isn't Andrew. *Dang, my stupid heart!*

I blow a wispy curl out of my face, buying time to come up with an answer. "First, we would get pizza together because I love pizza more than most things in life." A knowing smile slowly spreads across his face. "Then, I don't know. For a *perfect* first date, I guess there'd be some sort of gesture. It doesn't need to be grand, but it needs to be something sweet and romantic that shows he put some thought into the date and knows me well enough to come up with something I'd enjoy."

Andrew's deep blue eyes meet mine, and I swear I see something in them. There's a soft light like he's happy in this moment, and maybe, just maybe, there's a hint of something else behind those eyes.

Andrew checks the clock on his phone. "My mom should be here any minute. Let me call her to get an ETA."

He steps off for a moment to talk on the phone, and I reflect on our conversation. *Was it obvious I was talking about my feelings for him? No, because I don't feel that way about Andrew. We are just friends. How do I interpret his response? Is that just Andrew being his sweet self, or is Andrew giving me a hint?*

He returns and grabs my book bag. "Are you ready to go? She said she will meet us outside the bookstore in two minutes."

I take the last bite of my ice cream and toss my bowl in the trash. "I don't think I'll ever be ready to leave this place."

He laughs and slings an arm casually around my shoulder, walking us to meet his mom.

CHAPTER 11

Summer 19

"Emma!" Rebecca shrieks as she runs toward me for a hug. She wraps me up when she reaches me. I'm filled with such happiness to be back with one of my people. How am I here with her right now? I'm in shock. Before I can process what is happening any further, I'm bombarded with questions.

"How's collegiate running going, Emma? Are you showing everyone who's boss? I'm sure you're already traveling to the conference meet and regionals, just like you planned to. Are you still going to do the mud race this summer? I know I can't do it with you anymore" —she laughs, as if her death is just a minor inconvenience—"but you should still do it."

I sigh. "It won't be the same if I do it alone."

"Get my brother to do it with you! He needs something to do this summer, and you already know he said he'd do anything for you." She wiggles her eyebrows. "Speaking of my brother, you guys need to figure your shit out. You guys were so close to getting together last summer. I may not have heard his side of the story, but don't think for a second I didn't notice how smiley he suddenly was too. Not to mention the fact that Andrew was pretty much holding your hand in the UTV. That's right! I see everything."

I shudder at the memory of that day. Some good things happened between Andrew and me, but those quickly became a moot point after the accident.

"It's not that simple, Becs. So much has happened since then. We went nine months without speaking to one another."

"Emma." She pins me with one of her knowing looks. "You have both been in love with each other forever. It's been so painfully obvious watching the two of you, especially over the last couple of years."

"Clearly, you're wrong because a couple of years ago, Andrew was dating Angelina."

"No, don't bring her into this. That relationship was bullshit, and you know it. You guys were so close, and it's driving me crazy." She grabs both of my shoulders, forcing me to look her in the eye. "Figure it out already! You've both agreed you want to live your lives. Do you think skirting around how you feel and pretending to just be friends is living?"

She begins to step back. Little by little, she disappears into a cloud of nothing. I reach out for her. I'm not ready for her to go. We aren't done talking about this. I'm not done spending time with my best friend. I need her!

I awake with a jolt. Shooting upright, I throw my head into my palms and groan. I roll out of bed and get dressed in my bathing suit. As much as I want to go for a run again this morning to process everything that just happened in my dream, I know I'm going to have to settle for a swim in the lake. I haven't run in so long; I need to give my body time to recover. Running is a very high-impact sport and just throwing myself back into it as if I've still been running 40+ mile weeks this whole time would be a stupid idea, so I'll settle for the next best thing, swimming.

I rifle through the linen closet for a towel and walk out to the dock, thinking about what I'm going to do with my day. I'm not working this summer. My parents insisted I spend another summer at the lake with my family while I'm still young enough to have the flexibility to do so. They didn't have the heart to tell it to my grieving face, but I know they also think I'd benefit from spending the summer facing my loss rather than burying myself in work.

I was worried at first about falling behind, but the company I worked for during the school year encouraged me to take some time off. They even told me they'd welcome me back with open arms, come next fall, which was very reassuring.

I reach the end of the dock, toss my towel aside, and dive into the cool lake. The rush of the water fills my ears as I submerge my body, and it's a good feeling. It drowns out my thoughts for at least a moment, but as I resurface, everything comes rushing back. I don't even know what to think of my dream. I feel so overwhelmed. *Maybe if I break it down?*

Okay, the first thing she talked about was my running. That's an easy one. I've already given up my place on the team along with my scholarship. I've taken way too long off from running, let alone training. There's next to no chance of me ever coming back to running at the collegiate level. Oddly enough, I feel at peace with that.

I do want to get back to running for the joy of it though. There was a point when I genuinely loved the feeling. I want to get back to running just because it makes me happy. I can work on that this summer.

What else did she say? She told me to do the mud run this summer with Andrew. I could probably convince him to do that with me. Piece of cake! He already said he would run with me this summer, and the mud run is a pretty relaxed race. It's not like I'm going to be out there trying to get a personal best. If I tell him it's something Rebecca and I had been planning on doing, he will absolutely do it with me.

That's solved...well minus talking to Andrew, but I can do that later. *This is easy. I don't know why the dream made me feel so upset earlier.*

I reach the dock about ten houses down and decide to turn around. *The last thing she mentioned... oh. She was talking about Andrew and me.* My stomach flips at the thought of the events that played out the afternoon of Rebecca's accident. I shake it off and focus on what exactly Rebecca said. There was something about how we were so close and pretending to just be friends wasn't living life like we said we were going to do from here on out. Maybe I agree, but it's not like I have the first clue how to change our situation.

Things are so complicated. We just started talking again. Maybe it feels like no time has passed without us talking, but it doesn't erase the past nine months. Nor does it erase the past however many years we teetered on the edge of friends and something more but couldn't make the leap. Maybe Andrew and I aren't meant to be.

I reach my dock and set my elbows on the edge, resting my chin on my forearms as I catch my breath. I can't bring myself to get out of the water just yet and face the shiver that will come with the feeling of the cool morning air on my skin.

I grab my phone, which is resting on my towel, to check the time. It's just after eight. I've been out here longer than I thought. I mentally pat myself on the back for being in better shape than I realized. Then I notice the text.

ANDREW

Hey Em! You up?

I scroll to the next text, also from Andrew.

Sorry! That didn't sound how I meant it to. I was just going to come over and chat with you if you were awake...

I laugh a little as my thumbs start typing.

ME

> Yes I'm up. You can come over in 20. I just finished swimming. Need to shower and eat.

I drag myself out of the water, and, sure enough, the air hits my body, causing me to start shivering. Goose bumps cover my arms and legs as I bend over to grab my towel.

Andrew saunters down the dock. Surely my eyes are deceiving me because it looks like he just gave me the elevator look. You know, when someone starts looking at your face and then that gaze travels down your body? That's the look he just gave me. His throat bobs, and I know I wasn't imagining things. I quickly pull my towel around myself to cover up, blushing a little.

"Hey! I just texted you back. Let me go shower and then we can talk while I eat."

"Yeah, I saw your text, but then I saw you on the dock and thought I'd just catch you before your shower." There's still a heat behind his eyes that makes me want to bury my face in my hands. I'm not used to getting those kinds of looks from anyone, let alone Andrew.

I shudder as a bout of chills slither up my body. "Will it be quick? I have about two more minutes before my teeth start chattering and maybe three minutes before I get hypothermia."

He laughs smoothly and pulls my towel-wrapped body into his arms, rubbing my shoulders quickly to warm me. "I was thinking we could head into town today and hit the bookstore. Maybe we could grab some ice cream afterward?" For old time's sake?" He raises his eyebrows enticingly. "I know you just went to the bookstore, and I just got a new book, but I love to look." He quickly adds, "Plus, it'd give us a chance to make a plan for what we are going to do this summer to, you know, live our lives to the fullest or whatever." There's a hint of sarcasm in his voice but it's clear he's using it to keep from being too vulnerable.

"Sure, that sounds great!" I shiver again. "When were you planning on heading out?"

He squeezes me tighter. "Go shower before you freeze to death. You can text me when you're ready, and I'll drive us."

I nod in agreement and break free from his embrace. I immediately feel the tension break when I'm out of his arms. My mind may know that Andrew and I have been apart for a while and need some time to get back to where we were, but my body certainly doesn't.

"I'll text you," I say as I begin walking down the dock. He just stands there, watching me walk away.

Sitting outside the ice cream shop, Andrew has a double scoop in a cone with mint cookie and huckleberry, an odd combination to me, but they're two of his favorites. The huckleberry is a seasonal flavor only offered when the huckleberries are at their peak, and the mint cookie is supposedly the best mint he's ever had with "the most natural mint flavor I've ever tasted." I took a lick off his cone to taste it, and he's not wrong.

I spoon a bite off the top of my double scoop in a bowl. I savor the chocolate cherry chunk, before asking, "How was track this year?"

"I qualified for Nationals in the triple jump."

"Andrew, that's incredible!"

"And then I burst into flames at the actual meet. I did te*rrible*." He draws out the last word for emphasis.

"It's still impressive you made it that far, especially as a freshman."

He nods in acknowledgment.

I twirl my spoon around a couple of times before actually

taking a bite. When I finally swallow my ice cream, Andrew remains silent, leaving me nothing but room to ask what is really on my mind. "What made you decide to take me here today?"

He pauses, mid-lick. After a beat, he continues and then holds his cone down lower as he responds. "I just wanted a normal day with you again. Everything has been so heavy lately, and I've missed the bookstore and this heaven." He holds his ice cream up in the air to show me.

I chuckle. "Yeah, I've missed everything being simple too."

For some reason, the memory of my dream comes floating back. I still need to ask Andrew about doing the mud run with me. "Not to ruin it, but I had this dream last night, and it got me thinking."

He raises his brows with amusement and sits back on the bench, watching my face. "You had a dream that has been making you think? This should be good."

I shove his shoulder. "Oh, stop it, Andrew. I'm being serious!"

He holds his hands up in surrender. "I'm just teasing you. I'm listening. You know I'll always listen when you need me to."

"I do know." I start on my second scoop of ice cream, chocolate peanut butter brownie, loaded with fudge, peanut butter swirls, and big brownie globs. "Anyway, I remembered Rebecca and I were supposed to do a mud run this summer. It's not until mid-August, so there's still plenty of time before it." Avoiding his piercing gaze, and feeling vulnerable, I lower my voice a decibel. "I was hoping you'd do it with me since Rebecca can't anymore. I know you already said you'd be willing to run with me this summer, and you said you'd help me figure out how to start living my life again, so I thought maybe—"

Andrew cuts me off. "I'd love to do it with you, Em."

I smile. "Really? Are you sure?"

Andrew is nodding his head vigorously. "Of course! It's obviously important to you, and the fact that you still want to do it is huge. I'm definitely going to support that!"

"Thank you." I reach over to touch his arm, squeezing. He twists his arm around to grab my hand. He holds it for longer than expected. His touch sends an electric charge up my arm and through the rest of my body, resulting in a pink blush on my cheeks. Surely, he notices. I shy away, taking my hand back to scoop more of my ice cream. "It's melting."

He clears his throat and redirects the conversation. "Is there anything else you had in mind to do this summer so we can *really* live our lives to the fullest?" A smile cracks wide on his face.

I think of Rebecca's words from earlier. *I should ask him to take me on a date, or I should just lean in for a kiss. Maybe I should just lay out all of my feelings on the table for him and eliminate the confusion sitting between us.* We were so close before, like Rebecca said. Except that wasn't Rebecca. It was just a version of her that my subconscious made up. *Doesn't that still mean that's what I want to do, what I should do?* The little devil on my shoulder asks. She's a pesky little thing.

"Em?" Andrew looks at me closely. "Did I lose you?"

I shake my head a little, trying to understand what he's talking about. When my focus comes back, I mutter, "Sorry, I was just thinking more about that dream I told you about."

"Oh, were there other things it inspired you to do?"

"It was just a dream." I sigh. "I can't put too much weight into it."

He nods in approval, but I can't help but notice the look of disappointment that crosses his face too. "Were there any non-dream-inspired things you wanted to do?"

I relax, thankful for the change of subject. After thinking for a minute or two though, I come up blank. "I have no idea! I don't know what I want to do."

He pats my leg. "That's okay. Living life to the fullest doesn't have to be about the big things. I think it can be as simple as being open to new opportunities and taking them when you get them." He grows surer of what he's saying as he continues. "Maybe you drive past a restaurant every day that you've never tried but always wanted to. Now you make the time to try it. You've always wanted to try Krav Maga? Now you sign up for a class."

"I don't think I'm interested in Krav Maga."

"You get my point," he says with a light-hearted chuckle.

"I do. Did you have anything in mind that you'd like to do?"

He holds my gaze. I can feel his eyes assessing me. He's trying to stay nonchalant, but I can tell there's more going on beneath the surface than he's letting on.

"I think there's some life to be lived in spontaneity. Guess you'll just have to wait and see." His smirk that follows makes me melt faster than my ice cream in this sweltering summer heat.

"No fair! I told you something on my list!"

"You didn't *have* to do that."

"You asked me to!" I give him a teasing nudge.

"Should we head back?" He pulls out the keys to his truck, completely ignoring my irritation.

"Yeah, I guess we can do that."

CHAPTER 12

Summer 19

"What about a kangaroo?" I ask.

"I'd like to think I'd be something less basic than a kangaroo. Do I look like a kangaroo to you?" Andrew glances at me from his spot in the driver's seat, sees my face, and frowns. "Don't answer that."

I burst into laughter. "Alright, fine. You don't look like a kangaroo." I continue scrolling through a list of animals that jump. "What about…Oh, a klipspringer! It says they're five feet tall and can jump up to ten times their height! That's so cool. And look how cute they are!" I hold my phone out to him.

He stirs in his seat. "It looks small. I'm 6'3. I deserve a bigger animal than that!" He huffs.

"You came up with this game. We could've sat in silence as we drove home from the store, but you insisted we figure out what animals we would be."

"Well, I guess my game was stupid." Andrew's tone is annoyed but one look at his face indicates he's having just as much fun as I am. It's been a week since our trip to the bookstore, and we have quickly reverted to our old ways, laughing and teasing. The thought builds a soft warmth in my chest.

As I read the next animal from the list of jumping animals on my phone, I can't help but break the silence. "How about a kangaroo rat? They're even cuter than the klipspringer and can jump forty-five times their own body length, making them the strongest mammals relative to their body size."

"Why do I have to be something cute? Can't I be like a jungle cat? They're strong and agile. I'd like to think I'd be something like that."

I reach over and pinch one of his cheeks teasingly. "But Andrew, you are cute like this little guy." I hold up the photo of the kangaroo rat. "You don't look or act intimidating like a jungle cat. When I first met you, you were looking all sweet and innocent playing with one of the neighbors. Every time you open your mouth, your words ooze sweetness."

He looks appalled. "See, I know it's a compliment to say I'm nice, but I can't help but feel like that was meant to be an insult."

"No, it *was* a compliment," I clarify. "You're a nice guy, Andrew. I like nice guys. That's why we hang out."

He seems to be reflecting on my words and what they mean when I hear the song playing on the radio. "Andrew, turn it up!" I shriek in excitement as I reach over to turn the volume up myself.

"Why even bother asking me to turn it up if you're just going to do it yourself?" Amusement spreads across his face.

"Shhhh! Listen. Rebecca showed me this song last summer, and I love it. It's such a cute story."

I watch him glance at the song title across his screen. It's "Porch Swing Angel" by Muscadine Bloodline. "Who the hell is Muscadine Bloodline?"

I roll my eyes. "They sing 'Can't Tell You No' and 'Me on You.' They're not super big. Now shut up and listen, the good part is coming up, and it sets up the whole story."

Right as I finish, I hear the last words of the intro and the first verse begins.

I get lost in the lyrics. It's like this song was made for me. It perfectly describes how I feel about Andrew. The lyrics perfectly explain the fear and the aching need to put an end to the charade and be honest about how I feel. That's a big part of why I've always enjoyed books. They have the power to turn these abstract thoughts and feelings I experience into words. Rebecca has shown me over the years how music has that power too, and I've been thankful for that gift she has given me because I can't imagine my life without music now.

The chorus repeats to end the song, and Andrew's gaze meets mine and lingers.

"Rebecca showed you that song? It doesn't seem like her style." He chuckles to himself. "One time she lectured me on how this total hardcore metal song had a really deep meaning. I couldn't get past the first ten seconds of screaming to get anything out of it."

I burst into a fit of laughter. "Andrew," I pause, "you didn't know?"

He gives me a puzzled look. "Know what?"

"She was totally pulling your leg! She told me all about that during one of our Facetimes. I defended you! I insisted you knew it was a joke and were just messing with her right back, but I guess I was wrong." I shut my mouth for one moment and then burst out laughing again at the thought of Andrew concentrating on the song and trying to find meaning.

"Hey now! You can be pretty naïve too."

I lean into him teasingly. "Please enlighten me on how *I've* been naïve."

He straightens up in his seat and his voice goes up an octave. "Oh, there have been so many times!"

"Okay, then tell me about them."

"How about the time Rebecca and I convinced you we were going to get you a snake for your birthday? You were having an absolute meltdown at the thought of us shipping this snake to you and you being stuck with something that clearly would've freaked you out."

I shrug. "That's one. Good job. Way to highlight the *many* times I've been naïve." I give him a cocky smirk and throw in a slow clap for good measure.

His next words burst back. "How about every time you've believed we are just friends?"

I freeze, and I see him pale a little as he pulls off the road. *What is he talking about? What is he doing? Why are we pulling off the road?* It's then that I realize I don't even recognize where we are. We didn't go back the normal way. We should've been pulling into his driveway by now. I peer out the window, squinting in the early afternoon sun. "Andrew, what...where... what are we doing?"

He leaps out of his truck and comes around, opening the door for me. He grabs my hand to help me step down and closes the passenger door behind me. He locks the truck and starts walking up the path hidden amongst the bushes. The trail looks like it hasn't been used in ages. There are inklings of new growth in the dirt, and the branches from the bushes on either side grow across it. To add to its sketchy nature, the trail has a very steep incline.

"Andrew!" I stay close behind him, trying to grab his shirt so he will stop and talk with me. Not only does he owe me an explanation of what is going on right now, but he owes me an explanation of what he said a moment ago in the truck.

I finally get close enough to grab his arm. I tug him back, and he stops. "Where on earth do you think we are going?" I ask. "This is exactly how people get killed in horror films."

"No, it's not." He swats his hand at me. "There's still plenty of hours of daylight left. If this were a horror movie, it'd be pitch black out right now. We are perfectly safe."

He tries to spin around, but I grab him again. "Oh no you don't! You need to tell me what you think you're doing."

"*We* are going up this trail because I've always wondered where it leads to. Then we will see what happens."

My eyes grow huge at his nonchalant response. "What?"

He grabs my hand and starts leading me up. For some reason, I follow him. Clearly, my brain has turned to mush since his comment earlier about believing we are just friends. That's the only logical explanation for why I continue to follow him.

"You remember what I said a week ago about living part of your life spontaneously?" He doesn't wait for me to respond. "This is me trying to do that. I took Angie for a drive around the lake two summers ago, and I saw this trail. It was a lot more prominent back then, but I knew she wouldn't get out of the truck to check it out with me, so we didn't. Ever since then, I've wondered what we missed out on. It could be absolutely nothing, but I might as well go for it. Rebecca would've."

"Okay, let's go see it," I say, sounding much calmer and more confident than I feel. I'm still reeling over his remark in the truck earlier, trying to understand, but the moment has passed and we are focused on being spontaneous right now, which, surprisingly, I think I can get behind.

We quickly find the path only grows steeper. We practically have to rock climb to get up the darn thing. Andrew helps, following me and supporting me as I go up. At the top, it opens to a grassy patch, shrouded by trees in every direction. I can't help but feel disappointed. There's nothing here.

"This can't be it," Andrew insists.

I look around. "I think it is, Andrew. It's okay, you were still being spontaneous, even if it didn't go as planned." The look of disappointment on his face makes me want to wrap him up in my arms. He looks like a little kid who dropped his ice cream cone.

He wanders into the trees. I just watch him as he explores, but then he disappears. Growing paranoid, I quickly jog over to where I saw him enter the trees.

"Em, you've gotta come see this!" I hear him shout somewhere from the depths of the trees.

"Where'd you go? I don't like this. What if we get lost?"

"Then it'll be so worth it." He walks back my way to come get me. Once he knows I see him, he turns around again. "This way."

I follow him through the trees and reach another ledge. This one has a much better view than the grassy patch we just found. I take in the water below us, glistening in the afternoon sun. "You can see the whole lake from here. Where are we?"

"I think we are on the south side of the lake." He points off toward a cell tower. "We camped near there two summers ago."

I take it all in. This is incredible. This has to be the highest point on the lake. "It's too bad you didn't take Angie here. It would've been so romantic."

He nods. "Yeah, it is." I note his use of the present tense. I'm analyzing every word he says right now. "Do you think we can get down to the water from here? It's calling my name. It's so damn hot out." He begins fanning himself.

"We did just climb up a giant hill."

He starts scoping out the drop-off. "Oh yeah, we can totally get down there. Come on! It'll be fun."

Again, I don't know why, but I follow him.

It's easier to go down than it was to come up here. We have to scoot down on our butts a bit, but we make it to the water in just a couple of minutes.

Andrew immediately pulls his shirt off at the bottom and kicks off his shoes.

"What're you doing?" I blink my eyes in shock.

"What does it look like I'm doing?"

I look him up and down. "It looks like you've gone temporarily insane."

"Ha ha." He deadpans. "Are you coming?"

I shrug. "I think there's a flaw in your genius spontaneity plan. I don't have a swimsuit."

The smile on his face is immediately erased as the realization hits him. I can practically see the wheels turning in his head. "We didn't come all the way down here not to swim. I have a solution if you're up for it."

"Sure." I eye him skeptically.

"A 'sure' is binding under these circumstances." He mutters quickly.

"Wha—"

Before I can get off another question, Andrew launches into his solution. "You can just skinny dip. I'll do it with you if it makes you feel better!" He takes a look at the skepticism on my face. "There's no one here to see; the closest house is at least a half mile away."

"The nearest house may be far enough, but there's still another person awfully close by."

"Where?" Andrew begins looking out at the water for a boat or a swimmer.

I throw my hands out in front of me to gesture to him. "You, silly!"

"Oh, come on, Em! I won't look. You know that. You'd do it with Rebecca, right? What's the difference? You and I have been friends for just as long."

I note his use of the word 'friends.' This boy couldn't be more confusing, remarking on how I'm naïve to think we are just friends but then labeling us as friends fifteen minutes later.

"There's a huge difference, and you know it."

"Well, I'm going in. Feel free to join me if you'd like, or don't." He slips his thumbs into the waistband of his shorts, turning around. "I suggest you don't look." I don't even have to see his face to know he's baring that cheeky grin of his.

I quickly turn away and hear the sound of shorts drop, followed by pounding footsteps and a splash as he leaps into the water. I turn back to inspect the scene and find both his shorts and briefs sitting on the rock in front of me. He must've jumped off from there instead of climbing the rest of the way down to the sand, which surely would be a hard task without clothes for protection.

He treads water for a bit and then leans back a little with his hands behind his head. All I can see are his shoulders and bare chest, nothing I haven't seen before. "The water feels fantastic! Hurry up and get in!"

A twinge of a smile crosses my face. "Since when were you so much like your sister?" A mixture of love and sadness whirl inside of me at the thought. We were having such a good day until I had to go and miss Rebecca.

"This is what we said we were going to do," he explains, as if it's that simple to just suddenly throw caution to the wind and be spontaneous. "Someone had to do it, or our summer would be so boring."

"Hey, I like going to the bookstore and getting ice cream with you. And we still *would* go swimming."

He nods, agreeing. "I enjoy it too, but there's something about this that makes me feel so free. I can't believe I'm doing this because it's way out of my comfort zone, but I'm proud of myself for doing it anyway."

His words settle in, and I groan, realizing he's convincing me to do this. But I'm not doing this because of my feelings for Andrew or because I give in to peer pressure easily. I'm doing this because I know Rebecca would've loved it, and I trust Andrew whole-heartedly. Without Rebecca, he truly is my best friend, and I know I won't regret making another outrageous memory with him.

"Turn around!" I shout to him.

A huge smile cracks across his face, and he spins around swiftly. I tug my shirt and shorts off first. Then I unclasp my bra, using one hand to cover my top half while I slip my panties off with the other. I get a running start off the rock and dive in.

My head rises out of the water, and as I wipe the lake from my eyes, I find Andrew sitting about three feet away from me. "What're you doing? Don't get so close. If we are going to do this, we need ground rules!"

He laughs. "Relax, Em. I won't come any closer, and I can't see anything from here."

I peer over at him, testing to see if I can see anything too. Nope. My shoulders relax a little. "So, I'm in the water, now what?"

He splashes me. "Loosen up a little and enjoy the moment."

I scoop water into my hands and splash him right back. He pulls away. "You did *not* just do that!" A menacing smile crosses his face.

"You started it!"

I watch him wind up as he splashes me with twice as much vigor this time. I shriek and turn my head away, but the blow fills me with determination. I swoosh over toward him, reaching out to dunk him under. His eyes grow wide. "Okay! Okay! Let's call a truce. I can't properly defend myself when we're like this."

It's then that I remember we are both completely naked. I wrap my arm across my chest and back away. "I'm sorry."

On instinct, he comes a little closer to comfort me in my timid embarrassment, but he catches himself and stops. "It's okay." A grin creeps onto his face. "Most guys wouldn't complain about being in this situation, myself included," he admits. "But I'm a gentleman, so I have to draw the line somewhere."

His words sink in, and I can't help but be reminded of his earlier remark about us being more than friends. I'm reminded of the look he gave me while we listened to "Porch Swing Angel" and Rebecca's chiding in my dream a week ago. I think

about the moments we shared last summer when I was so sure
we were headed in the exact direction I've always wanted to.
The air is charged with electricity, and the words I say next just
slip out. "Andrew, can I ask you something?"

"Anything."

"What are we?"

CHAPTER 13

Summer 16

"Where the hell are you taking us, Rebecca?" Andrew leans forward from the back seat with a look of concern on his face.

I don't entirely blame him. We never come to this part of town, and as much as I love and trust Rebecca, she can still make some questionable decisions.

"I already told you guys it's a surprise," she insists, turning up the radio. "Just sit back and relax. You too, Emma. I can feel the tension in your body from over here." She laughs.

I glare at her and subtly try to let my shoulders relax, not wanting to validate her remark.

Suddenly, Rebecca flicks her blinker on and pulls into a dirt parking lot. There's not much here except for a few stands. One is for freshly grown cherries. The other is for fireworks. I immediately put two and two together. "Are fireworks legal here?"

"Nope," Rebecca and Andrew say in unison, Rebecca with a little more excitement and Andrew with a little more irritation.

"Everyone here does them anyway. No one gets in trouble for them. I think they'd be fun! You saw that family doing

Roman candles off their dock last year. Those kids must've been what, eight? If they can do it, we can do it!"

Andrew and I exchange a glance. With his shrug and small smirk, I get the message loud and clear. *This could be fun. There's no sense in arguing with her when she's already put her mind to it.*

I shake my head. "Can we at least get some of the big ones too? I don't just want those tiny ones that sound like a car backfiring."

At my acceptance, Rebecca's face completely lights up. "Absolutely! We can get whatever you want, within reason. I *am* on a budget here."

I laugh. "I think that's reasonable. I can chip in too. It doesn't have to be all on you."

She flicks the back of her hand at me as if shooing a fly. "Nonsense. This is my treat! We needed to mix up our Fourth of July routine."

"What routine?" Andrew asks.

"Exactly! We don't do anything special because we're already at the lake, and we don't need to go anywhere to see fireworks. It's time we start doing something fun on our own terms."

"Do you think your parents will be okay with this, Becs?"

We shuffle out of the car. "Are you kidding? My dad will love this!" Andrew interjects. "And mom will act disapproving, but the second we ask if she wants to set one off, she will be running over with glee like a kid in a candy store."

Somehow this all reassures me. "Well, I'm new to picking out fireworks, so how does it work?"

I see Andrew's and Rebecca's faces falter. Clearly, neither of them know either. Rebecca recovers quicker and approaches the gentleman at the stand.

"Here to buy some fireworks?" he asks eagerly. "You're lucky you came early enough. My stock will be completely out in another hour. What can I get started for you?"

Rebecca assesses the fireworks carefully and begins whispering with Andrew and me about which ones to get. She's immediately drawn to one in a box that is called Danger and Doom, apparently a specialty made just for this stand. All it takes is me showing her the price tag on the side of the box to persuade her those may not be the right fit for us.

"How about three Roman candles and a few bigger fireworks? How much will that set us back?"

He begins punching in numbers on a calculator and holds it out to her. I can't see the number properly with the glare of the sun, but I'm fairly certain it's in the triple digits.

She shrugs. "Throw in two more big ones then, and I think we should be set."

I quickly elbow her. "Since when were you made of money?"

"I think you've forgotten I spent all school year working at the country club. I served a lot of old people who were *very* generous with their tips, so I can afford to splurge a little bit this summer on fireworks." Seeing the weary look on my face, she adds, "I've already thought about this, Emma. It's what I want to do. Get out of your head, and let's have some fun tonight." She squeezes my shoulder.

I nod silently.

Andrew and the man at the stand begin loading up a box full of fireworks and carry it to Rebecca's trunk as she pops it open for them with the click of a button.

"That's a lot of fireworks," I say.

There's a scary look in her eyes as she replies, "Hell yeah! This is going to be awesome!"

"Settle down there, Pyro!"

Her mouth drops open, mocking insult, but I can tell I might not have been too far off. She looks *way* too excited about setting fire to these things and watching them explode.

~

It's kind of funny. One of my favorite parts about summer has always been how long the days are. At summer's peak, it doesn't even get dark until almost 10 pm, but on the Fourth of July, I've grown to resent the long days because they mean we have to wait that much longer to see fireworks. I should be grateful I get to spend my summers somewhere where the days nearly never end, but today I just don't have the patience to count my blessings.

"Someone check what time the sunset is. It's gotta be soon, right?"

I look between Andrew and Rebecca. Rebecca is on it. She's almost definitely more excited than me. I'm just excited to be surrounded by fireworks on all sides, but she is excited to light them off. I think I could do without our own fireworks. Naturally, I'm feeling a little uneasy about the whole thing, but seeing how ecstatic Rebecca is, I don't want to share that thought and bring her down.

"It says the sun should be setting in ten minutes," Rebecca answers. "I'd imagine it will get dark pretty quickly after that. Maybe we should start to build a game plan. What do we want to set off first?"

Andrew eagerly pitches in, "Best for last, always. We can start with the Roman Candles. One for each of us, right?" He doesn't wait for an answer before continuing. Andrew is in his element. He's always been good at planning things, which is a good balance for Rebecca who can be so chaotic and heat of the moment. "Then how many big fireworks do we have? I'm sure Mom and Dad will each want to set one off. Em, do you think Dani or your parents will want to get involved?"

"Definitely not Dani. My dad might if there's enough."

Andrew begins digging around in the box that's currently holding the fireworks on the Martins' beach. I watch him carefully count out the fireworks. "Looks like there will be enough for your dad to do one and still have one left over."

"I'll take one for the team and set off two of the big ones," Rebecca says, smirking devilishly.

"Yeah, that's just what you need, Pyro." Andrew rolls his eyes. "I'll do a second instead. I'm more experienced."

"Since when?" she challenges. "When have you ever set off fireworks?"

"Uhhh do you not remember Brendan's New Year's Eve party last year? He and I put on quite the show."

Rebecca crosses her arms, trying not to admit defeat. "So let your sister get some experience instead of hogging it. How else am I going to learn, Andy?"

I place my hand over my mouth, desperately trying to hide the smile that is spreading across my face right now. I love watching the twins fight. They are such a great match for one another. Between Rebecca's sass and Andrew's matter-of-fact tone, they are quite amusing to watch. I try to stay neutral, but when push comes to shove, I always pick Rebecca's side, even when she's wrong ninety-percent of the time. It's just how the girl code works, and I know without a shadow of a doubt that she'd do the same for me without even thinking about it.

"Maybe we should just let Emma do it. She *is* our guest, and she should get a say in the matter too," Andrew offers, turning toward me with raised brows.

"I don't know that I'd call myself a guest. I live next door three months out of the year," I correct, unsure why that matters. "I think I'm good though. One of you can have it."

"That'll be me!" Rebecca shouts.

Before Andrew can object, a firework explodes on the other side of the lake. We see the vibrant green light before we hear the bang a couple of seconds later. Just like that, the argument is over because it's time for the moment we've been waiting for.

Two more fireworks go off to our right and sparklers get lit a few beaches down from us. It's incredible.

I take a moment to just bask in the colors and sounds. One

firework shoots up, exploding with blue and then crackling in gold. I practically shiver at the sound. It's my favorite type of firework.

Andrew grabs the Roman candles out of the box, handing Rebecca one, and then turning toward me. "Ready?"

I shake my head. "I think I'll watch first."

Rebecca immediately pulls a lighter out of her back pocket as she heads closer to the water, eager as ever to set her firework off.

"Okay, seriously, you're only proving us right about the whole pyromaniac thing," I chuckle after her.

She rolls her eyes and shrugs. "I'm just being prepared."

With the Roman candle firmly in one hand, Rebecca lights the fuse with her other. There's a moment of silence as we all hold our breath and wait for it to go off. With a small kick, the first firework shoots up into the air. A tiny, shimmery red firework bursts open, shattering the darkness. A blue, yellow, green, and another red follow after.

When it's over, Rebecca calmly sets the Roman candle down near the water and dusts her hands off. "I'm ready for my next one."

What a badass, I can't help but think to myself. Our parents waltz out to the deck and come down to the beach, Dani in tow. While Andrew prepares to set off his Roman candle, I can see a glimmer in the eyes of my dad and Mr. Martin. They totally want to get in on this. I, on the other hand, am still content to just watch the show.

As Andrew's third firework goes off with a bang, Mr. Martin begins moving toward the box of goodies we brought home today. I watch him assess the box in the same manner I inspect all the flavors in an ice cream shop. He wiggles his fingers and dives into the box, coming up with one of the bigger fireworks.

"Stand back, kids! Let me show you how it's done."

He sets this firework down in a stand on the beach and

lights fire to the fuse. I see a small light fizzle up into the tube and then the firework shoots up with much more force than the Roman candles. It's a little startling. But with a bang louder than a gunshot, the firework makes everyone go still in awe. It's huge. I've never seen a firework so big. It must span the entire length of the Martin's beach and then some. It's fantastic!

"That. Was. Awesome!" Rebecca shouts, running back to the box to dig out another firework like Mr. Martin's. My dad is immediately in tow, and Andrew takes the two steps required to reach the box as well. It's a frenzy.

Fireworks are exploding on all sides of the lake, filling the air with snaps, crackles, and pops. It's just like we are in a giant bowl of Rice Krispies.

The next ten minutes fly by, and we are down to only a few fireworks left, but I have yet to set one off. Part of me is curious. I see the thrill in everyone else's eyes, and I want to be a part of that, but an even louder part of me is picturing me running away from the fireworks with my clothes set aflame and the Martins' dock going up in smoke. I know it may be crazy, but my creative brain can't decipher between what's realistic and what isn't.

Rebecca comes back from setting off another Roman candle. "Emma, are you going to take a turn?"

I shrug. "I'm not sure. It's been plenty fun watching all of you, though."

Rebecca moves in closer to me. "Come on. You should give it a try. Just one. Whichever one you want."

I give her a cautious smile. "I don't want to set myself on fire."

At that moment, Andrew joins the conversation. "You won't set yourself on fire. If it was possible, Rebecca would've managed to do it by now."

"Shut up!" she says with breathless laughter.

I can't help but laugh too. "I think I'm good to just watch. Thanks, guys."

Although I can see the disappointment on Rebecca's face, she doesn't push me too much more.

Mrs. Martin steps up to the edge of the beach with one of the big kahunas in hand.

I marvel at her bravery as she casually lights the firework in the stand and then immediately hobbles out of the way, shrieking with joy.

Mrs. Martin is doing it for goodness' sake! This one explodes not once, but twice, with a blend of colors unlike any firework I've ever seen, and I can't help but be amazed we picked these up from some stand on the side of the road. It's as that amazement fills my body that I realize I *have* to do this. I don't want to miss out on all of this! As if Rebecca is thinking the same thing, she turns to me and asks one more time, "You sure you don't want to light one?"

"I think I do," I whisper back, as if saying it too loud will set me ablaze on the spot.

She links arms with me and practically skips to the box. There's one firework left. "Looks like you don't get a choice, but I have a feeling this is going to be a good one."

I chuckle and shake my head, following her to the stand. Andrew joins us, eager to be a part of the action. "Nice, Em! You're going to set one off?"

I nod and give him a nervous smile. "I guess so. What do I need to do?"

"It's super simple. You'll set the firework in the stand this way." He shows me the bottom where the fuse is and how it needs to be sitting to get lit and set off properly. "Then you'll pretty much light this bad boy and stand back to enjoy it in all its glory."

"You guys better take a few steps back," I say, taking the lighter from Rebecca.

They follow my orders and I take a deep breath before setting the tube in the stand and flicking the flame on the lighter. The second it hits the tube, I turn and run as fast as I possibly can.

In those two seconds, I hear all the adults cheering and Rebecca whooping, but I can't help it as my eyes zero in on Andrew's beaming face as he shouts, "That's my girl!"

When I reach where Andrew and Rebecca are, I turn just in time to see the last of its flight before the firework shimmers to life. I swear I feel the ground shake with this one. It's beautiful and exhilarating, and I *cannot* believe I just did that. It's something so simple, and probably lame to almost anyone else, but I feel proud of myself. I almost missed out on this experience, and all the wonderful feelings that come with it, because I was too afraid.

As the smoke clears away, Rebecca elbows me and lifts her phone for me to see. "Check this out." She hits play, and I watch myself light the firework and run away, squealing with glee, just like everyone else did. Before the camera quickly turns to the sky to catch the spectacular colors contrasting against the black night, I hear Andrew yelling at me and see the look in my eyes as I gaze back at him.

I hope and pray he didn't notice that look, and that he doesn't now as he watches over my shoulder. *Wait? What am I afraid of? Him seeing me look at him like a friend? I'm just excited and wanted to share that excitement with him because he was the one who instructed me on how to do this. That's it.*

"Send that to me, please."

Rebecca nods and presses the share button, typing in my name in the send box.

That night, I watch the video at least five times before I finally close my eyes to go to sleep. As I slow it down, watching the proud look on Andrew's face, I swear I see a little blush on his cheeks.

CHAPTER 14

Summer 19

"What do you mean?" Andrew stammers. His earlier confidence is gone, and his summer tan has turned nearly ghost white.

I glide a little closer to him, looking into his eyes. "You know exactly what I mean."

His gaze shifts down nervously. I become aware of the fact that I just asked what we are to each other while we're naked in the lake with a fifteen-minute walk back to the truck and then a five-minute drive to follow. *Way to think.*

"Honestly, I don't know why you need to ask me that after all this time." He looks off at the mountains and then back at me. "I think I've been pretty obvious with how I feel. It's you that I can't figure out."

"What?" The word comes out shrill. "I think I've been pretty obvious." I laugh nervously.

"Hmmm…We both think we've been obvious, and we both think the other is confusing. Guess we have some things to work on."

"Like directly answering the question I just asked you," I remind him.

"Damn it, Em." He sounds exasperated, but he continues quickly. "You're my favorite person in the whole world. I just want to be around you all the time. When I'm with you, I forget about all the shitty things I've been through over the last year, and I'm the best version of myself. Seeing your smiling face every day is a true test of my self-control because, God, it takes everything in me not to grab you and kiss your sweet smile." He continues rambling as if he will lose the courage to say what he has to say if he takes even a second to think about it. "I've been stupid in the past, and this summer, I've tried to give you the space you need to heal. I know you've struggled with being back here. And I hope I don't have to bury my feelings to be your friend, but if I do, I will. I'll do whatever I can to keep you in my life because you mean the world to me, and it was hell without you for the last nine months. I didn't picture this being the setting of this conversation, but at least it's out there now."

Every part of my body is on fire at the sound of his words. I want to swoon right now, but if I value my life at all, and perhaps my dignity, I have to keep treading water. I want to kiss him more than anything else, but this isn't the right setting. We are skinny dipping in the deeper part of the lake for crying out loud! Instead of doing either of those things, I find myself frozen.

He likes me! How long has he felt this way? How long have we felt this way for each other and stepped around the issue because we were scared to ruin our friendship? How long would it have taken us to finally find this out if I hadn't said something to him just now?

"Em? Say something, please," Andrew implores.

I swallow. Even with him laying his feelings out like that, it's still hard to cross that threshold. It won't be easy to go back to the way things were once I do. I suppose it already won't be after Andrew's confession. I inhale and exhale. Here goes nothing.

"I feel the same way." I watch the wild smile spread across his face. Suddenly, the words I have left to say become easy. "I've felt this way about you for as long as I can remember, you idiot." I laugh. "You are this ray of sunshine in my life. I feel comfortable just being myself around you, but there's also something about being with you that makes me want to do everything I can to become an even better person. Somehow you make that so easy to do. I don't know where we go from here, but I hope there's some place for us to go because after all this time—" I stop, unsure what else to say, breathless from the combination of the last five minutes and still treading water.

"I think we can start by getting out of this water and getting our clothes back on because all I want to do right now is kiss you, but I need to get these groceries back to my mom. She's already going to whoop my ass for taking so long." He chuckles. "Besides, I'm still a gentleman." He nods toward my naked body.

A smile cracks across my face as I scooch away from him a little bit. "Who's getting out first?"

"You can go, and I'll watch from here."

My jaw drops. "What? Absolutely not! What happened to being a gentleman?"

He bursts into laughter. "I'm a gentleman, but I'm not blind. Seeing you in a bathing suit *kills* me." At the instant coloring of my cheeks, he quickly adds, "You can still go first, but I promise I will turn away."

My pounding heart settles as he promptly turns away from the shore. I find my clothes and get dressed.

Getting back to the road was no easy feat. We didn't talk much, too preoccupied with our thoughts and our attempt to make it back to the truck in one piece.

Now sitting in the passenger seat, I debate breaking the silence between us. "After both hiding our feelings for so long, I don't know what to do once they're out there. Now what?" I try to make it sound like I'm teasing, but underneath my façade, I'm panicking a little.

He peers over at me for a moment before returning his eyes to the road. "Listen, we can't let things be weird between us now. Nothing has changed because we both had the same feelings for each other before we shared them out loud."

I shake my head, agreeing. He's right. There's no reason for anything to feel different. My courage comes back. "Can I play 'Porch Swing Angel' for us again? I have it on Spotify if I can connect to your truck."

"I'd like that." He clicks a few buttons on the screen in the center of his truck. "It should be ready to connect to your Bluetooth."

I play the song, and it takes on a whole new meaning. I'm not listening to the same parts as before quite so much because I'm no longer burying my feelings for Andrew. Now, I'm hearing the parts that unravel the love story.

This song is poetry. I catch Andrew humming along, reveling in the moment as much as I am. I can't help the smile that blooms on my face at the sight of it.

The song ends, and I put on some random song from my playlist to get us through the rest of the drive. Andrew immediately twists the dial to turn the volume down.

"Hey! I was listening to that."

He smirks. "One of us needs to get a porch swing. It sounds romantic as hell."

I snort and roll my eyes. "You're such a dork."

"I'm serious," he insists. "Then we will be the perfect embodiment of that song. It can be our song."

My lips curve at the thought of us having a song together, even if it feels a little cheesy. Andrew interrupts my thoughts. "I have something to talk with you about."

I give him a weary look. "Okay."

He grabs my hand, resting on the center console. "Relax. It's nothing bad." He squeezes my hand. I realize this is a completely normal action from him, but it feels immensely different now that we have professed our feelings for one another. His hand lingers longer than normal, not letting go as he continues. "I want to take you on a date. I know we went to the bookstore and got ice cream a week ago, but I want to take you out to do something we haven't done before and be able to call it a date."

I feel the squeeze of giddiness in my chest that gradually bubbles up and shows in my face as I grin like a total idiot. "Yes…Yes, let's do that! I'd like that."

He returns my lame grin with a goofy smile of his own, as if he can't contain his joy either. He collects himself and responds. "How about tomorrow night? I'd do it tonight, but I have to be at the dinner my parents are hosting tonight. I can pick you up at five tomorrow."

"That sounds great. What'd you have in mind?"

We pull into the Martins' driveway, and he pulls out his key after killing the engine. "That, sweet Em, is for me to figure out."

I giggle. "No clue, huh?"

He walks me toward the front door of our cabin. "The problem is actually that I have too many ideas, and I have to settle for just one night's worth."

I gaze up at his beautiful blue eyes. "Play your cards right, and we can do everything you have in mind because there will be plenty of dates."

He gives me a smug look. "I already know there will be plenty. Now that we've made it this far, I'm not screwing this up. You're stuck with me."

"Oh, crap!" I tease as I open the door and take a step inside. "Thanks for a fun day, Andrew."

I reach out for his hand to give it a tight squeeze. He grabs it and pulls me in for a hug instead, and I feel myself sink into him. Despite spending an hour in the lake, he still has a clean, masculine scent to him. His body is warm and firm in all the right places. I could get used to the feeling of his strong arms wrapped around me.

We slowly peel our bodies apart, but his forehead remains pressed to mine. I can feel his warmth, and my heart is beating a thousand miles a minute. I can feel the soft puffs of his breath against my lips, and all I want to do is break the space between us, but he remains super still, and I'm careful to follow his lead.

"When I finally kiss you, it's going to be amazing. We aren't just going to kiss on your porch like some teenage cliché. I'm going to have something bigger planned for us."

His words take the wind right out of me. The combination of his lips this close to mine and his sweet words have made me forget about the most basic thing I need to live. He pulls me in for another squeeze before he finally pulls away.

He steps off my porch, heading back to his cabin. I walk into the house and head straight for my room to grab fresh clothes so I can shower. Dani is sitting on the couch, reading a magazine. Why on earth she isn't outside basking in the lovely afternoon sun is beyond me.

She peers up at me curiously. "Why are you wet? I thought you were getting groceries with Andrew?"

I run my fingers through my hair. "We did. We went for a spontaneous swim on our way back."

The look of shock on her face is priceless. "Since when were you one to be spontaneous?"

"Since now," I state, confidently storming off to my room.

I grab some running shorts and a T-shirt to put on after my shower. I have no one to impress. Andrew won't be around, and even if he were, he's seen me in running clothes countless times, and he still adores me. *Wow. Andrew feels the same way for me as I do for him. This is incredible!*

I can't wipe the smile off my face as I turn the water on and think about the fact that Andrew Martin told me how he feels about me today and is taking me out on a date tomorrow night. Rebecca would freak out if I could tell her.

That's when it hits me. The one person I want to talk about this with right now is Rebecca, and she's gone. I can't tell my best friend in the whole world about this exciting news. She spent so much time planning how to get the two of us together, and she doesn't even get to see it come to fruition.

Andrew and I both said we had cared for one another for a while before we professed our feelings, so what took us so freaking long? I'm not mad about the time Andrew and I missed together. Sure, it would be nice to have him be mine for longer, but I'm content to have found our way to each other now. However, I *am* angry at us for not getting our shit together for Rebecca. She wanted to see this happen as much as I wanted it to happen, and we took so damn long hiding our feelings because we were scared. Now, she doesn't get to be here for any of it.

At this point, I'm sobbing. I'm angry at myself, and I'm hurting for the loss of Rebecca. This should be a happy moment. I should be hugging Rebecca and giving her a play-by-play while she tells me "I told you so" right about now, but I'm not. I can't.

I get out of the shower and gain some composure while I get dressed and brush out my hair. I open the door, sniffling a little, and find Dani standing outside. She looks like she was just waiting there for me to come out.

"Sorry, did you need to use the bathroom?" I ask, wiping gently at the corners of my eyes, hoping she can't tell what I was just doing.

Dani opens her arms and wraps me up in them as if I'm a caterpillar and her arms are my cocoon. It feels good to be cared for like this. In college, I've been on my own. No one knew what I had been through right before coming to school, and my family was two hours away. Dani was even further because she's going to school out of state.

Rubbing my back, she asks, "What's going on? Are you okay?"

Just like that, the dam breaks, and I burst into tears all over again, balling in her arms.

CHAPTER 15

Summer 17

"This might be my best idea yet!" Rebecca practically shakes with excitement as we pack suitcases and a tent into Andrew's truck.

"I'm not convinced a weekend in the woods is your best idea ever," I grumble.

"Come on, Emma! You love the outdoors. Why are you being such a sourpuss?" Rebecca then dares to add, "You helped me plan this trip for weeks. I thought you'd be excited about this."

Why does she have to bring that up? As if I need a reminder about how excited I was for this trip before our plans changed.

Rebecca closes the back of Andrew's truck and stops to look at me. I think she's talking still, but I haven't been listening. My focus is on the driver's side of the truck, where the door is open, and Angelina is perched in the driver's seat while Andrew strokes her thigh and gives her a lingering kiss. He turns away from her and begins walking our way. "Do you two need any help loading things up? Angie and I packed the cooler. She even made cookies for us. Wasn't that nice?"

Rebecca gives me a concerned look before turning back to Andrew. "You know Emma already made us her grandpa's chocolate chip cookies. What are we going to do with two batches of cookies?"

Andrew looks at her funny. This Angelina, or Angie as Andrew so lovingly calls her (bleh), gets on my nerves. She wasn't even supposed to be a part of this trip when we started planning it. It was just going to be me, Rebecca, and Andrew, like it always is. Then Andrew decided that dating a girl for three months justified allowing her to crash our perfectly planned camping trip.

"I don't think we will have any problem putting those cookies away," Andrew replies. He's so annoyingly clueless, but I can't be mad at him. I don't think I've ever been able to stay mad at Andrew.

"It's fine, Becs. I'm sure Andrew and I will polish them off easily."

Rebecca still doesn't look convinced. She sees right through me. She knows the pride I take in these cookies, and I'm pretty sure she can see there's a little bit more bothering me than sharing the spotlight for cookies.

"Sorry, Emma. I know how much my Andy loves these cookies, so I just thought it'd be a good time to bring them along," Angelina, not so helpfully, adds.

I can't believe this is who Andrew had to pick as his first girlfriend. Yes, she's pretty, but everything she does is so irksome. First of all, she calls Andrew Andy, despite the fact that anyone who knows him is aware he *hates* that nickname. Second of all, she hates reading. I tried to make conversation with her, asking her about her interests, but reading was not on the list. When I asked her if she reads, she said, 'Eh, I read when I have to for class, but who can be bothered to read a whole book? They're boring.' *I* can be bothered. Andrew has no problem being bothered, and he should be with someone who appreciates books the same way he does.

I take a calming breath. Andrew is one of my closest friends, and I want to support him. He clearly likes Angelina, so I need to make more of an effort to like her too.

"Are we ready to head out?" Andrew asks the group.

Rebecca and I nod as Angelina hops into the passenger seat. "Let's get this party started!" Andrew cheerily hops into the driver's side of the truck.

The site we picked is not that far away from our houses. It's maybe a ten-minute drive and is just on the other side of the lake. The sunrises are incredible over here. I drag Rebecca out here at least once a week on our morning runs, which is how we initially got the idea for this camping trip.

Once we unload everything, Rebecca, Andrew, and I put the tents up. Angelina pretends to be useful by placing all the food out on the table, but come nightfall, that is all going to have to be put away because the raccoons will definitely get into it.

"Andrew, you could at least tell her that her work is absolutely useless," I mumble to him as we slip the cover over the top of my and Rebecca's tent.

"What do you mean?" *Since when was Andrew this stupid?*

"We aren't going to eat all of that food today, and the raccoons will get into it if it gets left out."

Angelina turns toward us and throws both her arms out, pointing to the table. "There, it's all organized by meal and everything."

"It looks great, Angie," Andrew encourages her with unnecessary enthusiasm. He walks over and plops a kiss on the tip of her nose. She pulls him in for a hug, nuzzling her cheeks into Andrew's chest.

I groan and turn away, catching Rebecca staring at me yet again. She grabs my wrist and begins pulling me away from the campsite. "Emma and I are going down to the water," she announces.

"But my towel is in my bag," I begin to argue, but she is quick to clear the air.

"We're not going to be swimming."

"Uh, Becs, I know we are close, but not like that," I try to lighten the mood. Why does she seem so grumpy all of a sudden?

She rolls her eyes and starts walking faster, still gripping my wrist. Her grasp is a little too tight.

When we reach the water's edge, she picks up a rock and skips it. I know what that means. She wants to talk for real.

I pick up a rock, skip it, and wait for her to start the conversation. I'm not even sure what she wants to talk about. It came on so suddenly. I don't see why she felt the need to discuss whatever it is now, while we are on the camping trip with Andrew and his little puppy dog. Sorry, I mean his girlfriend. *He's my friend. I need to try harder*, I remind myself.

"I know what's going on," Rebecca begins. "The reason you turned sour on this trip, the reason you're all of a sudden being an asshole to Andrew. It's because you're in love with my brother. Isn't it?"

I'm stunned into silence. I don't even know how to respond. I can't believe she would say something so ridiculous. I've always thought Rebecca in some ways knows me better than I know myself, but now? She clearly doesn't.

"I'm not in love with Andrew!" My bewilderment makes me sound less than believable, but I keep going. "Are we good friends? Yes. Would I consider him one of my best friends, behind you? Of course."

"Thank you for that," she interjects, sounding sincere.

"Do I love that we can talk about books and food and life? Absolutely. Maybe he's grown up to be kind of good-looking, and I feel all warm when we touch, but that doesn't mean I love him," I conclude.

Rebecca raises her eyebrows at me, her mouth going crooked. "I love you, but you are either way dumber than I thought, or you're lying to me, which we don't do."

Her words cut me. I've always appreciated Rebecca's brazen honesty. I suppose I do now too. I know she's only bringing this up because she cares about me; however, I'm just not sure what she's talking about. "You've lost me."

"Come on, Emma!" She sounds frustrated. "I've watched this happen for years, and I thought maybe I was overanalyzing things, or it was just a little crush that would go away, but I can see now that I wasn't wrong, and it's more than a crush. Before Angelina got here, and got your panties all in a wad, you lit up every time you saw Andrew, and you may not have told me, but Andrew is still my brother, so I know you guys have been texting and Facetiming throughout the school year. It's okay. You're my best friend. There's literally no one better to date my brother than you."

I sit down on the rocky shore. I don't even want to skip rocks anymore. "I guess I hadn't thought about my feelings for him. I've always felt kind of giddy around Andrew, but I haven't ever allowed myself to consider our relationship could go beyond a friendship." I put my head in my hands as I think some more. After a pause, I continue, "I hate Angelina. She's so wrong for Andrew. He could do better, and she's just so… dull."

Rebecca bursts into laughter. "At least you're starting to be honest!" She sits down next to me and pats my thigh. "I don't like her either. If it were up to me, we'd parent trap her ass on this trip and float her out into the lake on her tiny air mattress, but we aren't that lucky. She didn't bring an air mattress."

I snort. "Yeah, *that's* why we aren't doing that!" It feels good to be so brutally honest with Rebecca. I guess I had been holding back. "I thought Andrew and I were getting somewhere this year. We've been talking about so much more than just books, and I swear we had a moment. No, we had moments. Then all of a sudden, he has Angelina, and she's crashing our trip. It sucks."

"Andrew's smart. It may take him a little while, but he's going to realize Angelina is not the one. Mark my words, it's just a matter of time."

I hug her. "Thank you."

"You're welcome. I know we can't set her afloat on an air mattress, but is there some other way we can scare her off? She's going to kill the vibe of this camping trip!"

I bury my head in my hands as I laugh. "Gosh, I love you!"

"You think I'm kidding?"

"I know you too well to think you're kidding. That's why I have to be the sensible one and say we aren't going to do anything. You said it yourself; Andrew will figure out that she's not the one."

"I may have said that, but that doesn't mean I have the patience to wait for him to figure it out. Emma, she's going to drive us both mad. Please, we have to get rid of her." She emphasizes, "*Now.*"

"How the hell are we supposed to do that?" I ask, sure that this question will stop her.

She stutters a little. I was right. "We will figure something out."

"*We* will not do anything. I may like Andrew as more than a friend, but that doesn't mean I want to get involved in his love life like that. I want what's best for him, and meddling is not a good idea. That's a sure-fire way to piss him off and hurt him, which I want no part in."

"Ugh, Emma, you're the wor—" she's interrupted by the sound of crackling rocks and then Andrew sprinting down the beach toward us. He's in his swim trunks, showing off his lean muscles. His abs contract with each step down. He passes us by, runs off the dock, and dives right into the lake.

"What're you guys doing on the beach? You should be in the lake," he shouts as he treads water.

"Where's Angelina?"

"She's taking a nap. She said the sun was making her tired, so I thought I'd come and see what you guys are up to." He adds, "I guess I wasn't missing much."

"I was about to take your truck to the store. I forgot something, but you two go ahead. I'll be back in a jiff." Rebecca winks at me as she turns and walks off the beach.

"Geez, everyone is bailing! Em, you better come swim with me right now, or I'm going to be disappointed. I was promised this would be a fun camping trip, and two-thirds of you are being lame."

I roll my eyes with a grin on my face. "You're so dramatic."

"Em, get in the water now!" He draws out the 'w' sound. Even from here, I can see the smile that's plastered on his face.

I stand up. "All right, I'm coming!" I pull my shirt over my head and unbutton my shorts, pulling those off too to reveal my royal blue swimsuit.

I run out on the dock and cannonball into the water right next to him.

"Oh, that's how we are going to play it?" Andrew teases.

I smirk back. "I'm in the water. That's what you asked for. Now you're going to be picky about how I do it?"

He places his palms on the dock and lifts himself out of the water. I can't help but let my gaze linger on the rippling muscles in his back and his toned triceps as he pushes himself up.

He takes several steps back and then launches himself forward, running straight at me. I scream and duck my head underwater right as he leaps over me and cannonballs into the water.

I pop up, looking for him, just as I feel something grab my

ankle and tug. I shriek. Andrew shoots back to the surface and immediately begins laughing.

"What was that for?" I ask, splashing him in the face.

"Payback." The grin on his face turns devilish.

"I could've died."

"I wouldn't let anything happen to you, Em." He reaches out, caressing my cheek for a moment, then slowly drags his hand down and back into the water.

I want nothing more than to just crawl into his arms right then and soak up all the love he has to give to me. That's not how we work though, and Andrew has Angelina. Whatever he is doing right now, whatever I'm feeling right now, doesn't matter. He doesn't feel the way I do.

I internally curse myself before opening my mouth and asking, "Does Angelina know we're down here? I'd hate for her to wake up alone in the tent with no truck at the campsite and think we Meredith Blake'd her."

"Are you talking about that evil girlfriend from *The Parent Trap* who gets set off on a raft?" Andrew asks, narrowing his brows and scrunching his nose in puzzlement.

Of course, he knows exactly what I'm talking about. Rebecca and I forced him to watch the movie with us so many times! "Yeah…" I trail off with a laugh, hoping he won't think anything of it if I pretend I'm just being silly old me.

"You're so weird," he chuckles and pulls himself out of the water again onto the dock. "We can go check on her. I've got such a hankering for some Oreos and milk right about now anyway." He smiles, but it doesn't quite reach his eyes.

I swear he's disappointed we have to go back to his girlfriend, but I won't let myself think like that.

CHAPTER 16

Summer 19

I finish explaining the whole situation to Dani, the day I spent with Andrew, confessing our feelings for one another, and Andrew asking to take me on a date tomorrow night. Dani listened contently the whole way through, but now she looks at me confused.

"This all sounds so exciting! Why are you crying? Did something happen? What'd that idiot do? I'm going to kill him!"

"Woah, there! Settle down." I laugh. I have to be thankful for her willingness to throw down for me so quickly. That spark of spunk reminds me a little of Rebecca. The thought somehow comforts me. "Nothing happened. Andrew didn't do anything wrong."

My phone dings, and I glance at it.

ANDREW

Can't stop thinking about you and our date. I'm so excited!!

I blush a little and hold it out for Dani to see. "In fact, he's only doing things right so far." I set my phone back down. "It's just that I came home and realized how excited I was that everything finally felt like it was falling into place, but the person I wanted to tell all about it isn't here to listen."

Dani's eyes are full of sympathy and understanding. "Remember how hard it was when we lost Grandpa?"

I stiffen. "Way to kick me when I'm down."

She chuckles a little in exasperation. "No, I'm not finished. I just meant it was really hard after losing him, but you've gradually become okay with living life without him here with you." She adds, "You were way stronger than any of us expected during that time."

I nod. "Rebecca helped make me feel better."

She thinks about my response for a moment. "What did she do to help you handle it so well?"

I reflect on that moment nearly six years ago. "We skipped rocks. She talked to me about how it was okay to hurt, and I was lucky to be so sad over his passing because it meant I had someone worth missing. Then we baked cookies," I say simply.

I watch as her wheels begin to turn. "She's right. You were lucky to have her, even if it was shorter than expected. It doesn't make it easy, and obviously, there's no replacing her, but I hope you know I'm here for you. I can listen to you talk about your journey with Andrew or your memories with Rebecca. I can even go on adventures with you like she used to do if you ever want that."

I throw my arms around her. "Thank you, Dani!"

She hugs me back. "That's what sisters are for. Now, let's do something to honor Rebecca. What should we do?"

"I'm not sure. I've been trying to do that with Andrew the last week or so, but it hasn't made me feel better."

Dani bobs her head with compassion. "You said not being able to talk to her about what's going on with Andrew triggered your emotions, so maybe it's not the big things you miss about her, but the little things. We can do something small to honor her."

An idea immediately comes to mind, and a smile spreads across my face. "Do we have chocolate chips?"

Dani stands up and walks into the kitchen to check the pantry. "It looks like it. What're you thinking?"

I begin pulling out ingredients like flour, sugar, salt, and cinnamon. Dani's eyes linger on the cinnamon, knowingly.

"Let's make some cookies. But this time, can we eat some of the dough first and then eat the baked ones while watching *The Parent Trap?*"

Dani smiles. "That sounds like a perfect evening. Before we bake, you need to respond to Andrew, though. You can't leave him hanging."

I quickly pull my phone out of my pocket again and open the message. A giddiness erupts inside me and spills out as a goofy smile. "What should I say?"

She gives me a nonchalant look. "Clearly, you've done things right up to this point. Just be yourself. He's already told you he adores you for you. This is so cool. You get to start out already knowing each other. You don't have to worry about what he thinks of you without makeup or if he won't get your sense of humor. You're so lucky."

"Yeah, I guess you're right. I hadn't thought of that before."

"You get to skip past all the awkward getting-to-know-you stuff and jump right into the good parts."

"That also means there's more at stake," I say, growing anxious by the second.

"No, don't overthink it! That's exactly what I'm telling you *not* to do right now. This is exciting! Remember how giddy you were a few minutes ago?"

I smile, feeling a little more at ease. My thumbs start typing, and I don't let myself overthink it.

ME

Thinking of you too. Can't wait for our date! I
hope your dinner is the best you've ever had
since you're making me wait a whole day
longer to go on a date with you

He responds right away.

ANDREW

The food is great but there's very little that
makes being away from you worth it

A blush rushes to my cheeks and I feel my insides flutter to life. I am *so* in trouble. This boy is so easy to love. I just need to try not to mess it up.

With a knowing smile, Dani asks, "Ready to make the cookies?"

"Hell yeah! I can taste them already."

Dani and I slowly slither off the couch as the credits roll, our bellies full of warm, gooey cookies and delicious cookie dough. I glance at my phone for the time. It's late. Dani's and my best-laid plans were slightly thrown off when Mom came home not even two minutes after we pulled out all the cookie ingredients, insisting we needed to eat dinner first.

"Thanks for watching with me, sis." I nuzzle my head onto Dani's shoulder. I feel her stiffen the slightest bit. "Sorry."

"No, it's not you. We just don't do that much."

"Yeah, well we don't hang out much either, but we just binge ate cookies and cookie dough and watched a movie together."

She smiles softly. "I guess you're right."

I reach to flick the light on, and a mere five seconds after it turns on, my phone buzzes.

Dani gives me a knowing smirk. "Someone couldn't wait till tomorrow," she teases, drawing out the last word.

"It's almost midnight. I'm sure it's just a goodnight text or something." I wave her off, but she's already advancing toward me and grabbing my phone from my hand to read the text. She gives me an *I told you so* look and hands it back.

ANDREW

I know it's late, but would you and Dani be up for milkshakes?

Narrowing my eyes, I turn to Dani. "Why are you giving me that look? He asked if you wanted to come too."

She shrugs. "Yeah, but he's only inviting me because he wants to see you, and you told him you were hanging out with me tonight. It's called being nice. Andrew is like the king of golden boys."

"You're so dramatic."

"Tell him yes."

"We just ate a whole bunch of cookie dough," I argue.

"So? You can't tell me you're going to turn down a milkshake *and* an opportunity to see Andrew." My silence is enough to prove her right. "Ask if he wants to drive or if I should grab my keys."

ME

You and I both know the answer to that

ANDREW

Yes but I still had to ask. I'll drive us

"Andrew says he'll drive."

"Great! I think I might hit the hay. You two go without me." Dani makes a big stretching motion and fake yawns. "I'm *really* tired from that movie."

"You liar! Just come."

Dani shifts nervously. "No, I'm not going to impose."

"You're not imposing. Our date is tomorrow. This is just extra. I think it'd be cool to hang out with the three of us. Besides, Andrew and I are used to hanging out in threes."

I note Dani's small wince. "Fine, I'll come, but if the sexual tension gets to be too much, I'm getting out of his truck and walking home!" She waltzes out of the room.

"Oh, shut up!" I yell after her, a huge smile on my face.

She comes back down the hallway wearing shoes and carrying a sweatshirt. She leads the way to the door, and I slip on my flip-flops on the way out.

Outside, I can already hear the sound of Andrew's engine running. I start walking toward the Martins' driveway, but he scares the absolute shit out of me when he rushes up to me and swoops me off my feet, planting a kiss on my hairline. I look up at him with my eyes big as saucers, feeling nothing but joy.

I'm not sad about Rebecca. I'm not hung up on what is going to come next for Andrew and me. I'm not anxious about whether or not it will be weird to have Dani tag along with us tonight. I'm just happy. For possibly the first time since I was born, the wheels in my brain aren't turning so hard that steam is blowing out my ears. I'm actually present.

Out of the corner of my eye, I see Dani grab her phone and snap a picture of me curled up in Andrew's arms, and I'm immediately grateful to have a sister who loves photography and has such a good eye for moments that are worth capturing.

Andrew sets me down, with a goofy grin on his face, and I just feel so much warmth inside me as I take him in. He looks just as happy as me, and I know I could get in my head right now about how it isn't possible for us both to be this truly happy, but something about his presence grounds me. This all just feels right. There's nothing to question.

"Shall we go get some milkshakes, ladies?"

"I think we shall. I call shotgun!" Dani links arms with

Andrew and begins walking him toward his truck, turning back to me and sticking her tongue out teasingly.

I chase after them while Dani unlocks her phone to show Andrew the photo she just took.

"Em, you should come see this."

I look at the photo and horror fills me. "I look like a horse!"

"You do *not*." Dani insists.

"You look happy," Andrew says. "Look again."

With another glance, I move past how wide my mouth is and ignore how squinty my eyes are, and instead, I see a girl who has been through a lot but is managing to laugh and experience love and joy, gazing up at a boy she adores with wonder in her eyes. It's beautiful.

CHAPTER 17

Summer 17

Several minutes later, we enter our campsite, still dripping wet in our bathing suits and holding our clothes. The truck is gone, and there's no sight of Angelina. She must be in the tent.

Andrew saunters over to the plastic table holding all of the food and rips open the bag of Oreos. He grabs two and then looks around at the table for something.

"The milk is in the cooler," I offer, gesturing under the table.

"Thanks, but I'm looking for your cookies. Those things are the best I've ever had, and I think they'd complement the Oreos well." He winks.

I return his cheeriness with a frown. "Don't you think you should eat Angelina's cookies instead? You'll upset her if they go uneaten. Since I made my own cookies, and she's *your* girlfriend, the job of eating them kind of falls on *you*."

He frowns a little and lowers his voice. "Yours are so much better." Then he grabs two of my cookies and one of Angelina's.

I can't help but laugh. Andrew has always had a big appetite, similar to me. We've bonded over that throughout the years, but his has grown to be three times what it used to be, and he is still this chiseled masterpiece of a human. It's not fair.

He pours himself a small cup of milk, sits down in a chair, and dunks the Oreos in with patience as they soften. Then, in complete juxtaposition to his earlier patience, he shoves the whole Oreo into his mouth at once.

After he polishes off the last of his cookies, he gets up and moves toward the tent. "I'm going to check on her real quick," he explains.

I nod and just stand there, unsure of what to do with myself. *Why did Rebecca have to leave me alone at the camp with these two? Did she not realize I might end up murdering Angelina? Maybe she did realize and wanted to get out of the way so I could.*

I snag one of my cookies from the Ziploc they're sitting in and then head to the tent. I'll put some dry clothes on and maybe read a few pages of my book while I wait.

Right as I find my book, I start to hear kissing sounds in the tent next door. *Kill. Me. Now. This is not happening. No. No. No. This is not happening.* I rush out of the tent, determined to get as far away from camp as possible when Rebecca pulls back into the campsite.

She hops out of the truck perkily, but her face falls when she sees me. "What happened now?" Glancing at her phone, she's quick to defend herself. "I was only gone like half an hour."

I nod my head in the direction of their tent. "Andrew went to check on Angelina, but that turned into a makeout session, and I refuse to sit here and listen."

She immediately waltzes over to the tent and pokes it, then shakes it. She begins roaring, and I roll my eyes because she sounds more like a dying walrus than a bear.

Angelina starts screaming, and Andrew tries to console her as he yells at Rebecca, knowing it's his twin without even having to see her.

I have to throw both of my hands over my mouth to hide the laughter that is pouring out of me right now.

Andrew and Angelina come rushing out of the tent, and Andrew charges at Rebecca. "What the hell was that for? You freaked Angie out!"

Rebecca looks calm and collected. "I was just having a little fun. You both need to lighten up, or this camping trip is going to be miserable. You used to do this to me all the time. Remember, Andrew?"

Andrew backs off a little and the tension in his shoulders visibly releases. He turns to wrap Angie up in a hug, and Rebecca walks away, heading back toward me near the truck.

Her perky smile is back on her face already. "Dani bought us a bottle of tequila. Let's make some margaritas tonight."

I look at her confused and then burst out laughing. "That was a good one. Now why'd you leave me?"

Her face goes serious. "Dani *did* buy us tequila." She opens the truck and pulls out a bottle of Jose Cuervo, holding it up for me to see.

"Are you nuts?! Where did you get this from? I know Dani wouldn't buy it for you!" I feel my chest constricting as panic rises. It's not like I've never been around alcohol before. I have. I just haven't consumed it before, and I certainly have never illegally acquired it. Then the thought of *Dani* being the one to get this for us? No way! This is the same girl who won't even go on the tube with us because she's too afraid. There's no way she'd risk getting caught with a fake ID. Nope. Not her!

"I know you think Dani is some goody two shoes, but she's a college woman now, and she can get a little rowdy." She turns toward the truck again and grabs the bottle of margarita mix, setting it on the table.

"In case you've forgotten, Becs, we're only seventeen. We are a long way away from the legal drinking age. I haven't even had a sip of my parents' drinks at home. I'm not sure what you are thinking here, but it's a bad idea. You've got to take it back." I grab the two bottles and go to put them back in the truck.

She thrusts her arms out to stop me. "Emma, I just want to have a little fun. With Angie here and all this tension, this camping trip is a recipe for disaster. I want to make some good memories while we are out here."

"I just don't think alcohol is a good idea. I've heard it can make you more emotional. I'm already a bit insecure with her around."

She takes a deep breath. "Don't take it personally. Please. Andrew is super smart when it comes to school, but when it comes to life, he can be *so* stupid. I think what happened is he started to catch feelings for you and then went back to school and realized how inconvenient it is to not see you all school year. Then he found this little fox, and he felt somewhat happy. But Andrew's happiness with Angelina is nothing compared to his happiness when he's with you."

I blush a little at her conclusion, but then I brush myself off and get back to reality. Narrowing my eyes, I grumble, "Don't go around saying these things and getting my hopes up. I'm a big girl. I can accept the fact that Andrew isn't interested."

She gives me a sympathetic look. "I'm your best friend. Do you think I'd lie to your face like that just to spare your feelings? We are way past that in our friendship."

She walks over to the fire pit where Andrew is starting a fire for us and Angelina is sitting in a chair, scrolling on her phone.

Seriously, what does Andrew see in her? She can't even get off her phone for a camping trip? Her incredible boyfriend is right there surrounded by the best nature has to offer, and she doesn't even have the decency to enjoy it?

I shake my head, realizing that I am now staring at her boyfriend as he starts the fire. *Get it together.*

"Hey, you two!" Rebecca gathers their attention. Holding up the bottle of tequila, she explains, "I was thinking we could make this trip a little more interesting and have some margaritas with dinner tonight. What do you think?"

Angelina peers up from her phone and squeals in glee. "I love margaritas!"

Of course she does.

Andrew stops building the fire for a moment. I watch him look from Rebecca's hand holding the bottle, over to me, and then back to Rebecca. "I don't think margaritas fit the vibe of our camping trip."

Angelina groans a little and leans in toward Andrew. "Come on, Andy! Lighten up a bit. Margaritas are so good they'll go with anything." She takes a look at the bottle Rebecca is holding. "It looks like Rebecca even got us some good tequila."

Andrew's facial features sag a little. "Alright, I'm in. We don't need to go crazy though."

Rebecca nods. "Yeah, yeah, yeah. We'll be responsible." She moves back toward the table where the cups are and shouts over her shoulder. "You just worry about getting the fire started, and I'll make us some drinks to sip on while we wait."

I know better than to leave Rebecca alone with our drinks, so I follow her over.

She is already pouring some of the margarita mix into the first cup. Handing it to me, she says, "Here, this will be Andrew's."

I eyeball it. "How much alcohol did you put in here?"

"I only put about a shot in it. He's a big guy and this isn't his first drink ever, so he can handle a measly shot. Trust me." She waves her hand nonchalantly.

I watch her pour the other three cups. They seem heavy-handed to me, but I wouldn't know what a shot of alcohol looks like unless it's in a shot glass. She passes me another cup and then walks to give one to Angelina.

Before I bring Andrew his cup, Rebecca turns back to me.

"Oh, while I'm thinking about it, let's put the food back in the truck, so the raccoons don't ransack our camp tonight."

I bob my head and set the cups on the table for a moment as I fill my hands with the three different kinds of cookies out on the table. Rebecca joins me, opening the truck door for me before filling her arms with tomorrow's breakfast items.

I return to the table and inspect the cups. I don't remember which was which. The one on the left looks to be more full, so that's probably Andrew's.

I shuffle over to the fire and hand Andrew his cup and lean in to whisper in his ear, "I'd drink slowly. I don't know how much alcohol Rebecca put into this."

He nods. "I'll be fine. My parents make us margaritas at home sometimes."

I wince as he takes his first sip, which is more like a gulp.

Rebecca sips her cup and watches me as I just hold mine. "Come on, Emma! At least try it. I poured you a lighter one, and I had Dani specifically look for this mix, so it won't be too sweet."

I sip off my drink and am surprised to find Rebecca was right. I take another gulp and feel my insides warm. "It's pretty good." I hold my cup up in the air with a smile.

Rebecca gives me a pleased look, and I think worry crosses Andrew's face for a moment. I brush it off as I continue to sip on my drink.

A while later, I have no clue how much later, we finally clean up the last of our dinner as we each finish our third margarita. These things are so good! I don't know what I was afraid of earlier. I giggle to myself at the thought of earlier me being so opposed to this idea. The giggle quickly turns into full-blown laughter as I sit in the chair around the fire with the other three.

Rebecca looks at me inquisitively before her face splits into a huge grin. Her eyes are glossy, and her cheeks are a little pink. Angelina has the same look to her.

"Guys, I want to do something fun! What can we do besides play cards?" Rebecca asks.

"It's pretty dark to go do anything, and quiet hours start soon," Andrew replies rationally.

Rebecca gives him a pouty look, and I join in. Angelina speaks up. "I'm pretty tired, so I might go get ready for bed. Sorry guys."

"Buzzkill," I hear Rebecca mutter under her breath in her seat next to me.

I laugh, and it once again turns into uncontrollable laughter.

Angelina retreats into the tent, and I exchange a look with Rebecca. She shoots up from her seat and goes over to the table where the tequila and mix sit. She pours tequila into her cup and holds it up, squinting at it to see how much she poured. She shrugs and turns to me. "Give me your cup! Let's take a shot together." She wiggles her eyebrows in excitement.

I can't resist the eagerness in her eyes, so I stand up from my chair and feel the world tilt for a moment. Andrew grabs my elbow as I steady myself. I waltz over to the table and begin to set my cup down, but I feel an arm wrap around my waist. I'm lifted in the air, spun around, and set back down away from Rebecca and the table.

"No more tequila for her," Andrew growls.

Rebecca rolls her eyes. "You're not in charge of her. Why don't you go check on your girlfriend," she challenges as she reaches out for my cup and pours me a shot.

"Angie's fine." He looks me up and down, and I'm certain my cheeks heat. "She isn't. She hasn't drunk before, and three drinks is probably already overdoing it for her first time."

I ignore Andrew and grab my cup off the table while he's giving Rebecca a lecture. I tilt it back and slam it.

I place the cup back down on the table with a sour expression on my face. *Oh my God! No one told me tequila was this gross. It burns like hell, and the taste... bleh!*

Rebecca begins cheering. "Atta girl! You didn't even use a chaser! I'm so proud!"

Andrew whips around to find me holding my empty cup. "No, Em!" He turns back to Rebecca. "Are you trying to make her sick?"

I smile wide, despite the still disgusting taste lingering in my mouth and Andrew's scorn. *Screw him!* All that sinks in is Rebecca's praise. "What's a chaser?"

"It's something to make the shot burn less. Usually, you use salt and lime with tequila shots. We don't have that, so I was going to at least get you some lemonade."

I hang my tongue out of my mouth. "It's so nasty. Do you think the lemonade will still help, or will my mouth taste like this forever?"

Rebecca giggles as she goes into the cooler in the truck and digs out a can of lemonade. She cracks it open and hands it to me. "This will help. I promise."

I gulp it down and immediately feel better. After a few more sips, Rebecca swivels to Andrew, shoving his shoulder. "Why are you trying to kill the fun?"

"I'm not. I'm just being the responsible one, as always!"

Rebecca frowns and then struts off to the tent. I'm left standing there, unsure of what just happened. I look to Andrew for guidance. Andrew will help me. He knows what to do.

"Come on, Em, let's get you ready for bed." He tries to lead me to the tent too.

"I'm not tired though! I want to stay up and hang out with you. Please!" I beg.

I hear him blow a puff of air out of his nose. "I think we should just go to bed. It's getting late."

"We won't get into any trouble. I've been good all night."

He laughs a little at this. "I'll tell you what, we can go sit by the fire for a little while it finishes burning out."

I smile and begin to scramble over to the chairs, but the whole world flips over this time. I feel myself swaying. If I can just get to the chairs, I know it will stop, and it'll all be worth it because I can spend a little more time with Andrew. Andrew who I love so much but can't have. I let out a groan and take a staggering step forward, followed by another step.

I'm almost there! Then I stumble over one of the chair legs and fall forward. I throw my hands out, trying to grab anything that will help break my fall.

My hand makes contact with something warm. I hold it tight for a lingering moment before I hear Andrew yelling at me for the second time tonight. "Em, no!"

He yanks my hand off the warm metal grate surrounding the fire, and it's only then that I process the searing pain in my hand. "Ow! Ow! Ow! Andrew, help! It hurts so bad!"

He plops me down in a chair and grabs another cold can of lemonade from the cooler. "I don't want lemonade. My hand hurts too bad," I explain to him, a very logical answer.

He shoves the can into my hand. "How about you just hold this for me for a while?"

I slump into the seat a little bit. "Okay, for you."

He nods with encouragement. "Does that help?"

"A little bit," I admit.

"We can bandage your hand up with some ointment in a little bit."

I just shake my head silently. "I'm sorry, Andrew."

"It's okay! What are you apologizing for?"

My eyes get watery. "For everything. For not being better about telling Rebecca no when she got out the alcohol, for making you mad at Rebecca and me, and for hurting myself and making you have to take care of me now."

"You don't need to apologize!" He reaches out and rubs my shoulder, comforting me.

"Yes, I do. I feel so bad that I'm making myself sick," I tell him as my stomach turns.

I feel so nauseous. *I need him to forgive me, and I'll feel better.*

"Hey—" My sour stomach flops completely.

I leap up, dropping the lemonade can on the ground as I run to the edge of our campsite and crouch down to release the demons battling inside of me.

I hear footsteps and Andrew comes closer. I'm shaking and my brain is foggy, but I still know I don't want Andrew to see me like this. "No! Please don't look at me."

I feel his warm palm rub my back as I hurl again. Drinking was *such* a bad idea.

When I'm done, I step back and then sit in the dirt, tears streaming down my cheeks. I feel sweaty and weak, but at least my stomach is starting to ease.

Andrew scoops me up with one arm supporting my lower back, the other behind my knees. "I think it's time for bed. What do you think?"

I nuzzle my head into his solid chest in affirmation. He carries me to my tent and sets me down on top of my sleeping bag but pulls a blanket over me.

To my left, Rebecca is already passed out. Andrew begins to retreat from the tent. "Andrew, are you going to leave me here alone?" I look up at him with wide and scared eyes.

"I'm not leaving you alone. Rebecca is right there," he says lightly.

"She's sleeping deeper than the dead," I retort, giving her a poke to show him she isn't even stirring.

He deflates as he holds my gaze. "I can't just leave Angie alone in our tent."

I pout a little. "It's okay. I get it."

He peers out of the tent and then back at me with a

conflicted look on his face. "How about I lay with you until you fall asleep?"

I nod with a sleepy smile, satisfied with that solution.

I curl up under the blanket, warm and content knowing Andrew is right there to ensure nothing bad will happen to me. Sleep finds me quickly.

CHAPTER 18

Summer 19

ndrew is supposed to pick me up in half an hour for our date. I've already pinned my curls back into a half up-half down style that keeps my hair out of my face, and I've applied a light coat of mascara and a gold eyeshadow Rebecca bought me two years ago that I haven't used till now. She told me it would bring out the green in my eyes, but I never had an occasion for it. It turns out she was right. I hope Andrew doesn't think it's over the top. I never wear anything more than mascara.

I have three different outfits spread out on my bed. Dani helped me pick out each one. She's been living up to her promise to be there for me with these sorts of things.

It's impossible to pick an outfit though because I have no clue what Andrew and I are doing tonight. I can go casual in shorts with an off-the-shoulder floral top or jeans and a lacy tank top. But I can also dress a little more formal in one of my favorite sundresses, which also happens to bring out my eyes.

I check my phone for the time and any texts from Andrew. I still have twenty more minutes until he's supposed to pick me up. I haven't heard from him for the past hour, and I have to wonder what he's up to.

I shoot him a quick text.

ME

Can I have a hint of what we are doing tonight?
The suspense is killing me and I need to know
whether to go formal or casual

To my surprise, he responds a couple of minutes later.

ANDREW

Wear something nice but comfortable. I can't
wait to see you

My heart flutters as I reread his text. "Dani!" I call out. "I need your help again."

She comes in from her bedroom next door and stands in the doorway. "What's up?"

"He told me to dress nice but comfortable. What does that even mean?"

She leans against the door jam. "You guys are probably going to dinner since he's picking you up at five. Maybe it's a nice place, but he has something else planned for after?"

I nod absentmindedly. "So, what should I wear? Are jeans too casual?"

Her eyes flicker to my bed again. "Go for the dress. You can always put spandex underneath and then, knowing you, you can do anything in a dress."

I purse my lips as I consider her suggestion. "What about shoes? Oh gosh, I didn't even think about shoes!" She begins laughing at me. "Why are you laughing? This is serious. Andrew is going to be here in—" I glance at my phone again "—nine minutes."

She holds her hands out, giving me the universal *calm down* hand signal. "Take a deep breath. First of all, shoes aren't the make or break. Andrew is a guy. Do you think he cares what shoes you wear? He's just going to be happy to be with you. Second of all, you have plenty of time. Andrew will wait for you if you aren't ready."

I let out a breath after realizing I've been holding it the entire time she's been speaking.

Moving toward my closet, she asks, "What are your options for shoes?"

I flip on the light, and peer at my shoes sitting on the rack, blissfully unaware of the stress they're causing me. "I have Birkenstocks, fancier sandals, or I could probably even pull off Converse with this dress."

Dani's face scrunches up. "I know sneakers and a dress is your style, but veto if he said to dress nice. I'd go with the nicer sandals." I schlump my shoulders a little as I grab them out of the closet. "You better get going if you're going to be dressed when he gets here."

"You just told me I had time!" I shriek.

She smiles. "I'm giving you crap, but I still recommend at least getting your dress on."

With that, she turns, putting an AirPod in her ear and walking back into her room.

I grab the dress off the bed and a pair of black spandex from my drawer full of running clothes. I slip the two on and begin to strap my sandals on when I hear the doorbell ring. That must be Andrew. He's early!

I grab my purse from the hook on the back of my door and take one final look at myself in the bathroom mirror on my way down the hall. "Dani, he's here. I'm leaving."

She pokes her head out of her doorway, pulling an Airpod out of her ear again. "Have fun." She smirks.

I rush out the door and swing it open to find Andrew standing on the porch with a bouquet of vibrant indigo flowers and dainty white baby's breath. "Oh, Andrew, they're gorgeous," I exclaim, taking the flowers from his hands.

"You look…" he trails off, and I feel heat rushing to my cheeks. "Absolutely stunning."

I'm blushing now. I try to play things cool and brush off the compliment before I get embarrassed and start acting weird. "Can I put these in a vase before we go?"

He shakes his head in approval and takes a step inside the house. "Of course. There should be a packet of flower food wrapped in the plastic that you can pour into the water." He glides to my side, helping me find the packet and pouring it into the vase I just filled.

"I love how the bold color contrasts with the delicate baby's breath. What kind of flowers are these?" I ask, gently lifting one of the indigo flowers.

"The woman at the store said they're Bachelor Button flowers," he chuckles a little. "Quite the name. She said men used to wear them to indicate their love for their beloved."

I turn my head as I look at the flowers more. "That's sweet. Where's your flower?" I tease.

He quickly glances down at his bare wrist. "Will you look at the time! We are going to be late for our reservation. We better get going." The mischievous smile spreading on his face is hard to resist.

I return his smile and nudge his shoulder with mine. "It sounds like we are going to dinner! Do I get to know where we are going now that we are together?"

He moves his head back and forth. "Absolutely not! You'll see when we get there."

As we walk out the front door, he leads me straight to his truck. "Ha! I know we are driving somewhere now!"

He rolls his eyes. "That doesn't give anything away. I already told you I'd be picking you up today."

I shrug. "You could've picked me up on foot."

He opens the passenger side door for me, and I hop in. When he slides into the driver's side, he presses a few buttons on the screen on his dash. "Do you want to play some music?"

I smile. "Definitely. You have so much to learn about music."

"Hey, now! I may not be Rebecca, but I still listen to music. I think you'd even like my taste."

I press my lips together, unimpressed. "All right, tell me a song to play, and we will put you to the test."

"Look up 'Girl on Fire' by Kameron Marlowe. He's a smaller artist with a lot of great songs, but this one reminds me a bit of you."

I type the song title into my phone and queue it up. The first line alone sells me. His voice is smooth, and the lyrics are poetry. Chills grow on my arms. I continue listening as he tells the story of a young summer love between himself and a girl that he knew was going to do great things. He talks about trying to play it cool even though he doesn't know what he's doing and how his love for her never really faded.

"Which part reminded you of me?" I probe.

He turns right to exit the loop around the lake and head toward town. "It's a combination of little pieces," he explains. "The summer love, the girl on fire, who is you of course, and moonlight kisses in a Chevrolet bed, which I know I haven't gotten yet, but I hope I do soon." His dimple protrudes with his blushing smile.

I don't know how to respond to that. I'm not smooth like Andrew. He has such a way with words. I like to read words. I even like to write words from time to time, but actually speaking them is a whole other issue. I open my mouth. *Come on words.* "I...I hope so too."

I want to bury my head in my hands from my slow reaction time and awkward response, but a grin spreads on his face, and he reaches out to grab my hand on the center console, assuring me I said the right thing this time. It feels good.

"I have a song for you now, another song that reminds me of you," I share, giddy with excitement. At least a song can show him how I feel in a much better way than I clearly can. "Can I queue it up?"

He nods. "Tonight is all about you. Go for it."

"No," I interject. "Tonight is about *us*."

He squeezes my hand. "Us. I like the sound of that."

The song begins, and I find myself growing nervous. I'm practically pouring my heart out to Andrew through this song, and I hope he likes it.

I glance over at him and catch him tapping his free hand on the steering wheel as Abby Anderson sings about how this boy makes her lose sleep and how terrifying her feelings are, but she doesn't want to push him away because she wants to be with him. He's smiling. Thank God!

The song ends, and I'm still watching Andrew intently. I wait for him to speak. He turns to me, and I'm instantly enraptured by those gorgeous blue eyes of his. "I like it. I could get used to this feeling too," he gives me a cheesy grin, and I laugh.

"How much longer?" I pester him.

He tilts his head back and forth while he considers the question. "Pick four more songs, and we will be there."

"You pick two, and I'll pick two. That's only fair."

"Deal."

We each pick songs with stories to tell. I play one first, a sad song about a husband who stops recognizing his wife in his old age but remembers the memories of their youth. "Every time I hear this song, I want to cry," I tell Andrew

He scoffs. "Then why are you playing it for me?"

"Because it's a beautiful story," I burst. "Can't you hear how strong their love is?"

When it's his turn, he picks a more upbeat song, claiming, "This date needs to be salvaged from the depressing note you brought to it."

"Whatever," I cry, rolling my eyes as he smirks mischievously. Gosh, I want to kiss him right now.

We pull into the parking lot of a nice-looking restaurant. Andrew leaps out of the driver's seat and runs around to open my door.

"Thank you." I smile sweetly at him as he grabs my hand and walks me toward the front door. "What is this place?"

He swings open the heavy door. "You're going to absolutely love it, Em."

"So, biology, huh?" I ask Andrew between bites of the best brick-oven pizza I've ever had.

"Yeah, that's what I'm going with for now."

I nod my head pensively. "What do you want to use your biology degree for? I always pictured you doing something more creative."

"Honestly, I pictured myself doing something different too until last year." There's a pause, heavy with the unspoken truth of what must've changed the trajectory of his decisions. "I'm thinking I'll go to med school. I want to help people, and this seems like a good way to do it."

I furrow my brows a little. "What do you think of your classes? Can you see yourself as a doctor, or is that just what you think you have to do?"

I can see there's a twinge of dissatisfaction on his face at the way I'm questioning him, but I'm a little worried.

"The classes are fine, but it's a lot of introductory classes freshman year. I'm sure you understand. They're not all that relevant to what I'll be doing yet."

I finish chewing my cheesy bite of heaven before challenging, "You didn't answer whether or not you could see yourself being a doctor."

"I already told you it's not what I pictured for myself before, but I'm starting to see it." He grimaces.

"What did you picture yourself doing before last year?"

His face screws in concentration and he takes a bite of his pesto pizza to stall. This shouldn't be a difficult question to answer, but I think the conversation is making him uncomfortable. He knows I don't agree with following a career path just because he *thinks* it's what he should do.

"I guess I always pictured myself as a writer. I wanted to write my own books one day."

My face lights up. "Oh yeah! I remember you mentioning that before. I could see you doing that! Aw, Andrew, I love that for you! What's holding you back from pursuing a writing career?" Recalling a conversation we had about this topic last summer, I guess, "Is it what everyone else says about how much money you'll make?"

He tucks his chin into his shoulder, shying away a little. I rarely ever see Andrew in any state besides confident.

"Yeah, I'm not sure that it's a good way to make a living. Life as a writer would be harder."

I weigh out his response for a moment. "I mean, not all writers make it as huge authors, but it's not like you couldn't still make a living doing what you love. I've never read anything you've written, but I know you'd be a brilliant writer. A lot of people are having success with self-publishing these days." As excitement builds, I nearly shout, "You could even do smaller, more steady gigs like writing for a magazine or something to help keep you afloat."

A soft smile grows on his face. "You know, I wrote a lot growing up. I wrote a lot of short stories, but I never shared them with you because you were in most of them."

My jaw drops to the ground, and my stomach stirs. I don't have the soft fluttering of butterflies though. Instead, it's the furious flapping of hummingbirds bouncing all around in my stomach. "Andrew, you know I have to read those stories now! Tell me about them."

At my request, his whole body language changes. He is practically radiating light and excitement. "Well, they were mostly fantasy stories since that's what I grew up reading. You frequently made an appearance as the princess who didn't want to become queen. Instead, you helped this knight, me of course, on all his adventures. They grow to be friends, and the knight develops feelings for the princess after several adventures with her, but he can't be with her because she's royalty and, of course, she's already been arranged to marry another man who is brave and rich and hand-selected by her family. It's full of all the cliches, but it was still an escape."

"How'd you get the idea for that?" I always thought I knew Andrew so well, but here I am discovering there's a whole other side to him that I didn't know existed. It's not just a minor detail about him either. This is clearly something he's extremely passionate about. I can see it on his face the moment he opens his mouth to talk about it.

He shrugs and casually wipes his hands on the napkin in his lap. "I took a lot of inspiration from other books I read, and I guess elements of my own life. It's much easier to write about things you know. Wanting someone who doesn't want you back was my reality, and it was easy to write about. Yes, I know now that wasn't the truth, but in my head at the time, it was."

"When was the last time you wrote?"

He purses his lips and looks up as he tries to recall. "I think I started a story when I first got to school, but I didn't have any inspiration, so I gave up on it."

I reach across the table to squeeze his hand. "Maybe all the excitement from this summer will give you some inspiration."

A smile crosses his face. "Oh absolutely. I think the course of the stories will have to drastically change though. What do you think, should I have the princess call off the wedding, or should I kill off her husband-to-be?"

I laugh. "As great as it would be to read about his death, I think it will be much more meaningful if she realizes her feelings on her own, rather than it looking like she settled for the knight." I watch as he starts to sit straighter and exude both joy and confidence. "I like writer Andrew. If this makes you as happy as you look right now, I hope you'll consider pursuing it. Life is too short to not do the things you love to do."

I can see my words strike him because he immediately bites his lip and nods, thinking through what this all means for him. "Will you keep me accountable for my writing, like I'm doing for you with your running? It'll be the perfect trade-off."

"Sounds like a deal to me," I say, smiling.

I lick my fingers after polishing off my entire pizza. I love the fact that I've known Andrew for so long. He's seen me eat before and knows what my appetite is like. There's no judgment when he watches me eat the entire pizza, only a look of affection.

"Please tell me the night isn't over after this," I look at him with pleading eyes.

He beams. "Don't worry, Em. I have more planned for us."

CHAPTER 19

Summer 17

I wake with a throbbing in my head. I pull the blanket over my face to shield my eyes as the sunshine streams through the thin fabric of the tent. A groan slips from my lips.

I roll to my right. "Becs, I'm never giving in to your peer pressure ever again."

When I finally pull the blanket off my head and sit up, I find an empty sleeping bag where Rebecca should be. *Jeez, what time is it?*

I heave myself out of the tent and find my three camping mates fully dressed and ready to tackle the day. Rebecca sees me first and rushes to me right away. "Are you okay? Andrew said you were sick last night! I'm so sorry!"

I hold out a hand to her. "Don't yell at me."

She smiles a little. "Someone is learning her limits early. Don't worry. Andrew made some great breakfast burritos. A few bites of that, and you'll feel much better."

As I slouch into one of the chairs near the fire pit, Andrew rises from his spot. "How's your hand feeling? I didn't get a chance to bandage it up last night."

I look at him confused for a moment. I hold up both my

hands and find the angry red line that crosses my entire palm. Then I remember grabbing the fire pit and holding the lemonade can. "Let's just say it's the least of my worries right now." I grimace as the splitting pain in my head persists. "Do we have any Advil?"

Rebecca rushes to the truck and begins digging around while Andrew hands me a foil-wrapped burrito. "Angelina and I are going to head down to the water for a bit."

Unwrapping my burrito, I freeze at Andrew's use of his girlfriend's full name. I assess his face and can immediately tell something is off. I take a bite of my burrito and try to think back to the events of last night. *Is he mad at me?*

Rebecca comes back with a bottle of water and two tablets, interrupting my thoughts. "Here you go. You better perk up because we still have another day and a half out here before we head back."

I ignore her remark. "What do you think is going on with Andrew? He seemed upset. Did he say anything to you about last night?"

She sits down in the chair next to me. "He told me you were sick last night and that you were afraid to be left alone. I woke up about an hour after you went to bed, and he was still in our tent." After a pause, she notes, "He didn't seem mad at you, but I got a weird vibe too."

"Do you think it's because of something from last night?"

Rebecca leans in, even though no one else is nearby to hear us. "My twin intuition is telling me something is off with him and Angelina."

I pull back, my eyebrows raised. "Why would something be off with the two of them? They seemed fine last night."

She shrugs with a laugh. "My twin intuition only gets me so far."

"I'll give you this, you were right about the burrito and Advil helping my head."

"See! Would I ever steer you wrong?"

"Too soon," I deadpan.

She grimaces. "I said I was sorry! You did seem to have a good time up until after I went to bed. Maybe it was being around Andrew's toxic buzzkill vibes that made you sick."

I roll my eyes. "After our conversation yesterday, do you think being around Andrew is going to make me feel sick?"

"It might," she claims hopefully.

I finish my burrito in silence while I reflect on last night's events, trying to remember all the details. *Am I missing something?* I can't think of anything that happened between Andrew and Angelina. I'm fairly certain I remember everything before she went to bed. It's after that last shot that things get a little fuzzy.

I hear footsteps before I see Angelina and Andrew briskly walking back to camp. Angelina looks a little teary-eyed. I glance at Rebecca, sharing a curious look with her, and then turn my gaze toward Andrew. His face is completely expressionless. I'm so used to being able to read him, but I can't now. It's driving me crazy.

Angelina comes out of the tent a few moments later with her pillow under one arm and sleeping bag under the other. Andrew reaches out to help her grab her stuff, but she presses past him, opening the rear door of the truck and tossing her things in by herself.

Andrew looks visibly uncomfortable as he scratches the back of his head. "I'm taking Angelina home. I'll be back in a little while."

He hops into the driver's side and backs out of the camping spot before I can even process his words.

"What the hell just happened?"

Her disbelief is apparent. "I was right."

"Why do you look so surprised if you think you were right?

And how do you know you're right? Maybe Angelina had a family emergency."

She huffs as if to say *You're so simple-minded.* "Did you not hear him call her Angelina? That's a clear sign something is off with them. She was crying, and she looked pissed at Andrew. I don't know how else to prove it to you, but I'd bet you twenty bucks he broke up with her just now."

I know this news should make my heart leap with joy. I care so much for Andrew, and I know Angelina was not right for him. Even so, my stomach flips. *What happened to break them up so suddenly?*

I stammer, "You… You don't think Andrew would be so callous, do you?"

She narrows her eyes at me. "What are you talking about?"

"Couldn't he just wait until the camping trip was over rather than breaking up with her and sending her home early? She must feel so ridiculous for coming out here and getting broken up with."

"That's not callous. That's Andrew being his thoughtful self. I thought you knew him better than that." Her words cut me. "Andrew wasn't feeling things anymore and didn't want to waste any more of her time."

I find myself staring at my red palm as I think about Rebecca's insight. I guess she's right, but I still feel bad for Angelina. *This isn't your fault. You did nothing wrong.*

With that last thought, all of my memories come flooding back, Andrew taking care of me when I was sick. Me begging Andrew to stay in the tent with me so I wouldn't be left alone. *How embarrassing! Oh no, I hope Angelina didn't get mad at him for leaving her alone in the tent for an hour. That'd be such a silly thing to break up over.*

The look of unease must be apparent on my face because Rebecca interjects my thoughts. "You are not responsible for breaking up Andrew and Angelina. They were doomed from the start." She laughs devilishly. "We can ask him all about it when he gets back, but for now, we should be relishing in the fact that they're done."

"We *think* they're done," I add quickly, trying to tamp down my growing excitement.

"You and I both know they're done. We should be singing from the rooftops. Although, I'm a little disappointed we didn't get to Meredith Blake her ass."

I burst into laughter. "Alright, so how do we celebrate?"

She smiles broadly. "With more tequila."

I immediately frown and begin to protest when she erupts into laughter. "I'm kidding! We will keep you far away from tequila until at least college." She winks.

Andrew gets back about an hour later and finds Rebecca and I down at the water. Immediately, when I see him, I notice the gloom he carried this morning is gone. He seems like his usual laid-back self, maybe even happier than normal.

"What took you so long?" Rebecca calls out to him. She sits on an inflatable flamingo raft, sipping canned lemonade with her giant pink sunglasses perched on her face. Iconic. She's got her phone perfectly situated in the cup holder so she can control the music drifting off the dock from her portable speaker.

Andrew holds up a tub of something in his hands in response. "I stopped for ice cream at the little shop down the street. You guys better hurry. I'm going to eat it all by myself in the next five minutes, so it doesn't melt."

I don't even have to be right in front of him to see the grin spread across his face and feel the peace he is radiating.

"What kind of ice cream is it?" I call out to him.

He cracks open the top and sticks a spoon in, scooping a bite into his mouth before answering, "Oh, just a tub of ooey-gooey fudge brownie."

Rebecca and I immediately start paddling our floaties toward the dock. We are both huge chocolate fans.

When I hit the dock, I toss my floaty aside and take off at a sprint toward Andrew. I snag the tub right out of his hands and begin grasping for a spoon, but he pulls it away and holds it above his head before I can get to it.

"Andrew, you can't tease me like that!" I reprimand.

The smirk that crosses his face makes me want to kiss him right then and there. His blue eyes are sparkling with mischief, and his dimples are so prominent. I have to internally scold myself for looking at him like that when I don't know if he's a single man yet.

He lowers his hand with the spoon. "I'll give you the spoon if you will set the tub down for *all* of us to eat," he compromises, amusement coating his voice.

"Deal." I extend the tub out as he hands me a spoon.

Rebecca comes up from behind me. "What did you do that made you feel the need to get us ice cream?"

He scowls at her. "I didn't do anything. I just wanted ice cream."

Rebecca scoffs. "You and I both know you aren't that big of a chocolate person."

"There weren't many options at the store."

Rebecca takes a heaping spoonful from the tub. "I'll accept that answer for now, but I still have to ask what happened that made you take Angelina home early."

Andrew's shoulders sag a little. "We broke up."

"I knew it!" Rebecca exclaims. She turns to me. "You owe me twenty bucks, missy!"

My eyes grow as big as softballs. Before I can say anything, Andrew clears his throat, reminding us he's still standing there, fresh off of a breakup.

"I'm sorry you guys broke up," I say softly.

"Oh yeah, I'm sorry it didn't work out, Andy," Rebecca teases. "Maybe next time." She gives me a sly smile.

My cheeks immediately flush, and I have to pray Andrew didn't notice that. I give her a wide-eyed, raised eyebrow look to remind her not to be so obvious.

I go to scoop another bite of ice cream and bump Andrew's hand as he reaches in for a bite too. The small contact makes my heart flutter, and I let it.

"Can I ask what happened?" I inquire carefully.

Andrew digs into the ice cream, returning his spoon to his mouth with only a big brownie chunk. I can tell he's avoiding eye contact. *Come on, Andrew.*

Once he swallows, he begins to answer. "I guess I finally realized she wasn't what I wanted, and I didn't want to drag things out any longer than I needed to." Rebecca made a point of pinning me with a look as if to say *I told you so*. Andrew takes another bite, dipping his head down. Then he peers up at me through those beautiful brunette eyelashes and states, "I don't just want someone convenient."

His look is too much. I have to break the eye contact, so I quickly look down at the ice cream tub and peel a layer of chocolate off the top. "Thanks for the ice cream. This is hitting the spot."

A smile stretches across his face. "I knew it would."

Rebecca looks between the two of us, and I immediately recognize what she is thinking. She feels the tension between Andrew and I too. It's not a bad tension. Rather, it's this longing need to say what we are feeling right now and to touch and hold each other. But we won't do any of that with Rebecca sitting here.

With a large spoonful of ice cream, Rebecca stands up. "The only thing that could make this moment better would be eating my ice cream from my raft on the lake." Then she's gone, and it's just Andrew and me.

We take turns spooning ice cream quietly. Finally, I break the silence. "I am sorry about you and Angelina. I'm sorry about last night too. I'm never having alcohol again." I laugh with embarrassment. "I guess I do and say some pretty crazy things when I'm drunk. I'm embarrassed now."

He places his palm on my knee. "You never have to be embarrassed with me, Em. I hope you know that."

I nod. "I have to say, you can do way better than Angelina. I've always imagined someone better for you."

He looks at me with a playful curiosity. "What kind of girl do you imagine for me?"

I look down at my spoonful of ice cream. The tub is almost gone by now. There's just a melty layer at the bottom that I will very willingly slurp down if given the chance.

"Obviously you need someone who likes books and someone who can talk about them with you. You need someone who realizes how incredible you are. You're not just some pretty face. You're smart, and kind, and goofy. I hope you find someone who sees all of that and appreciates you for the gift that you are."

I cut myself off there before I make it too clear how I feel about him.

"Thank you, Em." He brushes a fingertip under my chin to tilt my head up and force me to meet his gaze. "I think I'm finally seeing clearly."

My heart pounds inside my rib cage, and I don't even know how to respond to his words. I'm melting into a puddle right now just like the ice cream left in the tub. *Say something*! I scream to myself desperately.

His smile begins to falter, and he pulls his finger away from my face. I try to smile softly back at him to convey my message since words are failing me, but it feels too late.

My heart breaks a little, and I curse myself for ruining this moment that could've been perfect. *Was that not the green light from him? Please don't screw this up, Emma! Say something! Anything!*

"I'm glad to hear you're seeing clearly again, buddy." I scruff up his hair a little as I speak.

Judging by Andrew's deflated look, I did, in fact, screw this up. *What is wrong with me? Did I seriously just say buddy? I've never called him buddy in my life! I'm an idiot.*

He stands up and begins walking down the dock to meet Rebecca. I can't even look at him right now. I just sit there with my head in my hands. *What did I just do?*

CHAPTER 20

Summer 19

"How'd you find this place?" I ask Andrew as we waltz out of the pizzeria. "I'm pretty full, but if I was offered another pizza to eat right now, I wouldn't hesitate to take it."

"I think you forget I grew up at the lake. I went to high school ten to fifteen minutes away from here." He explains, grabbing my hand as we begin aimlessly walking down the street. We still easily have another hour of light left.

"If that's the case, why haven't you taken me here sooner? You know how much I love pizza."

He chuckles. "Yes, I do. I've wanted to take you here for years, but it felt weird to take my *buddy* out to a nicer restaurant like this."

I don't miss his reference to nearly two years ago. I've wanted to give him an explanation for so long that the words burst out of me. "I didn't mean it the way it came across when I called you 'buddy.'"

He raises his eyebrows. "How else am I supposed to interpret the word 'buddy?'"

I groan. "I was seventeen. I'd never had a boyfriend before, and I panicked. Plus, you had just broken up with Angelina, and I didn't know how to read you. I was worried I was reading the situation wrong and would screw everything up."

He stops walking. "Never had a boyfriend? Past tense? You've had one? How did I not know?"

"I guess I still haven't technically had a boyfriend. I'd been on a series of dates with a guy in high school. He was nice, but I didn't feel the spark. I think I only had eyes for a certain someone." I look up at him through my eyelashes and find my words had the exact effect I hoped for. He has eased up and started tugging me along to walk more. "Don't dodge the topic, though. What happened with Angelina? Can I ask about that now?"

"Yeah, we can talk about it, but I thought you knew what happened."

I shake my head vigorously. "Clearly I didn't, or we would've been here much sooner."

He tips his head in my direction as if to say *fair point*. "Do you remember that night with the tequila?"

"Oh gosh! Do I? A disastrous night like that gets imprinted into your memory."

He laughs. "When you got sick that night and asked me to stay in the tent with you, all I wanted to do was curl up next to you and hold you, keep you safe. It was around then that I realized I didn't want to go back to my tent with Angelina and that I wasn't in love with her, nor was I ever going to be. I realized I cared for you as much more than just a friend." He squeezes my hand. "I thought you felt the same way after everything that happened, but then you went and called me 'buddy.'" He quickly adds, "I was going to break up with Angelina regardless of how you felt though. It wouldn't have been fair to be in a relationship with her after realizing how much I cared for you."

I tug him to sit down on the bench near us and look up at him with sorrow. "I'm sorry about that. I was an idiot, and had I been smoother, we could've figured things out so much sooner. Everything would've been easier."

He's already shaking his head in disagreement, and I'm taken aback. "Don't apologize. Sure, it would've been great to figure things out back then, but I think we have both grown a lot since then too. Who knows if we would've been ready for each other at seventeen? Besides, tonight, and really this whole summer, is about the present moment and moving forward, not about looking back."

I grin and squeeze his hand. "Okay, I can manage that. Do you want to keep walking for a bit?"

Andrew glances at the time on his phone and stands. "Yeah, we still have a little bit of time before the next part."

I give him a quizzical look, but he brushes it off, determined to keep the mystery alive.

We continue walking further from the direction of the pizza place for a few minutes longer as he points out different landmarks from his childhood.

"Do you hear that?" I ask him, eagerness flourishing in my eyes.

He pauses to listen, his forehead creasing in concentration. "Hear what?"

"Listen closely! I think I hear music playing."

"One of the restaurants probably has speakers outside. A lot of them do at this time of year," he suggests.

I shake my head. "No, it sounds like a live band."

I pull him toward the sound, the smile on my face growing with the volume of the music. Finally, we reach an open concrete area between two restaurants. There are lights strung overhead, and a band plays music at the front as people sit around, eating takeout while others dance freely.

I turn to Andrew with delight filling my face, just as he pulls me toward the band. "Will you dance with me? I'm not the best at it, but I'm better than the average guy." He winks.

I swoon a little and just beam in response as I let him pull me onto the makeshift dance floor. The song that is playing is a little more upbeat, so we wind up doing a quick two-step. As the song winds down, he twirls me around and dips me on the last note.

He pulls me back up, and I find our faces inches apart. His hot breath brushes my lips. God, I want to kiss him so badly. I've wanted to for years, and now that I finally know how he feels, it's nearly impossible to resist, but I know this isn't our moment.

Another song begins, and this one is slower. Andrew moves both of his hands down to my waist and pulls me in closer. We make eye contact, and I can see he's feeling the tension build between us too. He turns his head toward my shoulder, and I feel his soft lips graze my neck. Chills grow on my arms, despite the fact that it's still easily seventy-five degrees outside right now.

"I planned this date so perfectly, but this right here was a happy little accident," he admits.

"I'm glad it happened, and I'm glad we are finally going on a date. It was worth the wait." I add, "*You* were worth the wait."

I feel his breath hitch for a moment next to my ear. "You were too, Em. If I had the opportunity to do things over again, I wouldn't change a single thing. I'd take the jab of being called 'buddy' again—" He nudges me playfully "—and deal with the screaming ache to kiss you every time I saw you for nearly two years all over again because it led me to this moment with you. I'd say this moment right now is pretty incredible."

I nuzzle in closer to him as the song ends.

Andrew spins me around again just for the heck of it. Glancing up at the sky, he notes, "We better get going for part two."

"I don't suppose you'll tell me what part two is?"

Humor fills his face. "Sure, I'll tell you where we are going next, but that's it, okay?"

I assess his face hesitantly, wondering what he's up to. "Okay."

He whisks me back toward the direction of the restaurant, where his truck is still sitting. "We are headed to the grocery store."

I jerk my head back in surprise. "The grocery store? Is that code for something?"

He laughs. "Nope, I mean the grocery store. You'll see."

I glance at my phone while I wait in the truck. Andrew ran into the store and insisted I had to wait here. He said if I came in with him, it'd spoil the surprise.

I can't help but think about how things would be different if Rebecca was still here. She probably would've already sent me five texts during dinner asking for an update, and I'd have two more since then about how best friends shouldn't keep things from each other, even though the only reason she wouldn't have heard anything yet is because I'm having a good time and want to be polite on my date.

To my surprise, I have a text from Dani.

DANI

Hey sis! Thinking of you and hoping you're having a good time on your date. Don't do anything I wouldn't do

ME

Having a really good time. Too late... I already ate pineapple on my pizza. Whoops!

She responds immediately.

> The horror! And apparently you also text on
> dates. Strike 2! Get back to Andrew xo

I glance out the window, wondering if Andrew is headed back yet. I don't see him.

> Andrew ran into the store for some surprise that
> I can't see so I'm waiting

I see dots pop up on the screen and then disappear. I'm about to text her again when the doors unlock, and Andrew tosses a bag in the back seat. "No cheating. You can't look at what's in the bag. Promise?"

I scoff. "Why are you being so secretive? This better be good after the way you've hyped this up."

His eyes meet mine, and I can see he's being serious again. "It'll be good."

He pulls out of the parking lot, and in a matter of minutes, we are driving down a dirt road with no streetlights. The sun still hasn't gone down, but there's an orange glow beginning to tinge the sky.

"Oh my gosh! You're going to murder me! That's why you've been so secretive." I glance toward the mystery bag sitting in the backseat of the truck. "You stopped at the grocery store to get supplies!"

"Yes, because the mini-mart is famous for selling murder weapons," Andrew deadpans. "We are almost there. Just be patient."

I can't sit still. I'm glancing back and forth from the left to the right side of the road and back to the left side again, trying desperately to find something I recognize and get some inkling of an idea of what we are going to do.

Andrew brings the truck to a stop, and rushes out, throwing the rear door open and grabbing the grocery sack before saying, "Give me two minutes, and then you'll understand everything."

I don't even get the chance to acknowledge his words before he's hustling to the back of his truck, pulling the cover off his truck bed. I hear a lot of rustling around and then I begin to see little specks of light lining the back of his truck. *What is he up to?*

Andrew comes around to my door and opens it, holding out a bandanna. "What's that for?" I ask, pointing to it.

He pushes it toward my face. "It's a blindfold."

"What do you need a blindfold—"

"Just trust me, Em," he sighs, grabbing my hand and helping me out of the truck, then tying the bandanna to cover my eyes.

He walks me several feet along the length of the truck, and then his hands grip my waist to hoist me up and set me down on what feels like the tailgate. I let out a little shriek in surprise.

I hear him jump up next to me, and then he says, "Alright, you can take the blindfold off now."

He helps with the knot tied on the back of my head. When I finally see, I affirm I am in fact sitting on the tailgate, facing away from the truck.

I turn toward Andrew and see the pride radiating off of him. It melts my heart. He reminds me of a puppy sitting for his owner so he can get a treat, so innocent and excited.

I take in the scene around us. We are in a field that looks to be in the middle of nowhere. I catch a glimpse of the lights I saw earlier and turn to look at the truck bed behind me. It's filled with pillows and blankets, with a tub of chocolate fudge brownie ice cream seated perfectly against the pillows. Small tea lights are lining the truck bed. It's gorgeous. It's simple, and it's perfectly planned for me. I couldn't ask for a better date set up.

I open my mouth to say something to Andrew, but I'm speechless. This is so romantic, and I've never had someone put so much thought and time into something for me like he did.

"Oh wait! I almost forgot..." He trails off as he pulls his phone out and presses a few buttons. A speaker at the edge of the truck bed begins playing music.

I stammer, "I—I can't believe...you did this all for me? How did you plan this in less than twenty-four hours?"

He smirks. "I've had a lot longer than that to plan this one out. Do you remember when I took you into town for books and ice cream after you tried wakeboarding?"

"It was an amazing day, books and ice cream in one trip!" I reply.

"I remember you saying your perfect first date would involve getting pizza and a romantic gesture that shows thought and personalization to you. In a way, you planned this date out for us when you were fifteen, but I came up with the grand gesture idea last summer after that night under the stars. I saw how mesmerized you were by them, and we didn't even do things the right way, so we are doing it right now."

"You're incredible," I tell him. "I still can't believe all of this."

"We better eat the ice cream before it melts," Andrew insists, popping the lid off and grabbing two spoons from who knows where.

I happily dig into the tub of chocolatey heaven. Andrew follows suit.

"I know the stars aren't out yet, but they should be by the time we finish the ice cream," Andrew explains. "This is probably the best place to see them. There are no trees nearby to block the view, and there's no lights anywhere nearby to dull the shine."

"How did you find this place?"

He chuckles. "This was a pretty popular place to come hang out and drink in high school. I like this use for it a thousand times better though."

"Me too." I smile softly and lean my head against him.

He wraps an arm around my shoulders, and I love the feeling of being wrapped up in his arms. He's solid but cozy, like being wrapped up in your favorite blanket, only better.

The stars begin to come out as faint freckles of lights in the distance. "I hope you don't mind we missed the sunset," Andrew says as he licks his spoon clean. "I just couldn't bring myself to start us with any kind of ending, no matter how beautiful."

"What do you call this?" I ask, gesturing to the sky. "The night isn't the end of the day?"

He shakes his head vigorously. "No, we are watching the night just begin to unfold. Isn't it lovely?"

I can't help but wonder how I got here. When I woke up yesterday, Andrew and I were just friends, and somehow that changed so quickly. Now, we are here on a date. I've been dreaming about this for years! I know I haven't been on that many dates, but even if I had, there's no competition. This is the best date I've ever been on, and we haven't even kissed yet.

Andrew holds out the tub to me, offering me the last bite. I gleefully take it, and the urge to kiss him for that simple gesture nearly wins out.

"Thank you, Andrew. For all of it. The pizza, the grand gesture, the ice cream…this is easily the best date ever."

He grins. "I'm glad you like it."

He takes the empty carton from me and sets it aside, pulling me back to lean against the pillows and be able to take the stars in. They're very prominent at this point, shining with a brilliant radiance.

"Do you know any constellations?" I ask him.

"Do the Big Dipper and Little Dipper count?" he asks me with a self-deprecating chuckle.

"I suppose they do."

"Do you know more? Will you show me?" he urges.

"I only know a couple more than that. My grandpa was interested in astronomy and started to teach me before he passed." I point up at the sky, tracing with my fingers. "Do you see those five stars that kind of look like a slightly crooked drawing of a house?" I look to him for reassurance. "That's Cepheus."

I watch the childlike amusement in his eyes with adoration. "Where'd that name come from?"

"Cepheus was some king. He was married to Cassiopeia, whose father was Andromeda. Both of them are also constellations," I tutor.

"Dang. How do we get a constellation named after us?" he teases.

"Maybe you can start by becoming a king."

His eyes grow round. "I didn't realize those were the stakes. I'm only a knight who's trying to get a princess to realize I'm the one for her."

"Well, it's working," I turn toward him.

Our faces are so close as we both lie there, motionless. *This is your moment!* I scream to myself, but I'm frozen.

It's not like Andrew is my first kiss. I wish he was because it would be so much more poetic than my bumbling first kiss with that boy from high school who was only with me for the sake of being with someone. Even without this being my first time, I feel incredibly nervous. This is Andrew after all. I've wanted to kiss him for years. I've already messed things up in the past, and I don't want to do it again.

I catch him watching me intently. "You're overthinking things, aren't you?" he asks, running his pointer finger along my jaw.

When his finger reaches my chin, he pulls it in slightly, and then we are kissing. It's amazing. His lips are soft and full, and our tongues dance together.

We break apart for a moment, and our gazes meet again. There's a pause, and then he's pulling me back in.

When we separate, he speaks first. "Sorry, I wasn't ready for that to be over yet."

The hummingbirds with their rapidly flapping wings are back, but they begin to ease quickly because this is all starting to feel natural, meant to be.

CHAPTER 21

Summer 17

Music drifts lazily from Rebecca's Bluetooth speaker while the two of us bask in the sun on the Martins' dock, enjoying one of the few afternoons we have together, just the two of us.

Propping herself up onto her elbows, Rebecca turns down the volume. "So, it's been weeks since Andrew broke up with Angelina. I've tried not to push the issue, but I'm not very patient. What's going on with you two?"

I frown. "We were having such a nice afternoon. Do we have to talk about Andrew right now?"

"That right there is exactly why I'm asking! You haven't said much of anything about him since the camping trip. I thought you liked him. He's single now! What's holding you back?"

"It's complicated, Becs. I kept trying to get up the courage to talk with him, but we always get interrupted, or he says something that makes me think maybe I read everything wrong that happened that day. It's fine. We're in a good place now. I'm not going to mess with it. Andrew and I are never going to happen. I've made my peace with it," I say hoarsely.

Rebecca scoffs. "Yeah, right!"

"Please just drop it. I don't... I can't... it just won't work, Becs."

I meet her eyes, and her gaze softens. She sits up all the way, reaching out and wrapping me up in a tight hug. "It's going to be okay, Emma. I promise I haven't noticed anything off between the two of you. You just need to get out of your head. You overthink things way too much."

"Easy for you to say. You don't have any sense of crippling self-doubt."

"I don't have it because I won't allow it. When the doubts creep in, I tell them to get the hell out, and I keep moving. You should try it sometime." She winks.

"Maybe someday," I say dreamily.

Rebecca turns the volume back up on the speaker and scrolls through her phone for another song. "Okay, okay, one more song for you. You'll love this one. No question."

I settle back down onto my towel. "You seem very confident. What's the story with this one?" I ask, knowing Rebecca always has a story for the songs she introduces me to.

She shakes her head. "No story this time. I just heard it and immediately thought of you. Listen to the words carefully."

She hits play, and I listen intently. It's the story of a man who is in love with his friend. He wants to tell her how he feels, but he's terrified of ruining their relationship by exposing his true feelings for her. Eventually, he can't contain it anymore and asks her to be his. It's a sweet song, and it's beautifully done. From the singing to the music to the lyrics, it's all perfect.

The song wraps up, and I look over at Rebecca. "What's it called?"

"'Porch Swing Angel' by Muscadine Bloodline."

"Send it to me," I say eagerly.

She beams. "Will do." As she sits up, she assesses the scene around us. "Alright, I'm tired of lying around, and I'm out of new music for you."

I sit up too. "Okay, then what do you want to do?"

She brings her pointer finger and her thumb up to her chin to give her best thinking look, but I know her better than that. She has had this planned out for a while. I can see it on her face. "How about we climb the water tower?"

"Veto!" I cringe.

"Well fine, but you don't get any more vetoes." It takes her less than a second to suggest another idea. "There are these cliffs about a ten-minute walk from here that are a popular jumping off point. A lot of people from my high school go there, and I've always wanted to try it. We should go."

I give her a hesitant look. "Becs, you know I love you, and I surprisingly still trust your judgment most of the time, even after the tequila incident, but I'm not sure about this one. I'll openly admit I'm a chicken."

She sighs. "Come on! You already used your veto. Let's just go check them out, and then you can decide. It's not like we don't have the time to kill."

I tilt my head to one side as I consider it. "All right, fine. We can go look, but if I decide I don't want to do it, you can't force me."

She begins standing before I even finish my sentence. "Done. Absolutely! I promise!" I can practically feel the excitement buzzing off of her. "I'll text Andrew to meet us there. He should be wrapping up his training by now."

As I peer over the edge of the cliffs, my stomach turns into a gymnast, performing somersaults and cartwheels. It has to be at least ten feet down to the water. Standing at the top looking down, it looks like a long way to fall.

Rebecca scoots an inch closer to the edge, and panic rises inside of me, squeezing the air out of my lungs. *Yup, that's it. I'm not doing this.* "Okay, Becs. We saw it, and I say I can't do it. There's no way."

She schlumps her shoulders and gives me a pouty look. "Please! It looks so fun. How about you watch me and Andrew do it first? That'll show you it's perfectly safe."

My eyes grow round. "If I don't want to do it, what makes you think I'm okay with sitting by and watching you do it? It looks dangerous."

"I told you I've seen plenty of people come to this exact spot and jump. I have yet to hear of someone who got hurt here."

"Exactly. You haven't heard of anyone getting hurt *yet*. It's only a matter of time."

She rolls her eyes. "I'm such a bad influence on you. You're getting so dramatic." I can't help but laugh at her remark as she continues. "Andrew will be here any second, and he's going to tell you to do it too."

As if he had been waiting for his cue, Andrew pulls up right then. He throws his truck in park and hops out. Wearing a sweat-stained muscle tank and shorts that are cut several inches above the knee, his ensemble shows off every muscle in his back and shoulders. His triceps and his thick quads have a fresh post-workout pump. Realizing I've been staring, I immediately turn to look back over the edge of the cliff.

Under her breath, Rebecca mutters, "Wipe the drool off your face. Goodness, Emma! You've got it bad." As if she didn't just turn me speechless and redder than my still-damp bathing suit, Rebecca turns to Andrew without missing a beat. "Andrew, thank God you got here when you did. Emma doesn't want to jump off the cliff because she's too scared."

I whip my head in her direction. "I am not too scared! I said it looked dangerous. I'm not looking to finish my summer in the emergency room."

Andrew takes the two of us in and bursts into a fit of laughter. "Let me get a look at this cliff," he suggests as he walks in our direction.

As he looks over the edge, I watch his face closely. He looks completely unfazed. *That little daredevil! I should've known he'd betray me like this.*

He turns back to Rebecca and me. "It looks fun."

"See!" Rebecca erupts with excitement. "Let's go! I'll even go first if it makes you feel better," she says, getting way ahead of herself.

"I already told you that won't help," I mutter, my attention beginning to move toward Andrew who is tugging his tank top off in preparation for jumping in the cool water.

Rebecca snaps her fingers in my face. "Earth to Emma! Don't think I don't see what's going on here. Focus or you will end up getting hurt on these things."

"That's it! I'm out! You guys can jump to your deaths, but I don't want any part of this."

Rebecca laughs. "I'm just teasing you. Come on! Andrew, tell her she should do it."

Andrew nods. "Don't make me bribe you with books and ice cream again." He winks, and I feel my cheeks flush.

I casually laugh and swat at him. *We are just friends. We are just friends.* "I'm never going to live that down, am I?"

"Nope." The twins say in unison. I hate it when they do that. It freaks me out.

Rebecca begins shuffling toward the edge of the cliff, clearly eager to jump into the abyss.

Andrew teeters between wanting to be the first one in and trying to convince me I should just jump with them.

I see convincing me wins out because he steps toward me, reaching out for my elbow as Rebecca gets a running start and leaps out, shrieking with glee as her feet leave the ground. I hear the splash and rush over to the edge, watching anxiously for her to pop out of the lake.

She bursts up shortly after, sputtering water and wearing a huge grin. "You guys *have* to try that! The feeling when you think you should be hitting the water but still haven't? It's amazing!" Between gasps of air, she adds, "Emma, tell your doubts to go to hell and get in the water! You won't regret it."

Her delight and easygoing advice make me want to go, but there's still the part of me that is terrified of the drop. With all that distance, there's lots of room for things to go wrong.

Andrew's hand connects with my elbow, drawing my attention back to him and away from my chaotic thoughts. "Stop overthinking it. I promise we won't let anything happen to you." After a beat, he asks, "Will you do it with me? At the same time? I'll hold your hand."

My whole body feels tingly at the thought, but I'm still feeling unsure. He must see it on my face because he just grabs my hand. "Make room, Rebecca! We're coming," he hollers.

He pulls me slightly and I willingly walk toward the cliff. I move to peer over the ledge again, and he grabs my chin, pulling my face to look at him. "Don't look down again."

"I have to know where I'm jumping," I argue.

"Do you trust me?"

"Of course, I do, but this is about a little more than trusting you," I claim.

"There's nothing down there to get caught on. Just jump out, and you'll be fine," he instructs. I nod my head the slightest bit. He smiles. "Good. On the count of three. One…two…three!"

He leaps out with my hand still in his, and I have no choice but to jump too. Rebecca's right. There's a moment or two when I think I should be hitting the water by now, but we are still suspended in the air. Then comes the shock of the cool water, rushing up my nose and swallowing me up from my toes to my head.

I rush up to the water, gasping for air. "Holy crap!" *I just did that!*

Andrew comes up shortly after me, looking much calmer. He is beaming. "You did it, Em!"

Rebecca interjects, "We all did it, and not a single one of us died." I narrow my eyes in a glare at Rebecca, but she isn't deterred. "What'd you think? Want to do it again?"

"It was exciting, but I'm not going to tell you that you were right." I chuckle.

Rebecca begins splashing to get out of the water. She reaches a hand out to me as she gets to my side. "Come on. We are so doing that again."

Rebecca drags me out of the water to climb back up the cliff. Getting up is way harder than coming down. We are soaking wet and barefoot as we clamor up the dirt path, grabbing onto the occasional tree root jutting out from the ground to help pull ourselves up the steep slope.

At the top, Rebecca leans into me. "He looooves you," she teases.

"What are you talking about?"

She gestures out to the cliff edge where we jumped a couple minutes ago. "I know Andrew. He would've wanted to be the tough guy who jumped first, but instead, he stayed back and helped you get in. He held your hand and was patient with you. He adores you. I can see it."

I shake my head. "I told you, I already screwed it up, and things have been back to normal again between us, so I'm not going to try anything. Andrew and I are just friends, and that's all we'll ever be."

She smirks. "I can't wait to be the maid of honor at your wedding and tell everyone about this exact moment during my speech."

A smile breaks out on my face, and I lean my shoulder into her. "Alright, Miss Daredevil, let's see you jump again."

"Wow, you want to get rid of me that badly that you're

sentencing me to cliff-jumping now?" she says with a light-hearted tone.

I give her a look indicating she's being ridiculous. She reaches her hand out to me. "Alright, bestie, I want my turn jumping in with you."

"Do I have to?"

"Hell yes you have to," she insists. "If you'll do it with Andrew, then you have to do it with me." She pouts. "Please."

I grab her hand in answer, and she instantly becomes cheery again. "You know I only push you because you get in your head too much, right? I know you want to do these things but won't on your own. I'm proud of you. Look at all you've done just this summer."

Her words touch me and make me want to jump five more times just for her. I know Rebecca would do a lot for me, and I hope she knows I'd do the same. "Thanks, Becs."

She acts nonchalant as if she isn't an absolute gift in my life, and we walk a little closer to the edge.

"Should we count to three?"

"Yeah. One... two... three!"

We push off the edge. As we are falling, I notice Andrew still in the water. I had assumed he was following us up the trail, but there he is, treading water right where Rebecca is about to land.

The whole moment moves in slow motion, and yet it doesn't go slow enough for me to say anything.

I hear Andrew shout, and then I'm in the water. I rush up to the surface as fast as I can, desperate to find the aftermath. Rebecca is at the surface too, but I don't see Andrew.

"What happened?" Alarm fills my voice.

Cupping her elbow, Rebecca replies, "I think I bonked Andrew. I'm sure he's fine."

"Then where is he?"

Rebecca instantly pales, and I watch her calm demeanor turn

into pure panic. We part from each other and splash around searching for Andrew.

After a moment, I see Rebecca struggling to tug him up, so I rush to help. As I grab onto his arm, I instantly feel the dead weight, making my stomach sink. *Please let him be okay! How did this happen? I knew this was a bad idea!* But I can't say any of that. The fear and guilt on Rebecca's face is clear as day. I need to keep her calm.

We finally get Andrew onto the shore, and I take him in. He's pale, but it looks like he's breathing. *Thank goodness!*

"He's knocked out cold," I remark in surprise, careful not to say anything to indicate it was Rebecca's fault. It truly was an accident.

She turns to me. "What do we do?"

"I... I'm not sure," I respond, disappointed in myself for not being better in this situation. "Call 9-1-1?" I ask more than tell her.

With tears welling in her eyes, Rebecca looks at me with fear, an emotion I've never seen on her brave face. "This was a terrible idea! What was I thinking?"

CHAPTER 22

Summer 19

Rushing to step out of the shower, I nearly slip. I can't be bothered with the time it takes to towel off as I drip down the hallway. I grab my phone from my nightstand. Still wrapped in a towel, water droplets slithering down my arms and back, I type out my message.

ME

Andrew! Andrew! Andrew!

While I wait, I slip on my daily summer wardrobe, which, in a nutshell, is shorts and a tank top.

ANDREW

What? What? What?

I have an idea

And what is that?

It's a surprise. Come over in 15 mins. I'm driving

Ooooh a surprise for me? Do I get any hints?

> Just that I'm holding us both to living our lives
> to the fullest

Dani knocks on my door as I pull out my makeup bag to begin applying my usual coat of mascara.

"Come in!" I cheer.

"Someone is in a good mood," she remarks. "Oh, and is that a new tank top I see? Who are you trying to impress?"

I glower at her. "Yeah, it's new. What's up?"

"I was just wondering what you were up to. I swore I just saw you run down the hallway in your towel."

I snort. "That's because I did. I'm taking Andrew to the water tower."

"Really? The big ugly yellow one right by here?" She scrunches her nose and narrows her brows. "Why? Is that your idea of a romantic date, hanging out around the water tower?" She not-so-subtly tries to choke back a laugh.

"This isn't exactly a date. It's just us creating memories and life experiences. We're not going to just hang out around it. We're going to climb it. I've always wondered what the view from the top looks like."

She blinks. "Since when were you adventurous?"

"Hey! I'm adventurous."

"You must really be into Andrew. I'm guessing this is something he's always wanted to do?"

I shrug. "No. It's something I've always been too scared to do, and I think Andrew will be the perfect person to support me while I do it."

"Okay then," she says, her words dripping in doubt.

"Don't talk me out of this. Rebecca asked me to do it a few summers ago, and I said no. That's one more experience I could've had with her, but I was too afraid. I'm trying not to be afraid anymore."

Realization crosses her face, and she just nods, looking down at her feet. "I think it could be fun. Send me a picture from the top, will you?"

I give her a soft smile. "The view is going to be *amazing*. I know it."

I finish getting ready and give Dani a quick hug as I hear the doorbell. "Andrew's here."

"Good luck! You better hope this doesn't scare him off. You guys only went on your first date five days ago. It's not too late for him to change his mind."

"Shut up before I change my mind about you!" I yell back.

"What does that even mean?"

"I don't know!" I chuckle as I close the door behind me.

Before I can even turn around fully, I'm swept up into Andrew's arms, and the excitement I had when I first got out of the shower is instantly back. Something about being around Andrew just makes me want to do all kinds of crazy things. This boy could probably get me to jump out of a moving train with him if he set his mind to it, but I'll settle for climbing a water tower today.

Setting me down, he asks, "So where are we going?"

"I was thinking we could take a little drive to the ugly duckling," I say, using our given nickname for the hideous yellow water tower.

"For what?"

"To climb it. Duh."

He arches a brow. "That doesn't sound like something you'd be into."

"Well, today I'm not letting my fears hold me back."

"I like this new side of you."

I purse my lips. "Don't get used to it. I can already feel the panic welling up inside of me with each step I take toward getting there."

He swirls me in his arms. "Don't panic! I'll be right by your side the whole time. This will be fun!"

As he releases me from his embrace, I find my keys, twirling them in my hands, stalling. "Maybe we can do it tomorrow instead. The clouds might ruin the view."

Andrew glances at the clear blue sky above us and laughs. "It's too late, Em! You've already convinced me to go."

Standing at the base of the water tower, I'm beginning to realize just how crazy this idea was. I understand now why I had avoided this experience in the past. This is nuts. It must be at least a few stories high. I know the second I get on that ladder, the ground is going to feel a million miles away.

Andrew nonchalantly asks, "Do you want to go first, or do you want me to?"

"Uhhh." Sweat beads on my forehead.

"Do you want to see how easy it is for me to do it, or do you want me to go after you for support?"

"If you go first, there's a ninety-nine percent chance I don't follow you. I recommend you go behind me." I grab one rung of the ladder and turn back to him. "My life is in your hands now, Andrew. If I fall, you have to catch me."

"I didn't realize we brought Rebecca along," he teases, his smile quickly fading to a somber frown.

"We always bring her where we go."

He nods, his lips pursed. Then he kisses me on the cheek. "You've got this, Em. This is for Rebecca, right?"

His last sentence gets me moving up the ladder quicker than a spider monkey. Okay, not really. Slow and steady *did* win the race after all, but at least I'm moving now.

As promised, Andrew carefully follows behind me. When we reach the halfway point, I do what every rookie does. I begin to look down. With that one look, the world immediately plummets another fifty feet lower. I suck in a breath and stop moving, paralyzed. There's nothing for me to do. I can't just give up now. I'm halfway. It's not like I can just go back down easily. Andrew is in the way, and I've already come this far, but the prospect of going up any further makes me feel like I've inhaled thumbtacks.

My breath quickens, and my heart pounds furiously in my chest as if it's trying to escape the prison of my rib cage. I meet Andrew's gaze, pure panic in my eyes, but his own reflect nothing but peace. "We're almost there. Just one more rung at a time. Think of the view from the top. Think of the thrill when you get to tell everyone what you did today."

I nod, still frozen. He releases his grip on one of the rungs, reaching up toward me.

"Andrew, what're you doing? No! Are you crazy?" I argue.

But when his hand meets my waist, I can feel the panic ease a little. The prickling in my lungs is gone, and my throat opens up enough to allow a sliver of air in.

"Another step, Em. For Rebecca."

I slowly pull one hand from the safety of the ladder and then grab the next rung. My opposite foot follows, shakily, and when it touches the ladder again, the clanging sound makes me freeze again.

"No, keep going. Your steps are making music."

"What?" I ask, hardly able to hear his words right now over the rapid pounding of my pulse in my ears.

"Take another step. The sound is like music."

His words fill me with enough curiosity to allow me to make another movement. I hear the chime of the metal again.

"That's my girl!" Andrew cheers. Then he proceeds to sing the lyrics to "My Girl."

Laughter bubbles up unexpectedly inside of me, but my fear still keeps me plastered to the same spot. Andrew continues singing, pausing briefly between verses to insist, "Sing with me, Em!"

"I can't believe you're singing at a time like this!"

"Well, we can't exactly skip rocks from here, now can we?" he challenges.

I press my lips together in defeat. He's not wrong.

"Come on. You know the words." He picks up exactly where he left off, this time singing louder. "I want the birds to hear us and be jealous!"

Again, the smallest hint of laughter slips from my lips. Seeing the traces of a smile on my face, he begins singing even more ridiculously, adding animations with his one free hand, and projecting his voice out into the trees. When he runs out of lyrics to sing, he begins creating his own to the same tune. "Emma! Emma! She's going to crush the ugly duckling!"

He gives my butt a light encouraging tap. "Come on, Em! We have to finish what we started. Take one more deep breath and then take another step."

Silently, I follow his orders. I fill my lungs with as much oxygen as they will hold, allowing it to sit for a couple of seconds before I finally exhale.

"There you go. Now just one movement at a time."

I move my right hand again, then my left foot.

"Don't forget to breathe!" Andrew reminds me as he follows closely.

When we reach the top, all the tension and tight squeezing feelings release. I feel like a sponge that's finally allowed to soak up water again.

"Andrew! We did it! Thank God!" I've never smiled so big as I drag myself off the ladder onto the tiny ledge surrounding the water tank at the top.

"I told you you could do it." He holds up an imaginary mic. "I'm here with Emma O'Dougherty, the first girl to ever climb the ugly duckling. Emma, tell me, how does it feel?"

"It feels pretty freaking great!" I beam, taking in the view around us. The lake shimmers like it's laced with a million diamonds as the sun reflects off the water. The evergreen trees have never looked so full and vibrant... or small.

"We sure are high up, and this ledge is pretty narrow," I note as my smile turns into a grimace.

Andrew doesn't miss a beat, wrapping his arms around me. "I guess that just means I'll have to stay extra close to you since there isn't much room up here and all."

I kiss his forehead, which is currently pressed right up against my cheek as he smushes himself into me the best he can. The kiss draws his attention up to me, and he straightens up, eagerly reaching to meet my lips. When our mouths touch, I immediately recognize how much trouble I'm in. I've been so far gone for this boy for much longer than just the last several days since we went on a date. With his charm, those eyes, and that dimpled smile, he's impossible to resist, but then you throw in the way he cares for me and patiently helps me do things I'd never do on my own. There's no way I would've come up here alone today. If I had started this journey with anyone else, the fire department would've had to come and get me down from the ladder, but instead, Andrew managed to not only get me the rest of the way up the ladder, but he had me laughing a little while I did it. Andrew is amazing, and he can get me to do just about anything. That's terrifying.

Ignoring that profound moment of vulnerability, I whip out my phone. "I promised Dani a picture."

Andrew snags my phone from my hand and holds it out in front of him. "Smile."

He hands it back, and I take in the photo of the two of us with the whispering pines and the sparkling lake as our backdrop. It's amazing.

I send it to Dani.

ME

The view from the top

DANI

No freaking way! You did it! I'm so proud!

You sound surprised

I had my doubts

Well I wasn't even scared

I'm sure Andrew will confirm that 😌

He will

Only because he's your bf and he has to

It's beautiful up there. I hope you're taking a
moment to enjoy the beauty

I put my phone back in my pocket and allow myself to treasure the moment. I'm with Andrew, and I just climbed a freaking water tower. If you told me a year ago that I'd be here, I would've laughed hysterically. But here I am.

"I bet you've never had a date like this."

Andrew shakes his head. "The only other person I've been on a date with before you is Angie. I can assure you we never went on any dates like this."

"Did she ever take her nose out of her phone long enough to enjoy dates with you?" I ask, wincing as I process the amount of cringey jealousy I managed to pack into that question.

"You didn't like her much, did you? Were you jealous?"

"What? No!"

Andrew looks like he just heard the juiciest gossip. "Now *this* is refreshing to see."

"What do you mean?"

"Well, you've seen my jealous side, so it's nice to know you have one too," he says, sidling up to me.

"When have I seen you jealous?"

"Last summer."

"I did?"

"Yeah, when Brendan came and hung out with us that night. He was looking at you like you were some kind of dessert."

I scoff. "No, he wasn't. Besides, he wouldn't do that to you. You're his best friend. Wouldn't that be breaking some kind of bro code?"

He presses his lips together before responding. "Well, he didn't exactly know how I felt about you."

"Why not? I thought he was your best friend?"

"He is."

"Why would you keep that from him?" I press.

"It just didn't feel important to tell him."

As the silence settles over us like a damp blanket, he quickly amends, "I mean you're of course very important to me. You always have been. It's just that I'm not the greatest at telling people how I feel all the time. I cut a lot of people out last year when I was grieving Rebecca's loss because it was easier than talking about it. It's not about you, Em. I promise. This is a me thing."

I nod thoughtfully. "I guess that's something you'll need to work on."

He smirks. "Yeah, I guess so." He presses a kiss to my lips, assuring me in the best way he knows how.

"So, how the heck do we get down from here?"

"I'd recommend the ladder."

"Smart-ass."

He chuckles. "I'll be with you every step of the way."

CHAPTER 23

Summer 17

Rebecca's panic continues to rise by the second. I've never seen her so scared, but I can see the possibility of her twin not being okay is completely shattering her.

I carefully put on my best brave face, recognizing for once I have to be the one who isn't terrified. For Rebecca.

I grab Andrew's wrist and lean toward his chest. "He's breathing, and he has a pulse. Those are great signs!" Despite my best efforts, my voice shakes a little as I report the news.

"How do we get him to wake up? Oh God! This is all my fault. I'm such an idiot! If I had just slowed down..."

"Becs, this isn't your fault. He's going to be okay. I promise."

I swear God himself was looking out for me at that moment because Andrew wakes up, coughing up water.

Rebecca quickly wraps him up in her arms. "It's okay. Your big sister is here. It's okay. I'm so sorry, Andrew. Are you okay? Do we need to call 9-1-1?"

He looks incredibly disoriented. His pupils are huge, his eyes are glassy, and his movements are slow.

I nudge Rebecca a little, indicating we should give him some space. "I think he's going to be okay, but he almost definitely has a concussion. We should take him to the hospital to get checked out."

Blinking rapidly, Andrew pushes against Rebecca and me, forcing himself to stand. "I'm fine. Thank you, but it's going to take more than Rebecca's elbow to take me out."

"Clearly not! She just knocked you out cold. We are going to take you to get looked at."

"Yeah, I smashed your skull in with my elbow! You don't need to be Mr. Tough Guy right now," Rebecca croaks.

One look at Rebecca's face is all it takes to get Andrew to settle back down to the ground. "Fine, but I guarantee you a doctor won't tell you anything I can't already tell you. I'm fine."

Mr. and Mrs. Martin join us in the waiting room as Andrew gets checked out. They've been grilling Rebecca and me with lots of questions since they arrived, but they've finally quieted down. Now we all just sit in anticipation of the doctor's opinion.

Andrew steps out of the doors with a piece of paper in hand. He holds it up. "The doctor said it looks like a concussion, but I should be fine. She said to monitor for nausea or memory loss and to expect headaches and trouble concentrating or reading." He frowns. "No working out for a little while, and I'll check back in with the doctor in a week."

Mr. and Mrs. Martin nod vigorously. "Maybe I should go talk to the doctor myself." Mrs. Martin eagerly begins walking toward the doors Andrew just came through.

He grabs her by the arm holding her back. "It's all right here, Mom. She even gave me a number to call just in case. If you really feel the need to talk to her, you can call her when we get home."

The tension in her shoulders visibly releases.

We begin to walk out to our cars, and it's then that Andrew seems to notice I'm here. He does a double take. "You didn't have to stay here and wait, Em. Did no one offer to drive you home? It's been a couple hours. Do your parents know you're here? You probably missed dinner." His words spiral in concern, and I'm incredibly impressed he's able to recognize and process all of this information after what just happened.

I wrap one arm around him in a half hug as we continue through the parking lot. "I just wanted to know you're okay, Andrew. I texted my parents I was here, and I'll just eat leftovers when I get home."

He turns to Rebecca. "Can we stop for some food on the way back?"

She nods anxiously. I can tell she's still flooded with guilt. "Yeah, whatever you want! Are you hungry? We can pick up a pizza or sandwiches."

Andrew swivels in my direction. "What do you want, Em?"

I wave my hands out in front of me. "I'm not hungry. I can wait till we get home. It's not that far."

Andrew furrows his brows. "It's after eight o'clock, and you haven't had dinner yet. I know you're starving. Let's get some food." He assesses me. "I'm going to say you're in a pizza mood. Who am I kidding? You're always in a pizza mood!" The smile spreading on my face gives me away.

Rebecca hops in the driver's seat, and he places his hand on the small of my back as he guides me into the bench seat of his truck. "There's a Domino's close by. We can order it now and it should be ready by the time we get there," he insists.

My stomach growls, and he meets my eyes with a knowing look. I have no choice but to let him take care of me, even though the roles should be reversed after today's events.

The pizza is really good though, and Andrew was right; I'm always in a pizza mood.

CHAPTER 24

Summer 19

As we round the corner onto our street at the end of our run, I turn to Andrew and excitedly shout, "I'll race you to your house!"

I begin to take off, but he hollers back at me from behind. "Wait! No!" He gasps for air between words. "That's not fair. Get back here. Besides, I'm much too tired to—" My pace falters a little, but as soon as he catches up with me, he takes off at a sprint. I should've known better than to trust Mr. Track Star!

I push off and try to catch up. We reach his driveway, and I'm only a pace or two behind him. "You are such a cheater!" I shove him as a smile spreads across my face.

"What do you want to do with the rest of the day? We are supposed to have thunderstorms this afternoon." Andrew glances up at the sky. "It looks like the dark clouds are already rolling in."

"I think we should sign up for the race today. It's already almost the end of July. The race is in two weeks."

He groans. "Oh, I don't know. I don't think I'm in good enough shape."

"You just ran five miles with me. The race is only a 5K. That's barely over three miles," I argue.

He gives me a very serious look. "The mud adds at least three miles to the distance of the race. Everyone knows that."

"Oh, is that so?" I inquire, glaring at him and trying hard not to let through the smile that's attempting to creep onto my face.

He nods matter of fact, and my face betrays me as that dang smile shines through. As if that isn't enough, a giggle slips out too.

He swoops me up into his arms and twirls me around for a second, and my laughter grows. I watch as his face goes from very serious to filled with elation in less than a second.

Things have been going very well for us over the last few weeks. We've been training hard for the race, ramping up our distance to well beyond what we will be running just because we both enjoy being out here so much. We've exchanged lots of books and music recommendations and spent almost every waking moment with one another. Andrew even began writing again and shared part of his stories with me. They're amazing.

The only issue is we have about three weeks left until Andrew and I have to go back to school, and we have been completely avoiding the topic. We have done long-distance before as friends but not while we are in a relationship, and our schools are a six-hour flight apart. It's not the same as living next door to one another all summer.

I think we both realize that, but we have been having such a great time together this summer that neither one of us wants to bring it up.

"We can sign up for the race today. But that will take what... Five minutes? What about the rest of our day? Anything you have in mind?"

I think about it for a moment. "There's nothing on my 'really living list' that we would do indoors."

He nods. "I have an idea. My parents are leaving in a couple of hours for a client meeting in New York. I'll have the house all to myself until tomorrow afternoon, but I'd like some company." He looks at me with sweet puppy-dog eyes.

"I think I can help with that."

A sly grin blooms on his lips. "I have to get everything ready, so you can come over around four."

"Four?! It's only nine o'clock. What am I going to do with the rest of my day?" I challenge.

"Alright, you can come over and I'll make you some eggs, but then I'm kicking you out! I have big plans!" He winks.

About ten minutes before five, I wrap on the Martins' door quickly. The rain begins seeping through my coat despite the fact I was only out in the rain for about twenty to thirty seconds.

The sound of music drifts through the door, followed by Andrew's footsteps coming toward me. He swings the door open, and I throw myself into his arms, squeezing him tight and covering his lips with mine.

"Gosh, I missed you," I say to him.

"You're early! And you're soaked!" He laughs heartily and then kisses me back. "It's only been a few hours since I've seen you. You missed me already?"

"Is it so bad if I did?"

He shakes his head knowingly. "No, it's definitely not. I missed you too," he admits as he places another lingering kiss on my lips before grabbing my hand and immediately taking me to his bedroom to get a shirt that isn't completely soaked through.

As we walk back upstairs, he hesitates before bringing me into the kitchen. "Now bear with me. I lost track of time, and things aren't really ready."

I immediately become aware of the smell throughout the house. *Is that bread?* Then, I see the mess that is the kitchen. My mouth drops open and my eyes pop out of my skull like in the cartoons.

"Oh my gosh! Your mom is going to kill you!" I burst into laughter.

There's flour all across the counter and the floor. It is even tracked from the kitchen to the front door. There's a mixer on the counter, what looks like a pasta maker, and several open jars of tomato sauce that have dripped across the counter and stove.

Andrew gives me a sheepish grin. "I'll clean it up."

I take in the scene once more. "What are you making?"

He gives a self-deprecating chuckle. "What haven't I made? I started off trying to make pasta from scratch, but that appears to be a total failure. I was going to make homemade bread and then make garlic bread with it, but now that the pasta is a failure, I just have a loaf of plain bread that may or may not have way too much yeast in it."

He pulls a mountainous loaf out from the fridge of all places. Just from seeing it, I can tell he definitely let some instant yeast over-rise in that bread.

He looks at me with sorrow in his eyes. "I'm sorry. This was supposed to be a perfect homemade meal for you, and I'm ruining it. I would've asked you to come later if I had noticed what time it was."

I caress his face in reassurance. "It's okay, Andrew! Honestly, seeing you mess something up makes me feel a little better. I've been kind of spoiled lately." I give him a teasing smirk. "How about we make something together? That would be fun!"

He perks up slightly. "Okay. What would you like to make?"

I look around the kitchen and begin checking the fridge and pantry for ingredients. "I know we already had pizza on a date, but it looks like we'd have all of the ingredients to make a pizza from scratch."

He nods excitedly. "That sounds great! Hang on, let me at least get the mood right in here, the way it was supposed to be."

I watch him glide across the room to grab a lighter out of the drawer. He begins lighting some candles sitting on the windowsill that I hadn't noticed before. He lights more on the kitchen table and across the entertainment unit in the living room. Then he shuts the kitchen lights off and closes a few blinds to shut out the last bit of light slipping through the stormy clouds. We are left enveloped in just the soft glow of candlelight.

"It's beautiful."

I can see the pride shining through on his face. "What do we need to do first for the pizza?"

I inspect the ingredients already on the counter. I grab the yeast, flour, oil, and salt, setting them close to the mixer. "I'll measure out the yeast. You get me two cups of hot water."

"Yes, ma'am!" He salutes me and goes to fill the water.

The edges of my mouth turn up as he turns away.

After the yeast mixture turns frothy, I have him begin measuring out cups of flour while I measure out the salt and oil and search for a pizza stone.

Giving Andrew sole responsibility for the flour was my first mistake. He pulls a cup out of the bag, overflowing with flour, and levels it off, spreading more flour across the already powder-covered counter.

"Do you need help?" I laugh.

"No! No! No! I've got this," he insists.

As he scoops the last cup, he takes his powdered hands and flicks them at me, caking me in flour. I shriek in shock and narrow my eyes at him as he grabs my waist and pulls me toward him, pressing a big white handprint on the waistband of my joggers.

"Andrew! You're getting flour all over me!" I reach past him for the bag, sticking my own hands in the flour and then pressing them to his cheeks as I kiss him.

The look of shock on his face makes me giggle. "Oh, that's how it's going to be, huh?" He scoops another handful of flour and flicks it at me, covering my entire front side.

I gasp and try to reach for more flour from the bag, but he blocks me. I settle for scooping flour off the counter and swatting it in his direction just as he grabs me by the hips and lifts me onto the counter. He steps between my legs and kisses me tenderly, making me completely forget the intense flour fight we were just having.

I swoon as he says with a sly grin on his face, "I like making pizza with you."

"Me too," I reply, pulling him back to me for another long, slow kiss.

An hour later, we have mostly cleaned up the kitchen and ourselves. We devoured our pizzas. They were nothing fancy, but they were made with passion and love, making it some of the best pizza I've ever had.

I pull the plastic cleaning gloves off my hands. "I have another song to show you. Can I queue it up?"

"Sure," he hands me his phone between drying dishes.

I quickly search for the song I'm looking for as I realize the one currently playing is about to come to an end. I swipe over to add it to the queue and tell him, "Listen to the words. I think you'll like the song, but the words remind me of myself." I laugh nervously.

The song begins. Several lines in, I quickly interject, "Here comes the part I like!" I sing along.

Andrew's grin breaks wide as he watches me lovingly. "Is

that all you need? A little dancing around the kitchen? Some hugging and kissing?" He quotes the song.

He wraps me up in his arms again, and we are dancing along to the song. The song is too upbeat for slow dancing, so Andrew has a little hop in his step that's awkward but cute. I giggle with him as he spins me around and then pulls me in for a kiss.

"I like the song."

I beam softly, ignoring the fluttering feeling in my stomach as he takes me in with his beautiful blue eyes. I swear they can see into my soul, but the amazing part is, he sees my whole soul and still thinks it's beautiful.

"I have a song for you too. Hopefully, you don't know it because it isn't very new." He queues up the song and sings along with Tim McGraw about how I'm both his lover and his best friend.

My heart swells as I listen to the sweet words. There's something about that song that resonates with me. I think it has to do with the way Andrew and I are even better in a romantic relationship *because* we are best friends.

We continue going back and forth for almost half an hour before he finally pauses the music. "It's about time for the grand finale," he announces.

"What grand finale?"

He scoops me up and carries me piggyback into the bonus room where I see for the first time a huge pile of pillows and blankets on the couch.

"We are going to build a fort," he says, clearly trying to hold in his excitement.

I look back and forth between the pile of blankets and Andrew. "Are you serious?"

"Yeah, I'm serious. I remember how excited you were when I told you the story last summer about building a fort to read in. I thought it'd be fun to do together sometime, and seeing how the weather outside is absolutely crummy, there's no better time than now."

I give him a big smile and a tight squeeze before rushing to attack the pile. "Okay, you go grab some chairs, and I'll grab some chip clips to hold the blankets up," I say, hardly containing my excitement.

He kisses me on the forehead before rushing to the dining room.

CHAPTER 25

Summer 18

"I've been thinking about the speech I'm going to give at your wedding when you and Andrew get married."

I nearly choke on a piece of brownie from my ice cream, but Rebecca is completely unfazed, her focus on the road ahead, as it should be I suppose.

"I just think as your maid of honor, and the groom's sister, I can give a lot of great insights into the way your friendship blossomed into an eventual relationship."

"Becs, I love you, and you will of course be my maid of honor one day—"

"Awwww!"

"*But* Andrew and I are not together, and we are not even remotely close to being together. I love that you have so much confidence in us, but I think it's time to drop it. I can't take thinking more about something that will never happen."

"But it will!" she insists. "You need to work on your confidence, girl. You've got a kind heart and a sense of humor that catches many people off guard. Your big green eyes and freckles are *stunning*. When you walk into a room, people stop what they're doing to notice you because you just radiate light."

I open and close my mouth, unsure how to respond. When the shock finally settles, I answer, "Becs. You just described yourself… minus the green eyes and freckles part."

"Well, you're that way too. Andrew sees that. I see it in his face every time he looks at you. He's a goner for you!"

I churn my spoon in my ice cream, putting all my focus into getting the perfect bite. "Thank you. I appreciate the pick me up. I just want to be realistic. Andrew and I have been just friends since we were nine years old. If that was going to change, I think it would've by now."

"No! I'm going to prove it to you. Andrew just needs a nudge because he's scared of telling you how he feels, but if he saw there was a chance of losing you, I guarantee you things would change. You just have to let me prove it to you."

"The floor is yours," I tease.

"Well, I don't have the proof right now, but coming soon to a theater near you. Don't you worry!"

She pulls into the driveway behind Andrew's truck. I guess he's finally back from the gym. It's *only* 1:30 in the afternoon! We hop out of the car, and I'm still clinging to my ice cream cup, enjoying each cool, creamy bite.

"I will never understand how you manage to make your ice cream last the *entire* car ride home! That's at least twenty minutes!" Rebecca muses. She polished her cone off before we even started heading back.

I shrug. "I just like to savor it."

"Well, it shows both talent and patience. You should put that on your resume."

"Oh yeah, I'm sure employers would *love* to see that I can take more than twenty minutes to finish a couple scoops of ice cream." I chuckle.

As we saunter in through the Martins' front door, we find Andrew standing in the kitchen, wearing gym clothes and shaking up his protein shake. He still has a slightly sweaty sheen to him.

"Hey!" He nods at us as he takes a sip of his shake. "What're you two up to?"

"We just went and got ice cream. Can you believe Emma made hers last the entire car ride home?"

"Yes," he deadpans. Andrew has gone to get ice cream with me enough times to know better. Rebecca knows better too. She just gobbles her ice cream up in five minutes flat, so she can't comprehend it.

With a distasteful glance in Andrew's direction, Rebecca continues. "How was your workout? I can't believe you and Brendan spend *that* many hours working out. How do you not pass out?"

Andrew raises a brow at her. "It's what athletes do."

"Emma is an athlete, and she's not MIA for half the day."

"I don't know. Brendan and I like to have a little fun sometimes too. He's my best bud."

"I can't believe I still haven't met Brendan," I interject. "He's like this enigma. I hear about him all the time, but I've never met him, even though he's supposed to be your best friend."

"I guess I could see if he wants to come hang out with us tonight," Andrew offers.

His words make me feel like I'm floating. I'm suddenly desperate to meet this guy who is such a big part of Andrew's life outside of our summers at the lake.

Rebecca straightens up a little, and a light begins to shine in her eyes. She has an idea. Our eyes meet, and she gives me a little smirk. Giving her the benefit of the doubt, I tilt my head ever so slightly toward her as if to say *lead the way*.

"That'd be so fun! We can go night swimming and check out his *ah-mazing* abs and maybe make some s'mores or something." She gives me a quick wink.

I blush, rapidly looking between the twins.

Unamused, Andrew flicks his phone out of his back pocket. "I'll text him. Em, he makes the best burgers ever. You've got to try them! It'll ruin all other burgers for you, but it's worth it."

"Excellent! It's settled then. You two can cook burgers for us, and then we can swim later!" Rebecca chimes.

I give Rebecca a curious look.

Andrew rinses the shaker out in the sink and then turns to us. "I'll have him come over a little before five."

As soon as he's left the room, Rebecca turns to me, wiggling her brows. "This bodes well for you."

I'm not sure what I expected from Brendan, but I've found myself a bit surprised. Not in a bad way. He's kind and charismatic. He's a bit more outgoing than Andrew, and I'd be a fool not to notice how attractive he is. Even though he's just wearing a t-shirt and shorts, I can tell he's got a muscular build like Andrew, and there's something about his messy blonde waves that's both endearing and, dare I say, sexy?

I like him a lot. He's not Andrew, but I'm happy to see this person Andrew spends so much time with is a likable, respectable guy. It only makes me adore Andrew even more to see he picked such a good friend.

We're all sitting on the back patio, post-burgers, chatting. It's nice. I'm starting to wonder why we haven't done this before. Having an even number is a game changer and adding Brendan into the group has felt very natural. Granted, he has known Rebecca and Andrew since long before I came along. Leaning back in my chair, I place my palms on my full belly. "Andrew was right, I'll never be able to eat another burger again without thinking of this one. You've ruined all other burgers for me, Brendan!"

Before Brendan has a chance to humbly respond, Rebecca

interjects. "That's not the only thing he's good at. He's a runner like you too. Brendan, did you know Emma runs track and cross country? She's going to compete D1 this year, and she's going to be a superstar!"

"No kidding?" Brendan lights up. "I ran the mile a bit in high school but only for training purposes. I'm no long-distance runner. That's impressive!"

"What's your main event?" I ask, thoroughly interested.

"I'm going to college because of my 800-meter time. I dabble a little in jumping too, but not like Andrew." He slaps his buddy on the back.

"How did I not know you ran the 800?" I ask in shock, looking toward Andrew for an answer. "I've been running everything from the 400-meter to the 3200-meter. I think I'll end up running the 5k next year, though. My coach was already trying to talk me into it on my recruiting visit."

"The 5k? That's brutal! Isn't that twelve laps around a track?" I nod in reply. "Good for you! I'm the opposite." He chuckles. "My coach is trying to convert me to a 400-meter runner."

"You two need to stop throwing out random numbers," Rebecca interrupts.

"One lap around a track is 400 meters. Four laps convert to about a mile, and the 5k is 3.1 miles. Did I miss anything, Emma?"

"I think that about sums it up!"

"You guys have so much in common. Andrew, why have you been hiding Brendan from her?" Rebecca says, turning to Andrew with a pointed look.

"You *had* to have known we'd hit it off! Not too many other people know the world of distance running. He's a rare gem," I add.

Andrew scowls. I swear I can see steam coming out of his ears as his face grows redder by the moment. Why does he seem mad? Two of his good friends are getting along really well. That should be the dream!

I brush it off, looking to Rebecca for guidance. "Are we going swimming tonight?"

"Hell yeah, we are! Let's clean up the dishes and get to it." She abruptly pushes from the table, grabbing dishes with one hand and me with the other. She sweeps me into the kitchen with her as the boys slowly move toward the grill, scrubbing it down and collecting the rest of the dishes.

"So, what do you think?"

"Of what?"

"Of Brendan! Or the fact that Andrew is so clearly extremely jealous right now? I wish I had planned this myself because this is amazing."

Realization washes over me. "That's why you looked at me like that earlier?"

"He's gorgeous, and you guys have things in common. I'd be jealous of him if I were Andrew. It was just a happy accident that this all fell together, and he seems genuinely into you. This is so great!"

I stop what I'm doing. "You think Brendan is into me? Oh, this is bad. This is weird. Becs—"

"Calm down! All this is going to do is make Andrew realize you aren't just going to sit around waiting for him to act on his feelings."

My stomach churns.

The slider opens and closes behind the two boys. Brendan claps his hands together eagerly and asks, "So, should we get into our swimsuits? The water is calling to me."

Rebecca's words echo in my mind as his eyes flicker to me briefly before he turns to Andrew to say something. Andrew frowns and shoves Brendan's shoulder before his gaze flits over me too.

No freaking way! Was Rebecca right?

I turn to her, and it's impossible to miss the smug look on her face. She sees it too. I try to stifle the giggle bubbling up inside me, but it slips out. She leans into me as the boys leave the kitchen to get their swimsuits. With sheer glee, she murmurs, "This is going to be so much fun."

Excitement and hope rush through my veins as I grab my bag off the floor next to the couch and head to the bathroom to change into my suit. It's the suit I just bought with Rebecca in town today before we got ice cream. It's navy blue, and the bottoms have a little lettuce edge ruffle. She told me it made my butt look good, and, honestly, I feel pretty good in it.

I unlock the bathroom door and step out, wrapped in my towel. I may feel good in this, but I still have my modesty. Brendan and Andrew sit on the bar stools in just their swim-suits. *Damn,* they are a sight to see with their broad shoulders, taut chests, and perfectly chiseled abs. Feeling suddenly shy, I pull my towel around me even tighter. Meanwhile, Rebecca struts into the kitchen in her pale blue bikini.

"Ready?" Andrew asks.

Rebecca and I nod, and we all head out to the backyard. The juxtaposition is unreal as Andrew responsibly turns on the dock lights and carries towels for everyone while Rebecca grabs my hand and starts rushing to the dock, leaping off, leaving me with no choice but to follow.

We pop up with laughter just in time to see Brendan throw himself off the dock, curling into a cannonball. Before he surfaces, I feel a tug on my ankle, causing me to shriek. He bursts free from the water right in front of me with a huge grin, and I splash him in playful frustration. "Don't you ever do that again! You scared the crap out of me."

"Get a room, you two," Rebecca teases from over my shoulder.

I look to her, trying to hide my embarrassment and find

Andrew still standing on the dock, holding the towels and fuming. His eyebrows are narrowed, and his mouth is in a crooked line. I don't know that I've ever seen him like this before.

"Are you getting in, Andrew?"

That seems to break his train of thought, whatever it is. He throws the towels onto the dock and leaps off to my right.

Brendan continues to tread close to me, but Andrew lurks close by too. I can see his wheels turning before he finally speaks. "Hey, Brendan! Bet I can beat you to Emma's dock!"

"No chance!" Brendan calls back before rocketing in the direction of our property.

The second they're out of earshot, Rebecca bursts, "I'm a genius!" I can't help the laughter that follows her words. "What are you laughing at?"

"You *are* a genius, and I will give credit when credit is due, but I think you're reading into this too much."

"Emma! I promise you, I'm not. Andrew is so ticked that another guy is giving you attention. He just tried to use Brendan's competitive side to get him away from you. I told you earlier I'd prove to you that the prospect of losing you would trigger something in Andrew, and it's right here for you to see if you'd just open your eyes and stop being so humble!"

The boys hit the dock at about the same time, and I can hear them arguing over who got there first. I can't help the smile that grows on my face.

"I don't know, Becs. He's only ever treated me as a friend, and I don't see that changing."

"That's not true, and you know it."

When Brendan and Andrew come back to our company, they're both out of breath. In between pants, Andrew prods, "Em, tell this ass I beat him fair and square."

"Oh, shut up!" Brendan argues back. "You know I have the stamina to outlast you."

"This wasn't about endurance. It was a sprint." Andrew gestures toward the dock about 50 meters away.

"I don't know, I think you two will need to go again for me to determine the winner," I tease, shrugging my shoulders with nonchalance.

Andrew narrows his eyes at me as the corners of his mouth turn up ever so slightly. He reaches out and swoops me up. "Here, I'll give you a better view this time!" Then he pushes off the dock. I squeal with laughter, and he lets go.

Both laughing, we turn toward one another, and I catch Andrew's gaze. There's something soft behind his eyes. I can't help but think there's no way I'm imagining this. The look in his eyes. The tension between us. *I can't just imagine that, can I?*

We are broken apart by Brendan's loud remark. "Ohhhh! I get it now," he says, facing Rebecca. She simply nods with a soft smile. "Why didn't anyone tell me?"

Andrew turns back to me, saying something about a hankering for Oreos, but I don't miss Rebecca's response. "I'm not sure if he even realizes it yet, but he will soon."

CHAPTER 26

Summer 19

Lying in the fort, glued at the hip with my head on Andrew's chest and his arm wrapped around my shoulders, I'm beside myself with just how happy I am right now. Over a month ago, when I was thinking about my summer here, this is not what I pictured. I can't say this summer has been all sunshine and rainbows, but Andrew has helped make it a thousand times more manageable than I ever could have expected.

"We haven't talked about that night."

Instantly, Andrew's face falters. I don't need to tell him what I'm talking about for him to know what I mean. There's only one night. The night that changed our lives forever.

He must feel the difference in me, the tensing in my shoulders, and the way my breaths grow shallower and quicker because he presses me closer to him. I know this was my idea, but I'm already starting to regret it a little.

"I know it's not exactly a fond memory, but I think it'd be really good for both of us to talk about it." I laugh casually, trying to lighten the mood, but it does little to remove the suffocating tension that has settled over the entire room.

It's weird. I've talked about that night once before with Dani. It didn't feel like this. There were tears, and I had to stop here and there to compose myself before continuing, but I didn't feel like I do now, like I can't breathe. Somehow, maybe because Andrew was there, this all feels different. Maybe it's his energy. I can feel this dark cloud emanating off of him, and something tells me not all of it has to do with talking about Rebecca. Maybe part of it just has to do with him talking about how he feels, one of the few areas I've found him to be inadequate in. Everyone has their flaws!

"I don't remember much before or after the accident. Everything feels fuzzy when I try to remember. I do, however, remember her scream, vividly," he starts.

I burrow my fingers into Andrew's shirt, grabbing onto him both to show my support and ground myself.

"Going to the hospital is still a blur. I remember waiting for what felt like hours, but it wasn't long before we received news. I remember the doctor coming out, and I remember the brief pitying glance he gave our family before he leaned into the minister and started explaining what happened so he could break the news to us instead. The doctor couldn't even do it himself." I feel Andrew tensing up. I'm stunned to silence. Andrew has been so brave this summer. He's led me to believe he's healed, but here's proof right in front of my eyes that those scars are still there.

He continues, "The minister told our family the news, and I exploded. I grabbed the doctor by the arm before he could leave the room and unleashed all my anger and sadness on him. I can't even tell you what I said to that man. I regret it now because that poor man was probably just trying to hide his trauma after having seen the state of my sister. I know now he was just letting someone more qualified share the news. It just felt better to be angry than it did to be sad. But it didn't change anything. I still woke up the next day without my sister."

A single tear forms in his eye, and I'm desperate to ease his pain.

I press kisses to his jaw, his neck, and his cheeks. He nuzzles into me and gives me a soft smile. "I'm okay, Em. It's been almost a year. Time has helped."

I stare into his eyes, assessing. I want to make sure he's okay. As I stare into the depths of his vibrant blue eyes, I believe him, and it feels good. I press a final kiss to his lips and pull away knowing it's my turn. He shared a vulnerable piece of him, and now he deserves a piece of me.

I take a deep breath, trying to keep my breathing under control. "My sharpest memory is the vision of you asking me to call 9-1-1. The panic in your voice, the fear in your eyes, it will stick with me forever because I've never seen you look so afraid." I cringe a little as the memory replays in my head.

The tightening in my chest is back, but I power through. I'm stronger now. Andrew is here, holding me closely. I'm okay. "I remember the sound of the sirens in the distance and the feeling of complete helplessness in that moment and then the memories are pretty much gone until your dad called a couple hours later. I had been sitting on my bed, practically curled up in Dani's lap, and the news just broke me. There was this awful feeling in my chest, like my heart was trying to crawl out of my body because it couldn't take it anymore, and I sobbed until I didn't have tears left. My family practically dragged me out of the house the next morning to go home. I was in shock, but when I got to college and couldn't text her about all the new things I was experiencing, it all settled in. It felt like my life was over."

Andrew swipes at the tears on my cheeks, gentle tears that I didn't even know were there. "We've made it through it all. Look where we ended up," he says softly.

I nod and add, "We did. I wish Rebecca were here to see it, but it doesn't change the fact that I'm so happy to be with you."

We sit in silence for a long time. There's not anything else to say right now. All the feelings that got muddled up from our discussion need to settle back down. But lying with my head on Andrew's chest and his arms wrapped around me, I feel safe.

After some time, who knows how long it truly is, I feel us both start to relax again, and Andrew takes it as a sign to break the silence.

"I think that was important for us to do."

I nod in agreement. "Maybe, another time, I can hear more about what things were like for you after everything."

"Yeah, I think we can arrange that."

Satisfied, I glance at the clock on my phone.

"I need to go home. It's almost one, and my parents are going to be asking why I was out so late," I begin to pull away from his grip.

He immediately pulls me in tighter. "Can't you stay?"

I laugh at the craziness of his idea. "You may not have parents to watch over you tonight, but I still do. I can't get away with staying."

"Do you really think they will notice you're still gone? It's got to be well past your parents' bedtime. I know them, and they are not late-night people."

"When I'm out with a boy until late hours of the night, they are surprisingly alert." I scramble to my hands and knees, beginning to crawl out of the fort. "I can come back over tomorrow to help you take this down, but I'm already probably going to be in the doghouse."

"Okay, we will get you back, but at least let me walk you home. It's dark out."

I agree as I fold a blanket up, dying inside just a little bit at the thought of this fort being left overnight without being cleaned up. At least we cleaned the kitchen after our flour fight.

"Come on, Miss Neat Freak. You said we have to get you

home." He chuckles, placing his hand in mine as he guides me toward the front door.

Outside, the rain has stopped. It's peaceful as water silently drips off the rooves, and the air smells like fresh rain. We walk the hundred feet or so between my house and his, and he turns to kiss me before I walk up the stairs.

Gosh, his lips, the feeling of his taut muscles beneath my hands, him. It all makes it hard to say goodbye, even if it is just to go to sleep.

I pull back first and blow him a quick kiss again as I walk into the house.

Sure enough, my dad is sitting on the couch, asleep. He was waiting for me. I cross the room to shake him awake and let him know I'm home so he can go sleep in his bed.

"Hey, honey. What time is it?" he asks groggily.

"Late. You can sleep in your own bed now."

"What were you doing out so late?"

I roll my eyes playfully. "Dad, we agreed I didn't need a curfew this summer. You know I've stayed out later than this at school."

He glances toward the kitchen to check the clock, but he's out of luck without his glasses. He can't see that far. Then he adamantly adds, "In my mind, you're home and in bed by nine pm every night. I'm going to bed, darling. See you in the morning." He presses a kiss to my cheek and slowly moves toward the staircase leading up to his bedroom.

I turn down the hallway to head to my room. I still feel like I'm walking on clouds, even with this being such a simple date together. We didn't go out, and we didn't dress up, but it was one of the best dates I've ever been on. That's a perk of dating your best friend, I guess.

My thoughts remind me of the Tim McGraw song Andrew shared with me earlier today, so I pull my phone out of my pocket and play it on low volume while I change, careful not to wake Dani up in the room next door. She needs her full eight hours of uninterrupted sleep, or she gets cranky.

As I'm tugging my pajama shorts on, I hear a tapping sound. I pause the music on my phone, listening. But I don't hear it anymore. I reach back to play the last minute of the song, but the tapping starts up again. It's coming from my window.

Peering out into the darkness, I see a light flicker on as Andrew illuminates his face with the flashlight on his phone.

He indicates for me to open the window. Bewildered, I pull the latch and slide the window open.

"Now that you've made it home for your parents, you're coming with me." That mischievous grin is back.

"Coming with you where?"

"To bed," he says simply.

I shake my head in disbelief. "You're going to get me in trouble."

"No, I won't. I promise. Your parents already know you came home tonight. If they find you're not here in the morning, they'll just assume you went for an early run, which is pretty much your routine all the time now."

I tilt my head, acknowledging he has a point. I meet his gaze and see the hope filling his eyes. He's going to convince me with that look alone!

The edges of my mouth turn up just the slightest bit, and he reaches through the window to help me out.

"I don't even have any shoes or a change of clothes for the morning. My cover story only works if I actually come home in running clothes, not pajamas," I explain.

"Sorry, I got too excited. I guess you have a point. Hurry up and grab your clothes."

Then I hear a knock at my door. No mistaking it. My eyes grow wide, and I shove his arm back through the window, closing it quietly behind me before I open my bedroom door.

Dani is standing there, her hair in disarray, squinting hard from the light. There's a scowl on her face.

"Sorry, Dani! I just got back from my date with Andrew, but he called me because I left something at his place. I'm going to bed now. I'll be quiet," I insist, hoping against hope it isn't obvious I'm lying.

I've never been a good liar, and I'm not very quick on my feet when it comes to making up excuses. Good thing I'm not an actor. I would be horrible at improv.

Dani slowly stops squinting as her eyes adjust to the light. She crosses her arms. "I'm not an idiot. I could hear every word you two just said."

I try to hide my panic as I face her. *Maybe I can come up with some cover? No way. She heard everything we just said!*

I sigh and shrug. "We only have a few weeks left before we go back to school. I'm trying to soak up my time with him," I offer, hoping I can get her to sympathize with me and not blab to my parents. Dani is a rule follower, but she's never been a narc.

To my surprise, she leans against the door jam, her arms still crossed as she asks, "Have you two talked about how you're going to handle long distance?"

I grimace. "Not really. I'm kind of waiting until the very last minute because things have been going so well."

"Just make sure you two are on the same page before you leave. Distance can be difficult, even with all the technology we have to stay in touch nowadays. You may expect to text all the time, and he may think you two are only going to check in a few times a week on Facetime."

I eye her, wondering when she became the expert on relationships. "Fine," I say. "I'll talk to him if you cover for me in the event mom or dad notice I'm gone."

She considers the deal for a moment too long. I know

Andrew is still right outside my window, waiting to find out what's going on.

"Please, Dani. You said you'd be my Rebecca. Rebecca would do it for me."

I grimace as I process the words that just came out of my mouth. Even if they're true, I feel dirty using Rebecca like that to get what I want.

"I don't feel comfortable lying to Mom and Dad, but it's not a big deal as long as you two aren't getting into any kind of trouble." She pins me with a glare. "You're going right to sleep in your own bed and running in the morning, you say?"

I pause a moment and then nod as I realize what she's saying. "Yeah, I'm going right to bed and then I'll probably go run early in the morning with Andrew because he has to lift with Brendan later."

She nods curtly. "All right then. Goodnight."

"Goodnight," I reply as I close my door and then open it right back up again so it doesn't look weird when I'm gone tomorrow, supposedly on a run.

I immediately rush over to grab running clothes and shoes from my dresser and closet, even making sure I grab my watch off my nightstand before opening my bedroom window again.

Andrew welcomes me into his arms, immediately cuddling me up, and then lifts me off the ground after I quietly shut my window behind me. He struts back to the Martin mansion very casually as if he isn't carrying around a one hundred twenty-pound weight.

When he swings open the front door, he sets me down but immediately wraps his arm around my waist and pulls me in for a fierce kiss.

What has gotten into him? He's usually so patient and tender, but now it's like he can't get enough of me. I pull back and tease, "I thought you said I was coming over here to sleep?"

He immediately takes a step back, and I can see how flustered he is, conflicted between desire and concern. "You're right. I said that, and I meant it. You know I would never pressure you into anything, Em. I'm in this relationship for you and everything that comes with you. We don't need to rush anything. I like the way things are going." He pulls me in for another kiss but quickly pulls back again.

It's funny how a man saying he will wait for you somehow makes you not want to wait. I follow him down to his bedroom as if my heart isn't pounding from that kiss and my body isn't buzzing with the same desire I saw in his eyes a moment ago.

He laces our hands together as we mosey down the steps, descending into the basement. Instead of heading straight for his bedroom, he stops at the linen closet.

"What are you doing?" I whisper, despite the fact we are the only two people in the entire house.

He turns around, holding a pillow and an extra blanket. "I wanted to make sure you were comfy."

My heart swells at the extra thought he put into this. I just expected to crawl into bed with him, curl up in his arms, and that would be that.

He flips on his bedroom light and flicks off the light in the hallway, stopping to look at me for a moment. "Are you okay?" he asks, concern filling his face.

"Yes, of course. I don't want to be anywhere else right now."

He puts a hand on each of my shoulders, looking me square in the face. "You look flushed."

I'm sure that only makes more color scatter across my pink cheeks. "That's because of you."

His brow furrows. "What did I do? Did I do something wrong?"

I hold one hand up to cup his face, softly moving my thumb back and forth across his cheek. "You didn't do anything wrong, Andrew. You have been so sweet and thoughtful, the perfect gentleman." I hesitate before I carefully phrase my next sentence. "Maybe, for tonight, it'd be okay for you not to be."

He frowns, looking confused. I look up at him through my lashes, and something on my face must finally register with him because the look in his eyes turns animal.

He sweeps me off the ground and lays me on the bed, still gentle Andrew, and it's the perfect end to an already perfect day.

CHAPTER 27
Summer 18

I check the clock yet again. It's 2:36 in the morning. I frown as I realize only two minutes have passed since I last checked the time.

I toss my covers off and sit up. I reach for my phone and am nearly blinded by the beaming light. I guess it hasn't gotten the memo that it's nighttime.

Without a second thought, I shoot off a text.

ME

Any chance you're awake too?

Andrew's response is instant.

ANDREW

Yeah

I just finished up a project.

What kind of project? You already have something for school?

No this is more of a personal thing.

Oooh a mystery!

Something like that haha

Do you want to come outside with me? I'd
enjoy the company

Be out in 2

I grab a sweatshirt from my closet and tug it over my head before heading to the back door and stepping out into the cool air. With it being late summer, it never really gets cold here, but it does get into the mid-sixties at night, which is cool enough to cover me in goosebumps without the warmth of the beating sun.

I see a shadow moving on the Martins' lawn. Then I hear Andrew's voice whisper, "Come here."

He pats the spot next to him and then leans back down on what appears to be a small blanket sprawled across the grass. I join him silently. When I lie back and gaze up, I'm surprised to see so many stars floating up in the sky. It looks like he turned the back patio lights at the Martin residence off, but I wonder what it would look like without the lights from our cabin or the little specks of light still glimmering from other homes around the lake.

We lie in silence for a while as I get lost in the stars. They're gorgeous, and they remind me of my grandpa. Part of me wonders if he's up there now. He used to say he wanted to be a star in the afterlife so he could help bring light to the dark and keep a watchful eye on me. I wonder if he's proud of me, if I've done everything he hoped I would by this time in my life.

Andrew breaks the silence. "What're you doing up at this hour?"

I turn onto my side and find myself face to face with him, his nose inches from mine. *How long was he lying there like that?*

I regain my focus and respond, "I'm getting anxious about leaving for college. You know how much I hate change and then there's the fact that I have to meet new people. I hate those orientation-type things, you know, small talk. I want to skip ahead to the part where I know who my people are. Then there's cross country. I am excited to compete, but I'm so nervous. This is a whole new level of competition. I'll be racing with elite athletes." I inspect his face, expecting to find overwhelm in his eyes. "Clearly, my mind is racing."

He nods his head with understanding. "I get it. It's hard to adjust to change. I'm nervous too." Grabbing a hold of my hand, he adds, "But I know you're going to be more than fine in college. You'll have a built-in support system right away with the team. Remember you couldn't stop talking about how great the girls were when you came home from your official visit? You've worked your ass off this summer, so you're going to absolutely crush everyone. Don't forget that *you're* one of the elite athletes that will be out there competing," he encourages.

A weak smile crosses my face, and I can tell he knows I'm not feeling any better. "Em, you're the most dedicated, hard-working person I know. When you put your mind to something, you make it happen. If you want to make friends, you'll do it. If you want to make it to nationals for cross country, you'll do that too. You're just that incredible. I'm honestly jealous of all the people who will go to college with you and get to experience your journey in person."

I squeeze his hand. "Thank you, Andrew. I'm going to miss you. I know it isn't all that different from the last nine years being apart during school, but—" I trail off. I don't know how to tell him it feels different saying goodbye now. We've been through so much, and each day it feels like we've only been getting closer and closer.

"I'm going to miss you too," Andrew murmurs. "We don't

have to talk about college anymore though. We are still at the lake together right now, so let's enjoy it."

He lies back down to stare up at the stars, and I follow suit. After a moment, Andrew asks, "If you could travel anywhere in the world, where would it be?"

I don't hesitate. "Italy. The food alone is an obvious draw. I mean, imagine getting to eat fresh bread, pasta, pizza, and gelato every day! Oh my gosh, I'm drooling just thinking about it! I read this book a while ago where the main character spent a summer in Italy, and it made me want to go so badly. I want to see all the famous architecture and the rolling hills of Naples."

He chuckles. "That is the most fitting answer I could've imagined for you."

"What about you?"

"I don't know if I have an answer," he pauses and I wait for him to continue, comfortable in the silence. "I've always wanted to go to Greece because of the gorgeous turquoise waters and those simple white cottages along the coast. They're like something out of a painting. I also think it'd be really neat to travel to Thailand though. The water there looks beautiful, and I've heard they have a beach where you can ride elephants. Plus, think of all the cool food you could try there. I heard everything is cheap in Thailand, so you could have all kinds of cool experiences on a budget."

"Well, minus the fact that it costs a thousand dollars for a round-trip plane ticket."

"Minor details."

I snicker. "You've traveled with your family, haven't you? Where have you gone?

"Yeah, we've gone on a few work trips with my dad. We went to Japan once and Paris. Japan was super cool!"

"Did you not like Paris?"

"Oh, Paris was incredible, but you know, it's the city of love. I swear everything is designed for couples. There's the lock bridge and the Eiffel Tower. Even the delicacies, like cheese and bread, have this erotic energy, like they're meant to be fed to your lover. I think I'd want to go back someday with someone special. I'm sure the whole city would be a different experience if I could share it with someone I love."

I nod, fighting the urge to imagine traveling to Paris with Andrew someday. Too late. I'm already picturing us eating dinner at the top of the Eiffel Tower, feeding each other cheese and chocolate croissants, and kissing under the streetlights. I sigh a little at the thought and then mentally slap myself. *I need to get back to reality.*

"If you could have any superpower, what would it be?" I start us off again.

"Super strength, duh."

I laugh at the simplicity of his answer. "Okay, why?"

"I feel like I couldn't do much by myself without supernatural strength but think of all the people I could save if I had the strength to just throw the bad guys through a wall or stop a moving train with a single finger. What about you?"

"I think I'd want invisibility. I'm not sure it'd be as useful as super strength, but I'd like to be able to disappear every now and then."

Excitement fills his voice. "You could be a spy and do all these super cool top-secret missions for the FBI or the CIA!"

A puff of air comes out of my nose as I hold back a laugh. "You're right. That'd be pretty cool."

"Tell me a story about you when you were little," he pries. Our sides are completely pressed against one another now. I can't move. I can't breathe. I'm afraid that any movement will wake me up from a dream or make Andrew realize how close he is.

"What kind of story?"

"Anything you want. It could be a favorite memory or something embarrassing that happened to you. I just like to hear about your life. I'm only with you for twenty-five percent of the year. I want to hear about the rest of it."

"I'll tell you a story if you'll give me one in exchange."

He purses his lips for a moment, and then they curve into a smile. "Deal. You go first though. I need some time to think of mine."

I scoff. "I need to think of one too. You didn't exactly give me many instructions."

"That was by design. I'm letting you be creative!"

"Okay, okay, I got one," I say finally. He nods at me, encouraging me to continue. I watch eagerness grow on his face. "When I was little, I had a favorite stuffed animal named Lucky. My grandpa got him for me when I was three. He was this plush black puppy, and I took him everywhere with me. I believed by naming him Lucky, he would actually give me good luck." I laugh a little with embarrassment.

"When I was six, I took him with me on a family trip to New York. I accidentally left him in the hotel room, and I wound up getting a double ear infection before the trip ended, which made the plane ride home absolutely miserable. I was in tears, and I insisted it was because I didn't have Lucky with me. Once we got home, my grandpa came to visit me while I was sick. He brought me soup, told me stories, and he even brought me what I thought was Lucky. I later found out he bought me a new Lucky, but he washed him a whole bunch of times to make his fur look worn like my original one. It was really sweet of him."

He smiles warmly. "When did you find out that wasn't the real Lucky?"

"I didn't find out until after my grandpa passed away. He didn't have the heart to tell me, but Dani did. She thought it was worth telling me the story to show how much he cared for me."

"You still miss him a lot, don't you?"

I hesitate. "It's gotten easier. You kind of start to adjust to your new life without that person, but it doesn't mean I don't still miss him all the time. You just get used to the ache, I guess? Certain times are harder than others though. Christmas is always harder. We used to go to my grandparents' house for a week around Christmas and bake cookies and open presents on Christmas morning."

"That's sweet," he says, without a hint of judgment.

"Your turn," I say gleefully, trying to turn the discussion back around after the serious turn it just took. *How'd we get from superheroes to losing my grandpa? Whoa.*

Joy breaks out on his face in response to my excitement.

"Let's see… oh, here's something you might enjoy. Did you ever have those days at school when you did nothing else but read?"

I nod. "Yeah, those were my favorite days! We got to come to school in our pajamas and bring blankets to curl up with, and we'd just read as much as we could in a day to encourage kids to read more and boost the number of books they read during the year." I buzz with excitement at the memory.

"They were my favorite days too! One year, probably fourth grade, the all-day reading day got canceled for whatever reason, so I pretended to be sick. My mom and dad both had to go in for work, so they left me home alone. The second I knew they were gone, I built a fort in the living room and spent the whole day reading."

I gasp. "You little rebel! I love that you built a fort though. That's so fun!"

He chuckles. "It was, until my mom caught me taking the fort down. She came home early, and she knew right away I wasn't sick. I thought for sure I was going to get in trouble, but I think she thought it was funny. She pretended like she was mad at me for skipping school because 'school is important,' but I didn't get grounded or anything."

"I guess it's kind of hard to punish your kid for enjoying reading."

"Yeah, I guess so."

"I used to read in my parents' bathtub with pillows and blankets," I tell him.

He bursts into laughter. "What? Why the bathtub? There's got to be more comfortable places."

"I'm not sure. I think one of my teachers who was really into reading had mentioned it to our class one time, so I was determined to try it. Honestly, I couldn't get it to be that comfortable, but when my teacher talked about it, it seemed like such a good idea."

"You're weird," he laughs, "but it's what I love about you."

Blushing, I ask him my next question. "What's a dream you have that you're too afraid to dream?"

I can tell he's taken aback. He blinks a few times. "What do you mean?"

"You know, the thing that you wanted as a kid, but growing up you were taught you couldn't achieve it, so that dream got pushed down into the deepest parts of you, but it's still silently there, begging you to make it happen one day."

"Well damn. I'm kind of speechless right now."

"Because you know exactly what I'm talking about," I reply confidently.

"You seem to know this pretty well. You must have one too."

I can tell he's trying to turn the conversation back to me, to deflect. I don't blame him. This is a hard question. I don't even know what made me ask it because I can't imagine saying my own out loud. I'm not even sure if I'm in tune with my younger self enough to know what the answer would be.

"It was my question. You have to answer," I say finally, making sure he doesn't get out of this one easily.

He shifts around a little in the grass and lets out a big sigh. "I guess if I had to pick one, it'd be to be a published author. You know I've always enjoyed reading, but growing up, I thought it would be so cool to be the person who wrote a story that touched someone else's life the way all the stories I've read have touched me. I was told pretty quickly that most authors don't make it, and even if you publish a book, you probably won't make any money, so I don't know that I'll ever end up doing that."

"For what it's worth, you'd be one hell of a writer, Andrew. I hope someday, even if it's when you're eighty, you're able to write a story and share it with the world. And when you do," I add, "I better be one of the first people to read it."

His pure smile melts me, and I swear he's looking at me like I put the stars in the sky.

We continue asking each other questions back and forth for a long time, talking about the past, the future, and completely random topics. The sky gradually begins to lighten, and the stars begin to fade before I doze off.

I wake to the sound of my dad's truck starting up. *That thing is unreasonably loud!*

As I open my eyes, I find my face buried in Andrew's chest. One of his arms is draped over me, and we are still lying on the blanket on the lawn. He continues to breathe heavily, apparently unfazed by the loud noise moments earlier.

I'm afraid to move and wake him. He looks so peaceful. I allow myself to watch him sleep for just a moment before I begin feeling around with the hand that's not currently pressed into Andrew's side, trying to find my phone and check the time.

I feel the smooth silicone of my phone case and grab it, bringing it around so that I can peek at the time without disrupting Andrew. It's almost eight. We should get up before someone sees us like this.

I shake him awake, muttering his name. It takes several

shakes and raising the volume of my voice several times to get him awake.

He stirs finally and opens his eyes. When he meets my gaze, a smile crosses his sleepy face, and millions of butterflies begin swirling in my stomach with the sweet look he gives me.

He pulls me in tighter, wrapping me up in both his arms, and I don't say anything. I'm too stunned to speak.

"We should do this more often. Despite sleeping on just a blanket in the grass, I slept great," he mutters cheerfully in my ear, sending chills down my spine.

As he pulls back, I watch him melt before my very eyes. There's no misreading the look he's giving me. It's filled with adoration. His eyes slowly drift from mine down to my lips.

I become aware of the way my body is completely flush against his. My chest is pressed against his, and his hand is resting on my lower back. If it moved one inch south, we could be in trouble.

He begins to lean in, closing the already small distance between our lips, and I feel my whole body light on fire.

Then his phone begins ringing.

Andrew pulls back, picks it up, and glances at the screen before muttering, "Shit!" I watch his body stiffen and then he shoots up from the blanket with alarm. "Brendan was supposed to pick me up ten minutes ago to go to the gym!"

Despite his sudden hurry, he still helps pull me to my feet and grabs the blanket, crumpling it into a ball in his arms.

I turn to head back toward my house and let him go get ready, but he grabs my arm and pulls me toward him. He wraps me in for a hug and presses his lips to my forehead. "Last night was amazing." He lets me go and starts to head back to the house. "To be continued," he says with a sexy smirk that makes me tingle.

This can't be real! I have to be dreaming. There's no way Andrew is saying this right now, looking at me the way he's looking at me. Did we almost kiss?

My mind is swirling, and my heart is soaring. As I calm down and head back toward the house, I think to myself, *I have to tell Rebecca!*

CHAPTER 28

Summer 18

Rebecca flips a pancake high into the air, and it retreats to the pan crippled and folded.

I choke out a laugh. "I don't understand why you continue to try flipping them like that. I'm sorry, Becs, but you haven't been close once, and you just keep wasting good pancakes."

She feigns offense, pressing her palm to her chest. "I'll have you know that pancake would've landed perfectly if it had just made another half-turn. Besides, they're not going to waste." She picks a piece off the top of the pancake, still sitting in the pan. "I'll eat them. I care about what's on the inside, unlike some people."

She gives me the side-eye, and I just laugh, giving her a little hip check as I pick off an even bigger piece of the pancake to prove a point. To my dismay, I got part of the middle that is still gooey. I make a face as the sticky goo touches my tongue.

Rebecca points to my sour face. "See! I told you."

I roll my eyes, the edges of my mouth turning up. "Oh, whatever. When can we eat?" I eyeball the stack of blueberry pancakes that must be twenty high by now. Even with my habitually ravenous appetite and Andrew's post-lifting appetite when he gets home in an hour, there's no way we will finish all of those.

She picks up the bowl and peers in. "I'm guessing we've got about two pancakes left in here and then we can dish up." She smiles with cheer. Pancakes are one of her favorites, both to make and to eat.

"Hurry up! I finished my run forty-five minutes ago. I'm dying here, and my recovery window is closing."

"Here," she thrusts the bag of blueberries into my hand. "Have a snack."

I snicker as I grab a handful and then lean on the counter, popping them into my mouth one by one.

"I have something to tell you," I finally announce. "I've been trying to wait until we sit down to eat, but at the rate you're going, we aren't going to eat in this millennium."

"You're so impatient!" She swats me with the spatula.

"Let me tell you what I have to say, and you'll understand why." I smirk and add, "I know how much you love your gossip."

"Well, geez, should I pull up a chair or something?"

"That's sort of what I've been waiting for, but it's fine. You don't need the chair."

"This better be good," she exclaims, excitement filling her face.

"Now I'm nervous. I don't think I can talk about it." I begin to retract.

She swats me with the spatula harder this time. "Emma O'Dougherty! Tell me what you have to say right now, or I will kill you. I'm armed!" She wields the spatula, a smug look on her face.

I laugh at her so hard my side begins to hurt, which only makes her grow more impatient with me. "Emma! Now. You've taken so long the pancakes are finished anyway."

I wipe a tear from the corner of my eye. "Oh, good! Perfect

timing," I singsong as I pull four warm pancakes off the stack and put them on my plate with a small puddle of syrup for dipping. It may not be as visually appealing, but the syrup-to-pancake ratio is so much better this way.

We sit down next to each other at the kitchen island. I take a bite, contemplating where to start. I've attempted to practice this conversation with her several times this morning on my eight-mile run, but none of the words seemed right.

I open my mouth, thinking I know where to start now, and end up word vomiting instead. "I couldn't sleep last night, so I texted Andrew. I would've texted you because, you know, I love your company, but I knew you wouldn't be awake, nor should I be disturbing you while you're sleeping, so he was my next option."

She nods. "Get to the point."

"Anyway, I texted Andrew, and he said he was awake, so he asked me to come out onto the back lawn with him for a bit. We stayed out there for hours just talking and looking at the stars until we both fell asleep. When we woke up this morning, I felt like he was looking at me differently. I could tell from his face that something was going on, and I am pretty sure he leaned in for a kiss, but we got interrupted because he was supposed to go to the gym with Brendan this morning. Andrew wasn't answering his texts, so Brendan called right as he was leaning in. But he did say last night was amazing, and he had this super sexy look on his face as he said, 'to be continued,' which makes me think he wanted to kiss. Maybe we finally will."

I take a deep breath and note Rebecca's reaction. She's beaming, but then her face turns serious. "I can't believe you waited this long to tell me! What's wrong with you? Am I not your best friend?"

I reach out to pat her arm. "Of course you're my best friend. You're the first person to hear about this and will probably be the only person to hear about this if it makes you feel any better."

She purses her lips, but it slips into a smile. "I suppose it does a bit." She sets her fork down and turns toward me. "Now, you know I'm the most supportive person of anyone as far as a relationship between you and Andrew goes, but may I just ask that you never, ever again call my brother sexy in front of me?" She cringes.

I burst into laughter. "I can work on that."

"No working on it. Just doing it," she insists before picking her fork up and devouring several more bites of pancake.

"What do you think this means?" I prod. "You know Andrew better than anyone. Do you think I'm reading things right?"

She nods as she finishes chewing. "Oh, my sweet, innocent Emma, I know you're not the most experienced when it comes to guys and relationships, but I've been trying to tell you for two years now that Andy is in love with you! You guys are totally going to get together and then you're going to get married and have beautiful babies. Oh, I can't wait to be an aunt!"

I hold up my palms. "Let's not get carried away here. I think you missed the part where we didn't even kiss."

She interjects immediately. "Yeah, but you said you were about to! It's going to happen. Tonight. Mark my words, Emma! Oh, I can't wait!"

Anticipation fills my stomach. I know Rebecca can be overzealous. She just cares so much. Her heart is so big and full of love. But even with her overexcitement, I can't help but believe that what she says is true. Andrew and I might kiss tonight. We can finally get together. It's taken us years and years, but it's finally going to happen. I can *feel* it.

CHAPTER 29

Summer 19

I awake to a gentle kiss on my forehead and the feeling of Andrew's arms pulling me toward him. *Can this be my alarm clock every day?*

I open my eyes to see his wonderful smiling face and his chiseled bare chest. *Ahhh, I could get used to this.*

"Good morning, sunshine." He smiles.

"What time is it?" I ask him, trying to copy and paste this moment into my memory. *Who knows when I will have a morning like this again?*

"It's 8. I'm meeting Brendan to lift at 10:30. I figured you might want to go for a short run and then make some breakfast before you go home."

What did I ever do to deserve him? I finally begin to wake up enough to assess our surroundings. His laptop is lying on the bed next to him. I point to it. "What's that for?"

He shrugs casually. "I had a little inspiration early this morning, so I wrote things down while the ideas were fresh."

I smile and kiss him on the cheek. "My little writer."

"Hey, I'm not little!" He crosses his arms. "I'm almost six-three."

"You're right. My big writer?" I give him a questioning look, and he nods in approval.

"We should get out the door. I need an hour to let my food settle before I go lift."

"Roger that! Let me get changed." I grab my running clothes from where they got thrown onto the floor last night.

He slips on a shirt, and I sigh a little in disappointment. He must see the look of despair on my face because he laughs. "Don't worry, you'll see me like this again soon." He kisses me on the cheek while I pull my hair into a ponytail. "Ready?"

I slip on my shoes quickly and strap on my watch. "Yeah, let's go. We can just do three miles today. I'm craving pancakes this morning, and I want some time to make them."

"Pancakes, huh?"

"Wait, do you have blueberries?"

"Yeah…" He gives me a weird look.

"Then yes. Let's make pancakes."

He smiles and guides me out the door. We cut across the lawn, and we wait a couple of houses down for my watch to load. I can't risk my parents somehow seeing that I am just now leaving for a run. One can never be too cautious.

The run is short and sweet. Andrew seems in a good mood this morning, being extra affectionate and smiley.

He somehow pulls me into a game of would you rather, but when he brings up college in one of his questions, I become distracted. I keep thinking of Dani's insistence that we talk sooner rather than later about how Andrew and I are going to handle being so far away from each other in a matter of weeks. It makes my stomach turn sour. I know we should have the discussion, but I'm afraid of messing things up. Everything is going so great now.

Andrew still seems pretty chipper, but his smile falters once as he asks, "Are you okay? You just completely zoned out on my last question."

"Yeah." I shake it off. "I was just thinking about the race and whether we will be ready for all those obstacles and mud. Do you think we should be elevating our training somehow? You know, army crawling in the middle of our run and stuff?"

He gives me an astonished look as if I've lost it. Maybe I have, but I wish he wouldn't think so too. "I think we will be fine. It's not like we are racing for a time. We already established this is supposed to be for fun, not a competitive race. I thought you were trying to get away from that?"

I sigh. "Yeah, I guess you're right. I just like to be prepared."

His rising smile nearly cracks me open, ready to profess everything that's on my mind. "I know you do. That's one of the things I adore about you."

Before I can start a conversation I'm not ready to have, I spit out, "We're almost back. I'll race you home!" By the time the last word is out of my mouth, I'm off at a dead sprint toward his house.

I peek over my shoulder to find Andrew right on my tail. I speed up until I'm sprinting as fast as I can for the last one hundred meters back to his house. Naturally, I cut across the yard again to the front porch and then raise my hands to cradle my head while I catch my breath.

Andrew follows along one second later, doing the same. "That was *so* not fair! You had already taken off before you even said anything about racing."

I shrink back and give my best 'I'm sorry' look. It seems good enough for him because he wraps his arms around my shoulders and brings me in for a hug before opening the door and walking us into the kitchen.

"Okay then! Pancakes!" he announces as he begins pulling out the box of pancake mix, followed by milk and eggs from the fridge.

I rustle around for the pan and bowl, knowing by now where the Martins keep most of the items in their kitchen.

Andrew turns on some music and dances me around the kitchen a little as the pancakes sit on the stove cooking. He pauses briefly to flip them and then always returns to me, pressing his lips to mine, placing his hand on my lower back, or caressing my cheek.

Things are so great right now. I don't want to mess with another happy memory by talking to him about being apart. I know I need to make an effort to talk with him about things. I've learned from the past that sometimes other things can get in the way, but it doesn't change the fact that I'm scared or that I don't know how to broach the subject. Nope, I'm going to do it. I need to tell him how I feel. Andrew will make everything better.

Andrew serves us each a plate of pancakes and pauses the music, so we can actually talk during our meal. *How did he learn to always be so thoughtful like that?*

Taking the silence as my moment, I begin, "Andrew—"

"My parents—"

"Oh sorry. What's up?" I nod my head in his direction.

"My mom and dad want to have a family dinner when they get back tonight, so I won't be able to spend the evening with you, but don't make plans for tomorrow night."

"Yeah? What'd you have in mind?" I can't help the excitement growing inside me.

"I've been trying to think of things I've always wished I had the guts to do, and I got an idea. Would you be okay if Brendan tags along for this one? He was kind of the inspiration for this."

"Of course!" I insist.

"He's promised to be on his best behavior."

"I didn't have a choice then, did I? You already talked with him about this."

He laughs uneasily. "Well, I had to get the low down before I dragged you into the plan."

"What's your plan?"

"It's something that will challenge us both, but we will be proud of ourselves for doing it."

"Will you tell me?" I prod, between bites of fluffy pancake.

"Would you still do it if I did?"

"Touché. Can we please not do anything that will make me fear for my life?"

He bursts into laughter. "Em, I promise I won't do anything that will put you in danger. I'd be lost without you." He bends down to press a kiss to my hairline, my hairline which is currently matted down with dried sweat from our run.

I try to hold up my hands to stop him. "Sweat! Be careful!" I urgently warn him, but he kisses me anyway.

He pulls back and shrugs. "I don't mind a little sweat. I'm sweaty too." As if to prove a point, he leans in and kisses my sweaty head again.

His insistence on kissing me, even when I'm a gross, stinky mess of a human being warms my heart. We're going to be completely fine when the time comes to say goodbye. Nothing can touch us!

CHAPTER 30

Summer 19

"Tell me how your night went," Dani says with a smirk before raising her camera to her eye.

I watch her carefully set up her subject, a shaded tree stump across the street from our house, and wait for the shutter of the camera before I respond. I know better than to interrupt her process. Dani is an amazing photographer, but she's very particular about how she takes each photo. I have no clue what she sees in a tree stump, but I know when I see the final photo, with all of the right edits and angles, I'm going to feel some sort of connection to that inanimate object.

Her camera flickers, and I respond. "There's not much to tell. He made me breakfast after our run this morning, blueberry pancakes. Normally he makes me scrambled eggs."

She pulls her camera down and glowers at me. "You're so full of shit, Emma! Tell me what happened. I know you didn't go over there and go straight to sleep."

I blush. Rebecca was always the one who did the talking when it came to our love lives. Rebecca saw everything that was going on in mine, and it was mostly nothing. It feels weird to talk about personal details of my relationship with Andrew, even if that's what girls always seem to do.

"We didn't have sex." Dani's eyebrows raise a bit. "I'm assuming that's what you were implying," I pin her with a questioning look, and she nods to confirm. "We came close, but I just wasn't ready yet. Andrew is incredible and I really want to share that with him, but I don't take something like that lightly. I think there's a part of me that hesitates because I know we only have a couple more weeks together before our relationship will primarily exist over Facetime and texts."

Dani nods along with me. There's no judgment in her face, and I feel comforted. For a brief moment, I feel just like I'm talking with Rebecca. She was always a big talker, but at the end of the day, I know she had the same values as me, which was why we got along so well.

"You shouldn't take it lightly. I'm proud of you for not rushing into things, and I hope Andrew was understanding about it."

I immediately jump to his defense. "Oh, Andrew was beyond understanding. He didn't pressure me at all. He told me we would take things one step at a time." I can't help the smile spreading across my face.

"You are *so* in love! I enjoy seeing you like this," Dani says, bursting with support.

"Thank you. I am, and it's terrifying. I don't see Andrew ever hurting me, but the deeper we get into things, the scarier it gets because I realize more and more of me is invested. I already know how much it hurts to lose the people you love," I trail off. "I can't even imagine what it would feel like to lose someone who is still here. It's one thing to not be able to see and talk to Grandpa and Rebecca now, but to love Andrew like this and then have to watch him live his life without getting to be a part of it anymore would be so hard."

Dani gives me a half-hearted smile. "That's how love works

unfortunately, but you can't have it without taking the risk, and it's so worth the risk."

Again, I find myself wondering *how the heck does she know these things?* I've never known Dani to be in a relationship. As far as I know, she hasn't even had her first kiss. She's always been immersed in her studies and her photography. But then again, she did buy that alcohol with her apparent fake ID for Rebecca two summers ago, so there's probably a whole side to her that I don't know.

"Is there something I should know? Since when were you the expert on love advice?"

She chuckles lightheartedly, brushing the question aside quickly. "All I'm saying is you took a risk to get Andrew in the first place, and love will continue to be a series of risks. You've already learned time is fleeting. Don't keep waiting to talk with him."

"You're right. I'm taking another risk tonight just meeting up with Brendan and Andrew. Andrew still won't tell me what we are doing."

Dani's eyes fill with hope. "Well, I hope they show you a really good time and get you to loosen up. Summer is almost over. Then it's back to the grind."

I whip my head around to glare at her. "I have loosened up! Andrew and I went skinny dipping this summer, and I'm about to do a mud run for crying out loud! You know what that kind of thing does to a neat freak? I'm starting to have nightmares about it already!"

The edges of her mouth quirk. "This is what I'm talking about. If you were truly loose, you wouldn't be freaking out about getting dirty on a mud run that's several days away."

I purse my lips, unsure how to argue back.

"Hey, do me a favor and sit on the stump. I'm trying to do more photos with humans. Inanimate objects are great and easy for me to capture, but I think it'd be a good challenge to start trying to do photos with people."

I arch an eyebrow. "How is it more difficult to take pictures of people than a tree a stump? You literally bring something dead back to life again when you take photos of a tree stump. Humans are already alive."

She tilts her head. "You're right, but with humans, there's movement and emotions, and I have to figure out how to perfectly capture all of that to tell a story. I only get one second before the movement or the emotion is gone."

She lifts her camera and snaps a photo of me quickly. I frown. "I wasn't even ready! You're horrible at taking pictures of people!" I tease.

"See, I told you. I need to work on it." She winks. Then she holds the camera out for me to see. "I was capturing the understanding on your face. It's kind of beautiful. Talk to me more about Andrew. Those photos could be great, a girl in love." There's a dreamy look in her eye.

I do as she says, and we sit there for at least half an hour while she snaps photos, and I talk about how much I'm in love with Andrew. *Can you believe it? I'm in love!*

"Emma! It's been way too long. Andrew literally won't shut up about you, but he hasn't exactly wanted to share you, either," Brendan teases.

I blush, and I watch as Andrew does too. "Oh, shut up!" He turns to me. "He's *such* an exaggerator."

"No, I'm not!" Brendan insists. "Dude, you already have the girl. It's not even embarrassing to talk about her all the time. If anything, it'll just make her like you even more."

I laugh. I forgot how fun Brendan is.

I glance at the building in front of us. It's literally called

Yeehaw's. I don't think I've ever heard a sillier name. "So, what is this? Why are we here?" I interrogate the boys, anxiety practically coming out of my pores.

Andrew turns to Brendan. "Do you want to do the honors?"

"Is this another one of your high school insider secrets or something?"

Brendan laughs. "No! Andrew hasn't been here before, either, but I go to college half an hour away from here, and all my friends make the drive out here just to come to this place on the weekends."

I glance at it again. It doesn't look like anything special. It looks like an old-time saloon, complete with a front porch and wooden slat siding covering the whole front side. There are some windows on the front that are decorated with shutters, and there's a tin roof keeping the elements out. It sort of looks like a cliché.

"What do you and your college buddies come here for?"

Brendan's face splits into a huge grin. "Mostly to binge drink and then get thrown off Benji twenty million times."

"What?" I look to Andrew with unease, hoping he will give me some guidance. This *was* his idea.

Brendan jumps to his aid. "Don't worry, Emma! You're going to love it! They have this drink called the trough that you share with multiple people. It's pretty cheap and gets the job done fast, which is awesome! I don't even know what's in it, but it's delicious, super easy to slurp down."

"And who's Benji?"

"Oh yeah, Benji is the mechanical bull out back. You'll love him!"

My eyes nearly pop out of my head when I hear his words. I turn to Andrew again. "What are you getting me into? Is this a bar? None of us are twenty-one," I point out as if that isn't already common knowledge.

Andrew pulls his ID out of his wallet. "Yes, I am," he says coolly, handing it to me.

I take a look at his Alaska driver's license. "You have a fake?"

He nods. "Brendan does too."

"I don't," I state, still confused. *What is going on in his brain right now? I know we said we wanted to live, but I didn't mean break the rules and all our bones!*

"Don't worry about it," Brendan eases. "It's super easy to get people in here. The guy probably won't even ask for your ID. That's why a lot of college kids come here."

Again, my eyes are bugging out of my head. "You want me to *sneak in?*" I give Andrew pleading eyes, silently begging him not to make me do this. *He knows me! He should know this isn't my scene.*

"It's not sneaking in. You'll walk right through the door," Brendan shrugs.

"I don't think I can do this. Can you just take me home?"

Andrew reaches for my arm, gently pulling me away from Brendan for a moment. His face softens. "I'm sorry, Em. I should've told you before, but I thought you might chicken out. I just thought this would be something fun we could try, a new experience. I've always been too afraid to come here and ride Benji when Brendan's tried to bring me in the past, but I thought with you by my side, I might be able to overcome my fear today." He pauses for a moment to inspect my face before jumping in again, "And you don't have to drink! I already made Brendan promise he wouldn't pressure you. I won't be drinking because I'm going to drive us home. All you have to do is come inside and be my cheerleader." He smiles hopefully.

I toe at the ground, kicking a loose piece of gravel. I pull my lower lip in and drag my teeth over it. "You promise I won't get in trouble for coming in?"

He immediately turns to Brendan for his expertise, knowing

his word is only so meaningful when he hasn't been here before either.

Brendan nods. "Yeah, the bouncer, Jimmy, is super cool. Honestly, even if you showed him your real ID, he'd still probably let you in. I don't know how this place is still in business, but it's great!"

"Okay, let's do it I guess," I murmur with little confidence.

Andrew's face breaks out into a huge grin, and he pulls me in for a kiss. Somehow that little piece of affection fills me with more confidence to walk into this bar and cheer for Andrew while he faces his fears.

"This is great! We will just go right up to the front. Jimmy's a couple of years ahead of us, but he did track with Andrew and me in high school." Brendan explains, excitement radiating off him, just like it is for Andrew.

"This is going to be so much fun, Em! I promise you'll have fun tonight!" Andrew insists, kissing me again, this time just a quick peck, and he grabs my hand to lead us toward the front doors of Yeehaw's.

At the door, a huge man, standing easily another two to three inches taller than Andrew, guards the door. My stomach does a little flip. I hate getting in trouble, and this guy looks like he means business.

When he sees our faces, his lights up. "Well look what the cat dragged in! Hey guys!" He gives each of the boys that weird universal bro handshake-hug thing and turns to me. "Who'd you bring with you?"

"This is my girlfriend, Emma," Andrew introduces me with pride.

I give Jimmy a shy smile and reach my hand out to shake his hand. Instead, he goes in for a hug, giving me a surprisingly gentle pat on the back. When we pull apart, I reach in my pocket to grab my ID, but he just ushers us right on in, stamping our hands as we enter. "Have fun you three!" With a glance at the watch on his wrist, he adds, "The band should be coming on within the next half hour."

Walking inside, I see the place is actually kind of cute. There's a neon blue sign over a stage at the front that says Yeehaw's. On both sides of the stage, there are picnic tables and a bar beyond that. Off in the corner, there are pool tables and what looks like a jukebox.

"No way!" I exclaim. "Is that a jukebox? Does it work?" I practically buzz with excitement.

Brendan chuckles. "Yeah, it's a jukebox. It's great because it takes credit cards, and the list of songs on there is three million miles long!"

I grab Andrew's hand and pull him over to the jukebox, eager to scroll through the songs and queue one up.

Brendan was right about the list of songs being extremely long. First, the songs are organized by genre, ranging from pop to classic to country. There's even a genre called techno, which I quickly avoid.

I select the country genre and continue scrolling, but I'm quickly overwhelmed with all of the choices. "Andrew! I don't know which song to play. There are too many to pick from."

He sidles up next to me and begins scrolling. "Oh, here's a classic," he says, sliding his card into the machine and hitting the select button.

I look at the machine and see the name "Don't Rock the Jukebox" by Alan Jackson. I crinkle my nose. "Way to be original."

"At least I made a decision." He winks then presses a kiss to my forehead and grabs both of my hands to swing me around to the upbeat melody. Brendan doesn't miss a beat, whipping out his phone and yelling, "Gross!" as he takes a video of the two of us, a bright smile on his face.

I'm so relieved this evening hasn't felt weird after the events of last summer. I think it helps that Brendan's attraction was likely more physical than anything, and his friendship with Andrew is much more important than any girl.

Once the song ends, we head outside to check out the back patio. Since the live music hasn't started inside yet, it seems like that's where most of the people are currently gathered. There are string lights overhead, a cornhole in the back corner, a hot dog stand right next to the door, and in the very center of it all, Benji, the giant mechanical bull.

Andrew and I take a moment to absorb the scene while Brendan rushes over to two girls to say hi. I can only assume he knows them from college. They both greet him with excitement. I watch him gesture over to Andrew and me, beaming with pride.

My attention is pulled away from him and toward shouting coming from the direction of Benji the Bull as a short, stocky male clings on to the bull for dear life. A group of five or six people, who I can only assume are his friends, rowdily cheer him on. He actually looks like he knows what he's doing! Until he doesn't, and he's thrown off Benji to the black mats below.

The guy leaps up to standing and gives a masculine cheer as he flexes his biceps and grabs his beer from one of his buddies.

I turn to Andrew with raised eyebrows, trying to hold back my laughter. "You want to do that?"

"Well, I might not do it with such a dramatic appearance," he defends.

"Alright, I'll believe you," I say, turning to look for Brendan. "What happens now?"

Andrew points out Brendan at the bar. "Whatever you want. We can just hang out and play a game of pool first. You can get a drink if you'd like, or you can even go get in line for Benji if you're feeling ready."

"Uh-huh." I pin him with a look, unamused. "I'll be ready after I see you and Brendan up there."

"Done!" Andrew says. "I'll sign us up right now."

"There's a sign-up?"

"More or less," Andrew squints his eyes and shakes his hand from side to side. "Brendan said they have one for when it gets crazy busy, but if there's no one there, you can just hop right on sometimes."

I fall into a daze as I watch a girl on Benji now. She's getting thrown around like a rag doll, but she's staying on. *Good for her. Maybe she can teach me her ways.*

Andrew interrupts my thoughts by waving a hand in front of my line of sight. "Earth to Emma. Are you still with me?"

"I need a drink," I state firmly, heading toward Brendan at the bar.

He looks over at us with a smile. "Hey! Do either of you want a drink? We can just put it on my tab and settle later."

"Tell me more about those trough drinks," I respond.

He raises his eyebrows. "Wow, I didn't think you had it in you! They usually recommend splitting it between two to three people. I think it's about five shots. It used to be more, but they had to cut it down a year or two ago."

"What's in it?"

He squirms and offers, "Tasty alcohol?"

"Is it tequila?"

"Oh God no! I won't touch that stuff."

"Great. Want to split it then?"

He turns to Andrew. "Are you not going to join us?"

"No, I have to drive. Plus, it looks like I'll be keeping an eye on this one," he explains, patting my shoulder.

"You don't need to watch me," I tell him. "And we could always get an Uber home if we need to."

He nods. "I know, but I'm trying to do what I should've done last time I was around when you drank."

"Andrew, you took great care of me! What are you talking about? Besides, it wasn't your responsibility."

"Yes, it was. I may not have been your boyfriend, but I was

still your friend, and I knew you'd never drunk before. I should've done a better job of paying attention to how much you had so you wouldn't have had that bad experience."

"It's in the past," I insist.

"You're right, but this is the present, and I'm going to do things right now."

I grab his hand to pull him in for a quick peck. "Well thank you, Prince Charming," I say with a wink.

"Soooo are we splitting the trough or not?" Brendan interjects awkwardly.

All three of us begin laughing as I say, "Yeah, let's do it."

CHAPTER 31

Summer 18

Rebecca has been glued to my side all day. Ever since I told her what happened with Andrew, she's been peppering me with questions. "What are you going to say when you see him again?" *I don't know.* "Do you think you guys will finally start dating?" *I don't know.* "What will you do about leaving for school tomorrow?" *I don't know.*

It's been exhausting and terrifying to realize with each question that I have absolutely no answers for her. I can't be frustrated with her though because I know her great interest in my love life is only because she wants me to be happy.

My phone buzzes in my back pocket, pulling my attention away from my conversation with Rebecca for a moment.

ANDREW

Where are you?

His text has no significance. He's not flirting or professing his love to me, but still, it makes my heart flutter. I curse my heart a little for being so easily moved.

"Is that Andrew?" Rebecca asks, leaning over to my side of the car and peering over at my phone.

I quickly push her back to her rightful place in the driver's seat. "You're driving! Watch the road, not my phone please."

She pouts. "I just want to know what's going on! Will you read it to me?"

I roll my eyes because the text is so completely insignificant, but I grant her wish anyway and read it aloud.

"Aww he wants to know where you are! Tell him we will be home in three minutes, and you two can meet up to talk then. You have to promise to fill me in on every word he says to you if he asks to speak to you alone. I won't be able to bear not knowing!" Her excitement is contagious, and I give myself a moment to appreciate all the support she gives me. I don't know what I'd do without Rebecca as my hype girl.

I laugh as I text him back.

ME

We are headed home from the grocery store.
We will be back in 2 mins

ANDREW

Oh perfect! I want to talk with you

Rebecca interrupts again as she makes a left turn onto our street. "What'd he say?"

"He just said he wants to talk."

Rebecca stares me down. "That's all he said?"

"Pretty much."

"Well then, what else did he say?" she prods.

"Nothing!"

Her lips form a straight line. "Fine, but you have to promise to fill me in on everything else."

I shake my head at her, but I'm smiling as I do it. "Alright, I promise. You know I can't keep things from you anyway."

"You didn't tell me what happened last night," she reminds me.

"I wouldn't call waiting twenty minutes while we make pancakes keeping things from you." I scoff.

When we pull into the driveway, I notice Andrew sitting on the porch steps. *Is he waiting for me?* Suddenly I feel nervous. *Should I be nervous? Oh God. What if he thinks this was all just a mistake? What if he wants to take back the things he said and did? Oh, I don't think my heart could take it.*

Andrew smiles and waves from the porch as the two of us get out of the car. I immediately feel my nervousness begin to subside. *Maybe everything will be okay.*

His dimple begins to show on his right cheek as he continues smiling at me. "Mom's pretty pissed you haven't started packing yet, Rebecca. If I were you, I'd get it done now before she gets home." Andrew warns with urgency. "I can keep Emma company for a little bit. I promise" he adds, giving Rebecca a look that I know is twin code for something. It's probably *please leave us alone* because she tilts her head in his direction as if to concede but rolls her eyes while doing it.

I laugh under my breath as I watch the two wordlessly interact. It's kind of fun to be wanted so much by both of them.

Rebecca hustles inside with the baking supplies as Andrew places one of his hands on my lower back, setting that singular spot, and in turn my entire spine, aflame.

He leans in to whisper in my ear. "I was hoping to talk a little about last night. I can't stop thinking about it."

I blush. Out of context, it might sound like more happened than we did last night. Even so, a lot *did* happen. I feel like the whole course of our relationship is going to take a turn at this point.

We walk around the house, heading down toward the beach. The shore can easily be followed for a solid mile before the cliffs briefly interrupt the rocky water's edge, but that should be plenty long enough for us to discuss everything.

We take a few steps in silence, and I look to him for guidance. He's the one who texted me he wanted to talk, so he should be the one to start our conversation.

I watch him swallow as if he's gathering courage, and the nerves from earlier quickly rush back. I catch myself gulping too.

He finally turns to me, carefully taking in my facial features, trying to read me. He smiles softly. "I just wanted to talk about last night and make sure we are on the same page before I get my hopes up."

I nod, eyes wide, anticipation buzzing around inside of me like a fly stuck in the house. "Okay, what page are you on?" I ask cautiously.

He smirks. "I think it's pretty obvious what page I'm on, but I don't want to be misreading you too."

I sigh. "I don't think you misread anything. I had a lot of fun last night. My only regret is not having more time with you this morning."

He stops abruptly and turns to me. I wince, instantly regretting my words. *Oh my gosh! I literally stopped him in his tracks. How did I manage to read him so wrong?* My stomach cartwheels.

Then he's moving toward me, sweeping a finger along the curve of my jaw and to my chin. He tilts my face up toward him as he softly says, "Me too. There's something I wanted to do."

Here comes the tingling again. I can't even breathe as I watch him carefully, waiting for what I think, and hope is going to happen.

He leans in, and my heart is pounding a million miles per minute. I've lost all control of my body.

I close my eyes as he gets closer and begin leaning in too. I feel his warm breath brush across my lips just before we are interrupted yet again by the ringing of a phone. Andrew stops, leaning his forehead against mine.

He sighs in defeat and mutters under his breath, "Damn it!"

I laugh a little to mask my disappointment. I look at him,

wondering if he's going to answer his phone now that we've been interrupted.

"I'm so sorry, Em. I want this moment to be perfect. I know *I've* waited a long time for this. I have to do this right. You deserve the world and then some." He pulls away from me and reaches down for his phone. "It's probably my mom. I better answer." When he looks down at it, he affirms, "Yup, it's Mom."

He turns away from me as he takes the call, and I try not to be disappointed. *At least I know for sure he wants to kiss me. That's something! As if that wasn't enough, he had to go and melt my heart by telling me he wanted it to be perfect for my sake.*

I pull out my phone to check the notifications, trying not to eavesdrop on his conversation. *What could Mrs. Martin possibly need right now that had to interrupt this moment?*

There are five texts from Rebecca. I breathe out a puff of air through my nose as I find myself both surprised and not at all surprised by the notifications. On the one hand, I thought she would leave me alone with Andrew, but on the other hand, I know better than that.

> **REBECCA**
>
> I hope everything is going well!
>
> I'm dying here wondering what you two are "talking" about
>
> OMG you two are totally not even talking huh?
>
> Get some girl! Except that's my twin brother… so that's weird but I guess I can get over it for you because I love you 🤍
>
> Hurry up and get back so you can fill me in!!!

I glance up at Andrew. He's still on the phone, his brows furrowed and his light smile from earlier completely replaced by a prominent frown. I guess he's probably just as disappointed as I am to be interrupted. That makes me feel a little better.

I take this opportunity to respond to Rebecca quickly. I know she will appreciate it. Plus, this way, she can't say I kept anything from her this time.

ME

Rebecca I'm dying! He tried to kiss me again but your mom called and interrupted us... AGAIN!

Her response pops up instantly.

REBECCA

Noooooo! I'm sorry! I tried to tell her it could wait. I thought I convinced her. This is all my fault

No it's not lol! Everything will be fine. We still have time

Not now you won't

What do you mean?

Before Rebecca has a chance to respond, Andrew comes back over to me, resting his hand on my lower back. I take a second to appreciate the warmth of his soft touch before he speaks.

"Em, I'm sorry, but we have to head back. My mom is freaking out about dinner tonight since it's our last family dinner for a while. She needs me to come help her cook."

I nod, acting agreeable rather than bummed out like I feel right now. "No problem. I understand. I didn't know you cooked though," I point out.

He shakes his head, and a laugh slips out. "I don't. I have no idea why she insists I need to be home to help out with this, but we better hurry because she sounded on the verge of a meltdown."

I jut my lower lip out a little. "Aww, your mom is going to

miss you two! She's going to have an empty nest for the first time. I'm sure it's really hard to lose both of you at once."

He squints at me a little as we briskly walk back. "She's hardly losing us. We will be back in a few months for Thanksgiving and then Christmas, spring break, and obviously next summer."

I tilt my head at him. "That's not the same as having you around every day."

"I know," he finally acknowledges. "I'm sure it will be hard for her. That's why I'm going back now instead of saying 'screw that' and staying here with you to finish what we tried to start."

I chuckle. It's odd how I went from being so disappointed to now feeling giddy and happy again. I guess just knowing we are close, and knowing Andrew is so set on making sure things happen between us, makes me feel like everything is going to be okay.

When we reach the Martin residence he turns to me. "This is going to happen, Em. I promise!"

I nod, giving him a hopeful smile. "I can't wait."

He wraps me up in his arms quickly, and I can sense his hesitation before he lets me go. He slowly slides his hands down my arms and takes me in with admiration as he pulls away.

He nods and says, "Yes, this is going to happen." This time he is talking more to himself than anyone.

He finally turns away and begins jogging up the stairs on the back deck. "I'll see you later tonight!"

"Definitely! Rebecca and I still have cookies to bake, and she wants to do something fun for our last night," I respond right before he walks inside.

The giddy feeling falters a little as I walk back toward my house. We didn't get to talk about anything. I don't know if we are going to be boyfriend and girlfriend now or how we will approach going off to school six hours away from each other, all things Rebecca had asked me about earlier. I *do* know he likes me and wants to kiss me and is determined to make that happen. Plus, we still have time to talk tonight, so I'm sure everything will be fine.

I shrug off the unsure feelings and allow myself to just sit in the joy for now.

CHAPTER 32

Summer 19

We've been here about an hour, and I have a delightful little buzz. This isn't like two summers ago when I drank the margaritas. The world doesn't spin every time I stand, but I feel a little lighter and giddy. I just can't stop smiling, and things that are only half funny seem funny.

Andrew has been carefully monitoring my drinking, insisting I pace myself. I could be annoyed with him for being overprotective, but I'm choosing to be thankful I have someone who wants to show me how to have a good relationship with alcohol.

The live band started a little while ago, and we pretty much haven't left the dance floor. Brendan has alternated between dancing with me and just about every other girl in here. He's so personable and the perfect balance between being flirty and a gentleman, that it's no surprise he's been able to get so many dance partners.

Even with the liquid courage running through my veins, I'm still anxious about the reason we came here in the first place. I don't think any amount of alcohol will make me want to get on a mechanical bull and ride it for fun, but I also recognize if Rebecca were here, she would've already ridden the damn thing five times… at least! Everyone who's done it so far has seemed to have a good time. I've watched closely. There is a part of me that is curious, which is infuriating because that only means I have to try it. But that doesn't mean I'm not terrified to do so.

The band begins a new song, and I watch Andrew's face completely light up. "No way! Do you know who this is?"

I squint up at the stage setup. "Rusty Boot? That's a weird name for a band."

He frowns. "No, the song they're singing. It's by Shane Smith & the Saints!"

Arching an eyebrow, I ask, "Am I supposed to know who that is?"

"I guess not. They're not the type of band Rebecca would've listened to and introduced to you. This is a great song though. Will you dance with me?" He bows down to me with an outstretched hand, looking like Prince Charming asking Cinderella to dance with him.

Smiling, I take his hand, and he pulls me in. "What's the name of the song?" I ask him, leaning into his ear so he can hear me over the music that is now picking up.

"'All I See is You,'" he responds, sending chills down my spine from the sensual brush of his lips and the sweet meaning behind the song title.

I tune in to the song as the beat picks up, making me want to do a little jig, but instead, I follow Andrew's lead, bounding and spinning around with glee.

Andrew twirls me around then pulls me in snug against him with his arms crossed over me. There's a brief moment when our eyes connect, and we exchange a look that says so much more than words ever could. The band plays their upbeat song, the neon lights in the bar flash on the walls, and people all around us drunkenly twirl and bound, but in that moment, it's like my surroundings fade. All that's left is Andrew's handsome face, radiating warmth and love. The look in his eyes is warm and soft. *He's in love too. I can tell.*

"This song is so cute I want to cry!" I shout over the music.

His already smiling face transforms into pure joy as he spins me back out. He releases me and links elbows with me, skipping in a circle, and I can't help but throw my head back and laugh at his goofiness. He's not the most amazing dancer, but I'd dance with him any day because he just lets loose and has a good time.

The song winds down, and I catch myself panting from the sporadic and goofy dancing we just did. Andrew grabs me by the waist, drawing me in closer for a soft kiss. It has all the gentleness that leaves me longing for more and makes me forget we are surrounded by people. Or maybe the alcohol is hitting me a little more than I realize, but anyhow, I go in for more, slipping my tongue teasingly into his mouth.

I feel his grip on my waist tighten and can't help but smirk against his lips as I begin to realize how my kiss is impacting him too. I'm almost certain he is about to pull me out the front door and take me straight home when he pulls away. "So are you ready to ride a bull?"

I wince. "Five more minutes?"

He steps closer to me. "You don't have to if you don't want to."

A wave of relief rolls over me, but it's quickly followed by guilt. *Why do I feel guilty?*

I straighten up a little. "I'll do it."

"What?"

Looking back up into Andrew's beautiful blue eyes, I repeat, "I'll do it."

"Yes!" He wraps me up in a bear hug. "I didn't want to push you too hard, but I knew you wanted to! You aren't going to regret this. This will be a story you'll tell your kids someday!" He rattles on in excitement. "Rebecca would be so proud."

His words crack my heart in two, but I plaster on a smile anyway. It must not be entirely convincing because his smile falters as he asks, "What's the matter?"

"Rebecca would be proud. That's all. I just miss her," I say, shrugging and trying not to let the alcohol get the best of my emotions.

Andrew pulls me back into his brawny arms and squeezes tight, rubbing my back. "I miss her too." After a moment he adds, "Somehow doing these things makes me feel a little closer to her, you know?"

I nod my head into his chest, and his grip on me tightens. When Brendan walks up, I pull away from Andrew with a renewed sense of determination.

"Is it time to ride Benji?" Brendan asks with glee.

"Hell yeah, I'm ready! I call dibs on going first!" Andrew beams.

Brendan is quick to argue, but after a well-fought battle of rock, paper, scissors, Andrew wins.

There's no line outside, so Andrew hops on right away. Watching him cling to the bull fills me with anticipation. For someone who has never done this before, he sure has a lot of confidence.

Even without experience, he seems to be doing great. I watch him squeeze the bull tightly with his knees, and he remains loose, letting the bull whip him around with his chin tucked to his chest while his center of gravity remains square on the center of Benji.

The bull gets faster and faster, and I begin to wonder if he lied about never doing this before. He's a natural, and he's clinging on longer than I've seen anyone last tonight. Granted, he is definitely the most sober person to ride Benji this evening, maybe ever.

Benji gives another violent thrust, and it's enough to break Andrew's grip. He flies off the bull onto the padding below.

Brendan and I rush to his side, checking on him. He looks fine, but his face is a mix of joy and sorrow. He's smiling, but I swear I see a tear forming in his eye.

Brendan helps him to his feet as Andrew asks, "Are you next?"

"I don't think I can follow that performance, man! I've tried before, and I always fall off five seconds in."

"That's never stopped you before."

Brendan tips his head to acknowledge Andrew's point and heads toward the bull, hopping on.

Still watching Brendan, I whisper, "You looked a little emotional."

He shrugs. "This is going to sound crazy, but I could *feel* her there. There was a moment when I could hear her cheering me on and saying how much of a badass I was." He chuckles.

I throw an arm around him. "That doesn't sound crazy at all."

As I finish my words, Brendan gets thrown off. He was right. He probably only lasted about five seconds.

"All you, Emma!" Brendan sings. "I'll warn you though. Benji is *not* very kind."

I nervously push past him toward the mechanical bull. I can still feel the buzz coursing through my body, giving me an odd sense of confidence, which somehow simultaneously makes me even more nervous. *I don't know the first thing about bull riding! Damn it! I should've done some research on my phone beforehand.*

I slip one leg over the big bull and slip my hand through the strap I'm supposed to hold onto. The bull begins to move, and I tense up, but it's not so bad. I have no clue how Brendan got thrown off so early. *This is easy.*

Then there's a clicking sound as the bull levels up and begins bucking harder. I fill with panic as I try to remember what Andrew did to stay on so long. I quickly realize I'm not afraid of riding the bull. I'm afraid of what happens when I can't stay on anymore.

I squeeze my knees as tight as they can go. I can't see them, but I'm sure they're turning white like the knuckles on my right hand as it grasps the strap. I try to tuck my chin, letting Benji throw me whichever way he pleases and praying I can stay on. I do, for a little while, but right as I grow proud of myself for staying on through the last buck, I get thrown off.

Andrew rushes over to me with a bright smile on his face. "You did amazing!"

I blush. "Thank you! I tried to mimic you as much as I could, but that bull has an attitude."

He chuckles and helps me up. "Are you ready to head home yet?"

I nod. "I think it's about time we call it a night."

We snag Brendan, who got distracted between his bull ride and my own with a beautiful, leggy brunette. On our way out the front door, Jimmy waves at us with a friendly grin.

"I think tonight turned out to be a success," I say as we drive home. Brendan is already passed out in the back seat.

Andrew gives me a soft smile. "It did. Thanks. I know this is far from your idea of a fun evening."

"I wouldn't say far!" I jump in, a little offended. "I got to spend the whole evening with you, dancing and playing around. I enjoy Brendan's company and seeing the two of you together. Plus, now we can both say we've ridden a mechanical bull. How cool is that?"

He beams back at me. "I can't wait to tell all my buddies at school I rode a bull. When I tell them the story, it's going to be a real bull, though. And it's going to have a scarier name than Benji... maybe Big Ben."

I roll my eyes. "Cause Big Ben really gets you shaking in your boots."

"Okay, I'll think of something better."

I laugh, but it's not quite a full-hearted laugh. My mind is racing at the mention of school. Our relationship is worth fighting for. I need to make an effort to talk with him before it's too late. "Hey Andrew, I'm scared about what comes next."

"What do you mean?"

"We're about to leave for school again. That means I won't get to spend every day with you. We'll have to try to stay in touch through texts and Facetimes, and deal with busy schedules and time differences."

"I'm scared too, Em. We'll be okay though. We've done it before."

"It wasn't the same."

He reaches out for my hand. "I know, but we aren't the same people we were in the past either. We are stronger and better. We've got this."

I nod, trying to reassure myself too. "You're excited to go back to school, aren't you?"

He shrugs. "I mean, I'll miss you, but I'm ready to get out of my parents' house and see my friends. Plus, I reached out to my guidance counselor about switching majors, and it looks like I'll not only be able to do it, but I'll be able to get into some writing courses for the fall semester!"

I pause. "You didn't tell me about that. When did you reach out?"

"Eh, about a week ago."

"That's great, Andrew!" My excitement for him dissipates. "How did this happen a week ago, and I'm just now hearing about it?" I try to sound casual, desperately ignoring the way my heart hurts because he failed to tell me such big news.

"I don't know. I got the email in between training sessions with Brendan, and then my parents bombarded me with chores when I got home. I guess I was just busy and forgot."

Andrew's tone is so casual, and it splits me in two. I'm reminded of last year when he didn't respond to my texts. I know that was an entirely different situation, but I'm beginning to wonder if we will be able to handle a long-distance relationship. *If he forgets to mention big news to me while we are seeing each other every day, how is he going to communicate with me when we are six hours away and not seeing each other for months at a time?*

I'm sober enough now to realize my thoughts are spiraling, but I can't help it. I'm scared. My feelings for him have grown so much stronger this summer. They are far from just a crush. Right now, I feel the kind of love for Andrew that I know can crush me if I lose it, and it's terrifying. I don't know how to prevent it, but I have to. I've already been through so much in the last year.

People try long-distance all the time, and it rarely works. My roommate last year had a long-distance relationship with her boyfriend until he cheated on her two months later. Andrew would never do that to me. I know that in my heart, but it doesn't mean long-distance won't find another way to tear us apart from one another.

We spend the rest of the car ride listening to Shane Smith & the Saints's version of "All I See is You." Andrew hums along gleefully, but I feel the summer ending, and the weight of it all is breaking me.

CHAPTER 33

Summer 18

"Cookie time!" Rebecca sings.

I laugh at her as I help her pull out the rest of the ingredients, including the chocolate chips and the bag of flour we purchased from the grocery store earlier today.

Andrew is sitting at the counter, watching us rush around to get everything ready for the cookies. "Are you going to help?" I tease.

He purses his lips, hiding a smile. "I already helped make dinner, and it was a complete disaster. Just ask Rebecca. I think it's best for everyone if I just supervise this operation… and taste test!"

"I'm not sure if you can be a taste tester if you aren't going to help." I shrug.

"Fine, then tell me what you want me to do. I'm at your mercy."

Rebecca eyes me, clearly picking up on the obvious flirting that is happening between the two of us. I haven't had time alone with either twin since my conversation on the beach with Andrew was cut short. We had to part ways for dinner time, but

I came over as soon as I could after both of our families had finished our meals.

"Andrew, I know something you could do to help!" Rebecca chimes in. "Can you go out to my car and check to see if I left my baking sheets in there?"

Andrew's face fills with amusement. "Why on earth would you put baking sheets in your car?"

"Just go look!" she insists. "I think I brought them over to Lily's house last week, but we didn't make cookies, so I forgot about them."

Still looking suspicious, Andrew challenges, "Since when did you go over to Lily's house during the summer? You only ever hang out with Emma."

"Obviously not because I saw her last week. Please just go, and then you can help taste test!"

He turns his back and begins heading toward the garage. "Where are your keys?" he shouts over his shoulder.

"Oh shoot! They're probably on my nightstand or my dresser."

Andrew huffs up the stairs to go to Rebecca's room. "Alright, we have a solid minute before he comes back down and realizes my keys aren't up there," she begins, pulling her keys from her back pocket and tossing them across the room onto the couch. "You have to fill me in on what happened earlier. You two seem happy… flirty." She winks at me gleefully.

I blush a little. She's right. I know *I* am happy, and Andrew sure seems to be flirty.

"I already told you over text what happened. We were out on the walk, and he said he wanted to make sure we were on the same page. I told him I wished we had more time together this morning when we almost kissed, and he agreed. He leaned in—" Andrew rumbles down the staircase at that moment, so I shut up quickly.

"They're not up there, Rebecca."

She bops her palm to her forehead. "Oh, you're right! I think they're over by the couch. Silly me. Sorry, Andrew."

He pins her with a glare as he walks over to the couch. He picks them up, remarking, "You're lucky these cookies are so good, or I would not be doing this." He turns to me before he walks out, and his eyes are sparkling. He winks quickly and heads out through the garage.

"Anyway." Rebecca prods me.

"He leaned in to kiss me again, but he stopped because your mom called."

"Why'd he stop? He should've just kissed you! That imbecile!" she shouts. "I ought to teach him a lesson or two in romantic gestures."

I laugh as I measure and pour the two kinds of sugar into the mixing bowl. "Please don't. I think he knows exactly what he's doing. He said he's been waiting to kiss me for a long time, so he wanted it to be perfect. He also said I 'deserve the world.'"

She pouts. "That's so sweet! Who knew my little Andy was capable of that?"

The garage door slams closed. "Capable of what?"

I feel my cheeks flush as I turn to Rebecca to wordlessly say *Don't tell him.*

She doesn't even meet my gaze and responds to Andrew without caring at all about embarrassing me. "Capable of being romantic."

His eyes grow wide for a second, and I can see his calm and collected aura has been temporarily compromised. "Why do you say that?"

She moves across the kitchen to wrap an arm around Andrew's shoulder. "Oh nothing, little brother. A little piece of advice for next time though, just kiss Emma when the phone is ringing. That in and of itself is a perfect romantic gesture because then it shows you care more about her than any other distractions, like your phone."

Andrew pulls away from her. "How about you just butt out?"

She laughs, and he nervously laughs too, meeting my gaze. I can tell he's only concerned about me and how I feel at this moment. He could care less about his sister's teasing. He just wants to make sure that I'm not uncomfortable. So, I laugh along with the two of them and change the subject. "Hey, Andrew, want to help me with the dry ingredients? It should be a super easy task for you. Rebecca, you can add the eggs and vanilla extract to this bowl."

Andrew nods and walks over to my side of the counter. "What do you need me to do?"

"Based on your horrible cooking skills, I say I'll measure everything. You just have to pour it into the bowl."

He nods in agreement and watches me carefully as I measure out the flour, leveling it off with the swipe of my finger.

I try to pretend I don't feel the heat of his gaze on me as I continue with the recipe easily. I've only made these cookies about a million times.

I hand Andrew the measuring cups and teaspoons as I measure, and he pours them into the bowl before handing me back the measuring devices. We work smoothly together as a team.

I make the mistake of allowing him to pour the dry ingredients from their separate bowl into the wet ingredients, and half of the flour mixture ends up all over the counter.

Normally my inner neat freak would be screaming at the mess, but this time, I don't care. Andrew looks way too cute trying to concentrate as he pours small amounts of the powder into the rest of the dough. I'm too happy right now to let a small mess distract me.

"Okay, add the chocolate chips and the dough should be ready for taste testing," I tell Andrew.

He reaches into the bag and grabs a fistful of chocolate chips. "Just like this?" he asks.

Horrified, I rush over to pry his hand back open and get him to release the chocolate chips back into the bag. "No no no! Use the measuring cups. The recipe calls for one cup of chocolate chips," I explain.

He laughs at himself a little, embarrassment turning his cheeks pink, a sight that I don't recall ever seeing.

Once he's poured the cup of chocolate chips in, he looks at me, waiting for permission to dig into the dough.

I pinch a clump of dough and hold it out for him to take. Instead of holding his palm out for me, he takes it from my hand with his mouth. I feel the brush of his soft, full lips and the brief warmth of his tongue, and it sets my soul on fire, leaving me wanting more.

"Mmmm, this might be the best batch yet, Em!"

I give his shoulder a light smack. "You're only saying that because you helped!" I giggle and then turn serious. "They're not even baked yet, so we will have to see how they taste when they come out of the oven."

"Trust me—" he holds my gaze "—this is the best batch I've *ever* had. I can tell already."

I hear Rebecca groan behind me. "Oh, please you two! Get a room already. This is going to get old fast," she complains, but as soon as Andrew rolls his eyes at her and turns away, she smiles at me and gives me two thumbs up. I can tell this makes her happy to see. She's been telling me for years now that this was going to happen between us, and I didn't believe her, but here we are, right on the cusp on something amazing.

"Hey, let's get the fire pit going on the back deck to enjoy our cookies while the sun goes down. Then I want to do something fun," Rebecca suggests with a smirk.

Andrew and I nod in agreement.

"I'll get the fire lit while you two finish up with the cookies in the oven," Andrew suggests.

CHAPTER 34

Summer 19

I sit in my pajamas with a clean body and full belly, reading a book alone in my room. I haven't seen Andrew much today, and the distance has given me perhaps too much time to think. I desperately want to talk with Dani about my conversation with Andrew last night and all the resulting feelings I've had since then, but for some reason, this just feels like something I need to tackle by myself.

Andrew's truth bomb last night about his courses shouldn't be making me feel this upset, but it's only sent me down a rabbit hole. This isn't the first time he's kept something to himself. *How are we possibly going to tackle distance together if he can't open up to me?* The thought constricts my lungs and makes my stomach do a few somersaults. In the past twenty-four hours, it's started to hit me just how much Andrew's silence last year left a scar on my heart. After Rebecca's accident, I lost two of my best friends in one day, and one of them was still alive. One of them *chose* to leave me. Then there's his other minute moments of secrecy which somehow hurt just as bad and cause my doubts to swirl like a hurricane inside my head. I know we've talked about it a little bit, but I'm still terrified that trying to put our relationship through long distance is only going to end in heartbreak.

I can't lose Andrew again. He's helped me so much this summer with overcoming my fears and healing in the wake of Rebecca's accident. *Were we being crazy for thinking this would work?*

We're only nineteen, which means we'd have to handle distance for at least three more years during college. That's ridiculous to try to tie ourselves down like that when we have so much life to live. I may love him more than I've ever loved anyone or anything, and he may bring light into my shadows, but sometimes love just isn't enough.

I know I can't take the heartbreak from losing Andrew again after losing his sister not even a year ago, and I definitely wouldn't wish that heartache upon Andrew either. He's been through enough in his lifetime. I should probably just end things now. We only had the summer together. It will hurt a lot less to end things now rather than draw it out. We can stay friends, and then I won't have to lose him for good.

I huff and set my book down. There's no way I can sit and read right now. I'm far too distracted. Grabbing my phone, I press shuffle on one of my playlists. Music will clear my mind. It will give me the clarity I need to figure out what's right for Andrew and me.

But the first song to play is "Porch Swing Angel."

"Are you kidding me?" I grumble to my phone, skipping the song and throwing my phone across my room to the soft protection of my bed.

My music shuts off suddenly. Growing more irritated by the minute, I drag myself off my window seat, tears forming in my eyes as I march across my room toward my bed to hit play again.

Except the play button isn't even an option because my music is being interrupted by a call from Andrew. My thumb hovers over the button, ready to slide it and answer it, but I hesitate. *I just said I needed some time to think. I don't need to answer his call right now. I can talk to him later,* I convince myself. Except, seeing his contact photo, a selfie with Andrew kissing me on the cheek, makes me completely ignore whatever thoughts I had. It's my sweet Andrew. I should just talk with him about all the things weighing on me. If there's anything I've learned from the past, it's the importance of communication.

"What's up?" I answer.

"Hey, gorgeous! I wanted to see what you are up to. I think I'm free for dinner tonight."

"Do you want to come over for a little bit? I've had some things on my mind, and I think it would be good for us to talk through them."

"I'll be right over."

I note the fear in his voice and rush to console him, but he's already hung up. Before I can even consider doing something with my hair or putting some Chapstick on my dry lips, he's knocking on my window.

I glance up to find Andrew crouched down and peering in. He's dressed in one of his university track and field t-shirts with his typical effortlessly messy hairdo. My heart does a little pitter-patter, and I can't help but think that maybe I was being irrational. Seeing him here in front of me, all I feel is love for him, even with his imperfections.

I crack the window open for him, and he begins popping the screen off simultaneously. As he steps in, I thoughtlessly reach for his hand to help him balance and immediately feel my palm light on fire from his touch.

He pulls me into him for a fierce hug, and I have a flash of saying goodbye to him in a week. It makes my already aching heart whimper in pain, but I tell it to shut up as I pull away from Andrew, putting distance between us again. I gesture for him to sit on the bed next to me.

He follows my guidance and reaches for my hands, placing both of them in the warmth of his calloused palms. I take a deep breath, recentering myself and not letting his touch distract me from my purpose.

Andrew's piercing blue eyes are analyzing me closely when he finally speaks, "Em, what's going on?"

"I know we talked last night about distance, but I think we need to revisit the subject. I'm absolutely freaking out that we aren't going to be able to make this work. I don't know anyone who has survived distance, and I just can't lose you."

He narrows his brows at me. "We aren't going to break each other's hearts. Don't let your doubts creep in now."

"But aren't you just a little concerned about distance? It's not an easy thing to overcome, and we've only been together for several weeks."

"But we've known each other for over ten years. That means something."

"I mean, yeah, I guess it does, but still. Andrew, can you really tell me you're not afraid?"

"Em, where is this coming from all of a sudden? You sound like you're trying to break things off."

"I'm not trying to break things off, but I *do* think we need to take off our rose-colored glasses and face the facts. Long-distance doesn't work. Look at last year. We were both going through things, and your way of handling that was by cutting me out. Last night, I found out you didn't feel the need to share a pretty monumental life event with me until almost a week later. I should be the first one you want to tell. Now, you won't even admit to me that you're scared of distance. You *still* can't communicate. We need to communicate better than we ever have when we're that far apart, and we are both going to get so busy when we go back to school. Maybe we don't make sense right now. If we just go back to being friends, all of this will hurt less. There's no breaking up, no losing each other, no resentment. We can still be us without all the pressure of a relationship. It will be just like the last ten years, which had been pretty great before Rebecca's accident."

"I'm not going to let you do this. I agree, we should talk about distance, and we can get real about it. It's going to be hard, but just because *you* haven't seen something work doesn't mean it can't. You know we can't just go back to the way things were." He clasps my hand tightly and pulls me back toward him, wrapping me up in his embrace, filling my nostrils with the scent of his rustic body wash.

I shake my head, refusing to look at him. "You might not understand now, but this is for your own good."

"You're right. I don't understand what could *possibly* be going through your head right now to make you think this is what's best for us. I thought we were going to talk about solutions to make this work. I didn't realize you already made up your mind." He pulls away from me as his nostrils flare.

"I haven't made up my mind, but I'm offering this as a solution where we can minimize the damage. Do you think we can last through all the obstacles we are about to face, Andrew?"

"*I* believe in us. We can handle anything that's thrown our way. You don't have any reason to doubt us. We've been great together. Maybe just take a deep breath and let your thoughts settle for a second."

"I don't need a second. I know I have a reason to doubt us." I growl. "Where did you disappear to when things got hard last year? You completely cut me out of your life. You had almost an entire year to heal and patch things up with me, but you waited until I was confronting you. You think we are going to survive long-distance when you shut people out like that? No."

I'm stunned by my sharp tone, but I'm sort of proud I finally recognized the way he made me feel so long ago and for speaking up for myself.

He shakes his head at me. "You're not upset with me. You're

letting your fears creep in. Don't throw us away because you're scared of what you're feeling or what you might be able to feel if we move forward. Don't let all of this come crashing down because you're afraid of losing me. You're just going to turn your worst fears into your reality if you do. I know I haven't been the best at expressing how I feel all the time, but I'm willing to work on it for us."

My lip is quivering now, and my lungs feel like they're being squeezed in the hands of a giant. "I think it's too late to work on it. I need you to be better *now*. I need to know I can trust you *now*. We are running out of time, Andrew."

A flash of hurt crosses his face. "I can't believe you'd expect me to just be perfect overnight. I accept you for who you are. I love every part of you, your vibrant, funny, smart, and kind side but also your scared, overthinking, reserved side. Love should be about choosing to work on things together and being patient as people grow, not demanding they be better right *now or else*. I thought you felt the same way about me as I did for you, but I guess I was wrong."

His words slice my heart in two. As he sits up from my bed, each of his movements is like a foot stomping on the remaining pieces of my heart.

"Andrew, no that's not—"

"Em, please stop. I believe in us, but you clearly need some space. I don't want to hear from you for a couple days until you've had some time to figure things out."

As he slams my window closed, tears stream down my face uncontrollably, and I can practically hear both our hearts shattering like glass. I can't help the thought that crosses my mind as I watch him walk away. *This is where we end.*

CHAPTER 35

Summer 19

I spent most of the day in bed since Andrew left. I sobbed myself to sleep about an hour after he crawled out of my window, and I slept until the next morning. My body certainly needed it after all of the emotional turmoil I've put it through recently, and the alternative is being awake where I can think about what happened yesterday and see Andrew hasn't called or texted me. Not that I've made an effort either. I'm hurt, and everything feels final. He doesn't want to be friends, and I don't know how to convince him to take me back after what happened yesterday. I know he said he wanted to talk things through, but he also stormed out. I'm not sure what to make of everything.

Maybe a run will clear my head and help me find solutions. It's the only thing I can think to do, and I don't want to spend the rest of my time here holed up in the cabin.

When I finally exit my room with my hair pulled back into a high ponytail, Dani looks up from her computer. She appears to be editing the photos she took of me before I left for Yeehaw's. The thought makes my stomach feel like it got thrown down a flight of stairs, tumbling and turning over and over again until it settles in a sour, painful ball. *How did everything change so quickly?*

"Are you okay?" she presses, puddles of worry filling her green eyes.

"Yeah, I'm fine. I was just really tired." I shirk off her concern, grabbing my watch off the charger on the kitchen counter.

Her watchful eyes follow my every movement. "Nuh-uh. Something's wrong. I'm not just talking about you sleeping in. I haven't seen you in over twenty-four hours, and now your eyes look swollen and red. Come talk to me." She pats the dining room chair next to her.

Part of me considers ignoring her and rushing out the door to some peace and quiet. I want to be left alone with my breaking heart and all the emotions that come along with it. I need this run to figure out my next steps. I already know what Dani's going to say. I don't need to sit through a discussion with her to know she's going to tell me this whole fight was stupid, but it doesn't matter because it's over now, and the only option I have is to figure out how to move forward.

"I don't feel like talking right now, Dani."

Hearing the screeching of Dani pushing her chair out, I refuse to turn around. I'm so emotionally drained. I don't think I can have a conversation with her right now, especially about my fight with Andrew.

She grabs my shoulder, turning me to face her.

"What's your problem?" I protest, my guard up.

Her eyes grow wide with confusion and maybe a little hurt. "What's *my* problem? What's *your* problem, Emma? I've told you I'm here for you. You can tell me *anything*. I don't know what else I need to do to prove to you that you can trust me." Her voice continues to raise an octave with each sentence. "I'm your *sister* for crying out loud!"

I wince as she manages to send a dagger or two right to my heart.

I lower my walls a little. "I'm sorry. There's just a lot going on in my mind right now, and I know you're not going to understand, but it's already done."

She furrows her brows. "Why do you assume I won't understand? Even if I don't, do you not trust me to at least *try* to understand your side?"

I purse my lips, trying to fight the guilt building up inside of me. Sighing, I explain, "Andrew and I had this massive fight yesterday. I don't think there's any coming back from it, but it's fine. We needed to go back to being just friends anyway. It's for the best."

I can already tell she's trying to hide her reaction. Her face remains stoic, but her eyes are searching. "Oh, Emma, I'm so sorry! What happened?"

"I told him I was afraid of doing long-distance, which led me to suggest maybe we go back to being friends instead, but it ended in a huge fight," I say, trying to act matter-of-fact and pretending like I am confident in the decisions I've made.

"Why did you tell him you should break up?" she asks, slowly, as if asking the question too quickly will scare me away. Maybe it will.

I take a deep sigh, growing irritated. Although my irritation has nothing to do with Dani or her questions. I'm realizing I'm irritated with myself for getting into this whole situation. Things were going great between Andrew and me, but I screwed it all up.

"Dani, I just couldn't do it. He is changing his major and didn't even tell me. I don't know how we could handle long-distance if we can't even communicate when we are together. Then I can't help but think about how he completely ghosted me last year after Rebecca's accident or how he wouldn't even admit to me yesterday that he was afraid of distance until I was practically in tears. I really, really care for him, but I don't know if we could make distance work. I can't take the heartache if we break up down the road, and I don't want to hurt him either."

"So your solution was going back to being friends and breaking both your hearts instead of allowing yourself the possibility of being happy?"

"No, that's not what I'm doing," I insist as my walls clamor back up.

"Emma, you can't just break things off when they're going great because you're afraid someone is going to get hurt. If everyone did that, no one would end up with a happy ending. You have to take a chance on love to have love. I can already see this is tearing you apart, and I'm sure it is doing the same to Andrew."

"That's my whole point," I argue. "I need to break things off now because it already hurts so much. It will only hurt worse down the road when we inevitably break up because I can't trust him. Plus, distance doesn't work."

"Why can't you trust him? Because of something he did while he was enduring the worst pain of his life? Don't act like you were perfect either, Emma. You completely shut out your entire family, the people that are supposed to be closest to you. You didn't try all that hard at making friends in school, either. You just threw yourself into work and pretended like the rest of the world stopped existing. You can't judge him for what he did then when you did the exact same thing," she challenges.

"But he still isn't being completely transparent with me. It's happened this summer, too."

"Can you honestly say you're perfect? Don't act like you have overcome everything that's held you back in the past. You've grown, but you're still scared of things. You're still not letting me completely in. It sucks. You've come so far. Don't let old habits creep back in just because summer is ending, and we have to go back to our old lives. You can let your life this summer be your new life wherever you go."

I'm speechless. I had no idea Dani felt this way. Honestly, I didn't think she noticed. It's not like Dani and I were ever that close until this summer.

"Dani, I'm sorry. I didn't realize…"

"It's okay. I know we weren't that close before, but I've always *wanted* to be there for you. I can't even imagine the pain you went through when you lost Rebecca, and it was so hard to watch you shut the world out. You became this shell of a person for months, but this summer you were vibrant again. You were letting people in, and you were healing. Don't throw all that away again and shut everyone out. You deserve happiness."

I chew on my lip, trying to keep myself from tearing up again, but these tears aren't sad tears. They're happy tears because I now know I have a sister who is willing to fight for my happiness.

"Don't deny yourself the possibility of staying together and being happy. You're not even giving the relationship a chance. I can only imagine that hurts *more* than if you try and fail. You both will have to live with the what ifs and the knowledge that you didn't even want to try," she continues, as if she hadn't already gotten through to me.

I choke on a sob. *When did I start crying again?* "I *do* want to try, Dani! It's just terrifying. I can't take more loss."

"Aren't you losing Andrew this way anyway?" she challenges.

"I—" I pause, her words hitting me hard. "I'll explain everything to him in a year from now. He'll understand. I can at least get my friend back. I'm sure of it."

"Even if that's true, do you want to go another year of your life without Andrew in it?"

I want to scream *No! Of course not! He's one of the best things to ever happen to me.* Instead, I shrug. "It doesn't matter anymore. It's already done, Dani. You may be right, and I may have made a huge mistake, but I've already said all those things to him. I've lost his trust now."

She shakes her head, a smile spreading across her face, instantly drawing my attention. *Why is she smiling? This isn't a happy moment or a funny moment. This is one of the low points of my life!*

"Emma, you idiot! You've been friends with Andrew since you were nine years old. You've both loved each other for years, much longer than just this summer. You're smart enough to know Andrew wouldn't just throw all of that away because of a fight. You just need to be honest with him."

I'm already shaking my head. "You weren't there during our fight, Dani. He was really upset with me. I said some really hurtful things and royally screwed up this time."

"Okay, so you make up for it. You tell him you messed up, and you prove to him how much you love him."

"It's not that simple."

"Yes, it is. Quit making everything so complicated. I know you tend to overthink things. It's okay, but don't let your mind play tricks on you and ruin your chance at happiness."

I swallow and wipe at the tears streaming down my cheeks. "I need to go for a run," I practically whisper as I turn away from Dani and head out the front door to let every part of these nightmarish last twenty-four hours sink in.

CHAPTER 36

Summer 19

I'm going to pay for this run tomorrow. I've somehow managed to run nine miles so far while averaging a pace of six minutes and forty-five seconds per mile. I don't know the last time I ran this far, especially this fast, but my mind is racing, and each mile passes swifter than the late summer breeze.

At this point, I've already decided I'm going to run ten miles. Once I made it to eight and a half, there was no point in trying to convince myself I'd go any shorter. Ten is just a perfectly round number. It makes sense. In a world where I don't currently know what's right versus what's wrong, I'm thankful for even numbers like ten.

I've spent the last hour wrestling with my heart and mind. My heart is screaming at me through tears, telling me I'm an idiot, and I need to get Andrew back as soon as possible. Screw the odds, I have to *try* to be with him. He's worth it. Meanwhile, my mind is still telling me we'd be in over our heads trying to stay together.

However, my mind is starting to side with my heart as I carefully analyze my discussion with Dani. She made good

points. I love Andrew, and I know he loves me too. Our relationship is worth fighting for, and I will always have to live with
the what-ifs if I don't try. I'm no saint, and I was being such a
hypocrite for expecting him to be perfect, especially after all
that we've been through in the past year. *But is that my heart or
my mind talking?* I just don't know.

My watch beeps at me, notifying me I hit ten miles. My last
mile was 6:30 pace. It's insane how fast I can run when my mind
is occupied.

I pull my phone out of my pocket. This is the longest I've
gone without talking to Andrew since we made up earlier this
summer. I know we both said some very hurtful things, but I
still can't believe he hasn't texted me. I thought he believed we
were worth fighting for, but here I am, alone. I guess he decided
it's not worth the fight if I don't want to be fought for. Here's
the thing, I know now that I do want that. I'll have to be the one
to fight for us now.

ME

Hey

It's pretty obvious you don't want to hear from
me right now but I think we should talk when
you're ready

I was absolutely right when I said I'd pay for my run. Stepping
out of bed the next morning, I moan, realizing how stiff my
entire lower body already feels. My shins burn, and my glutes
cease up as I walk down the hall to the bathroom Dani and I
share.

Despite my aching body, my mind is feeling a little better
this morning. The run thankfully helped me fall asleep the
second my head hit the pillow. I know what I want to do now,

what I *need* to do. I have to get Andrew back. I have to prove to him that I love and accept him just as he does for me.

I quickly glance at my phone to check for texts from Andrew. Still nothing.

I'll do whatever it takes to get him back. I'll buy him all the books in the world, even if I'm broke for the rest of my life. I'll grovel on my hands and knees. I'll tell him I'm the stupidest person alive. It's not like I'd be wrong because at one point I sincerely believed the best thing I could possibly do was break up with Andrew.

I hop in for a quick shower. I need to start the day fresh, and there's no way I'm working out today. Maybe a walk later would be good for my legs, but I know better than to push my muscles too far by going for a run or a swim.

As I rake the comb through my hair, I hear Dani saunter down the hallway. Part of me wants to tell her thank you for talking with me yesterday and being my voice of reason, but the stubborn part of me doesn't want to give her the satisfaction of knowing she was right. She is my older sister after all. I can't give her too much power.

Stopping by and leaning on the doorframe, she asks, "Are you feeling better today?"

I nod silently.

"What are you going to do?"

I set the brush down and begin to put on a coat of mascara. I can't look at her when I tell her this. "You were right. I'm going to talk to Andrew and prove to him that I love him."

She squeals with glee and wraps her arms around me. The force of her hug bumps my arm, causing me to smear mascara all over my right lid.

"Look what you did!" I scold.

She continues beaming at me. "You're making the right choice! How are you planning to do that exactly?"

Carefully cleaning off the unwanted mascara with a Q-tip, I answer, "I haven't exactly gotten that far."

"I'll help you come up with a plan."

"It's okay. You've done plenty already. I think I need to do this on my own. I'm just going to go over and talk to him. He's not returning my texts."

She raises her eyebrows. "No no no! You screwed up much more than just an apology. Remember when you bought him a book at the beginning of the summer? You pulled off a bigger gesture to make up with him then, and that was a much smaller fight."

I wince. I know I messed up big time, but hearing Dani say it makes me feel even worse. "What should I do then? I don't feel like anything can make up for our fight. I doubted us. I don't know how to show him that it was a mistake."

"You'll have plenty of time to figure it out because you need to give him some space first."

"Why? Shouldn't I be pounding on his door right now and letting him know how quickly I realized that I was being stupid?" I question.

"You flipped the switch on Andrew pretty suddenly when you shut him out. I think Andrew will appreciate knowing you put some thought into taking him back. For the sake of your relationship in the long run, he needs to know that you didn't just change your mind back again as a rash decision. Give yourself another day or two to sit on this and make sure it's what you want. Then prove to him that you're in it for the long haul, not to change your mind again in another day or two."

"Ouch," I mutter.

"I'm sorry, but you deserved that one."

"Whose side are you on?" I challenge, feeling betrayed.

"Yours," she states coolly, "but it's not my fault you were being a dumbass. I'm just here to make sure you fix it."

I can't help the laugh that escapes me. Her frank tone once

again reminds me of Rebecca. "Thank you, Dani. I'm really glad I've had you here for me this summer. I hope you know I'll always be here for you too."

She pulls me in for a warm embrace, and when she pulls away, her face turns serious. "That's enough sap for a couple days! Let's get to planning your grand gesture for Andrew."

Grabbing two grocery sacks from the back of the car, Dani asks, "Do you think he's just going to agree to meet up with you and hear you out?"

We've been talking about my grand gesture for Andrew for easily two and a half hours, including our entire trip into town for groceries.

"Uh, I guess I hadn't really thought about that. I'd like to think Andrew is reasonable enough to hear me out. I know I hurt him, but he has to know me well enough to know that wasn't my intention. He said we needed some space, but I still think he wanted to work things out."

Dani nods along. "So, what, are you just going to text him and arrange to meet? He hasn't exactly returned your texts. Maybe you should just show up at his doorstep and grovel for him to give you the time of day!" Excitement fills her face. "Oh, or will you need my help to trick him to come out? Maybe I can have a flat tire he needs to help me with and then you jump out and surprise him!" Dani's enthusiasm is growing by the second.

"No, I'm not going to do that. First of all, why would he be the one to help you with a flat tire instead of literally anyone else in our family? You don't talk to Andrew all that much as it is. Second of all, I don't want to trick him. I want him to talk to me because it's something he genuinely wants to do."

"Fine," Dani says, deflating.

I burst into laughter. "I didn't say you couldn't help! I just said I don't want to trick him."

"I'm not hearing the difference," she deadpans but not without cracking a brief smile afterward.

It's then, while we are both smiling and laughing together, that I look up to see a set of broad, muscular shoulders and a head topped with scruffy brown hair sitting on the porch of the Martin residence. My heart flits, and I begin to raise my hand to wave a peace offering. I smile at Andrew as he stares at the two of us from his spot on the porch with a book in his hand. Even from this distance, I can see the horrified deer-in-the-head-lights look he has on his face. My wave appears to break him from his train of thought. He frowns, no, scowls, and shuts his book, rushing back into his house.

"Andrew, wait!" I gasp, suddenly desperate to repair things right this second. *To hell with planning things out and giving things time. I need to fix this now.* I need him to know how much I care about him, but I'm too late. He slams the front door behind him with force. It's enough to send a chill down my spine because I have *never* seen Andrew act so cold, but I only have myself to blame.

Tears threaten the corners of my eyes. *I should go after him, right? I have to! I need to fix things.*

Dani is at my side in an instant, rubbing my back and telling me it's okay. "You're going to fix this. The sting is still fresh, and he just saw you laughing and smiling with me as if what happened between you two didn't hurt you. It's all just a misun-derstanding," she soothes.

I know she's right, and her words provide me with some relief, but they're not enough to stop the tears that are flowing. I'm just so exhausted from this whole situation. There have been so many highs and lows. The high of being with Andrew, the low of breaking up, the high of knowing I'm going to fix things, and now the low of knowing how much my actions hurt him.

I have to talk with Andrew, and I need to do it the right way. This whole experience only further reinforces what Dani said. I need to show him how much I care, and I owe it to him to make sure this is what I want because I can't go back on him again.

CHAPTER 37

Summer 19

Four days apart from Andrew has given me all the clarity in the world. I've stewed in the misery of not being able to send him a text or have him join me on my runs, and I've had time to reflect on his importance in my life beyond being right next door.

Andrew has been my friend for eleven years now, and he's been there for me through everything. He's encouraged me to try new things like wakeboarding and cliff jumping. He's supported, and encouraged, my book addiction over the years. He broke up with his girlfriend the instant he recognized that he might have feelings for me, and he's helped me heal from the loss of Rebecca. He's incredible, and a few small mistakes don't erase all of that trust we built or the friendship and eventual relationship we built.

"Are you sure this is going to work?" Dani asks me as she helps me load a few items into my car.

Her hesitation instantly increases my anxiety. "What happened to hyping me up? I liked it better when you were being supportive!"

"I know. I know. I'm just nervous," she says defensively.

"*You're* nervous? I'm about to beg the man I love to forgive me for saying some very hurtful things and shutting him out, and *you're* nervous? I need you to tell me how great this plan is, not be nervous for me." I'm panicking now.

"Everything will be great, Emma! I'm sorry for doubting you. This is a well-planned apology, and he's going to love it. Andrew hasn't stopped loving you in just a few days. He's going to hear you out, and you two are going to have an amazing reunion."

Even after hearing all of this, my nerves are still consuming me. This *has* to work. I will fight for Andrew as much as I have to, but I don't want to go one more day without him. I'm such an idiot for pushing him away. Dani was right. I have to be willing to put my heart on the line if I want any chance at experiencing love.

When we are finished loading the car, Dani gives me a quick "good luck," and I head over toward the Martin mansion. Instead of going to the front door, I head straight to Andrew's bedroom window.

When I peer down his window well, I see his light is on. I *knew* he'd be in there. I watch him for a moment before I announce my presence with a light tap on the glass. He's sitting on the floor with his back pressed against the side of his bed. He's got a book in his hand, surprise, surprise.

As I wait in the window well, I pray he will let me in. He looks up, and I see the hurt immediately cloud his eyes upon the sight of me. He sits there for a while, not moving. I knock again and gesture for him to let me in, but he still hesitates. After a moment, he shakes his head a little but comes to open the window anyway.

He doesn't immediately drag me into his arms or greet me with a kiss or even a smile. He just opens the window and quickly retreats to his bed, without giving me a second look.

I had built this moment up in my head as though we would

instantly make up. I thought for sure Andrew would see me at his window and know I was there to apologize. I pictured him welcoming me right back into his arms. I see now that I was wrong.

I change my original plans a little bit. Rushing through his window, I tackle him onto his bed and wrap him up in a bear hug. I'm not even in control of myself anymore. I'm just acting without any thought whatsoever.

I pepper his face with kisses and squeeze him tightly to me. After several moments, I feel the angry tension in his shoulders release briefly.

I want to beg him to forgive me right this instant, but I realize this moment isn't about me. It's about Andrew, so instead, I run my fingers through his hair the way he likes and squeeze him to me, trying to wrap him up in all the love and warmth I have to give, to show him how much I still care for him.

We stay like that for several minutes before he peels me off him to look me in the eyes. "What are you doing here? What's going on?" His stony demeanor is back, and his walls are quickly rising back up.

"Andrew, we need to talk. I had this whole plan for how this conversation was going to go, but now that I'm here, I don't even know how to start except to tell you I'm sorry for being such an idiot. I hope you'll forgive me. You were completely right. I still need to work on handling my fears, and I let them get in the way of our relationship. From now on, I promise to talk with you reasonably about my concerns. I'm not going to let my fears get in the way. I'm starting right now by putting myself out there, knowing that you might reject me. I understand you might not want to get back together with me, or even be my friend again, but I'm here to tell you I was wrong, and I want to do everything I can to fix things with you because you bring light to my shadows and joy to my sorrows. You continue to challenge me and make me a better person, and I don't want to spend another second of my life without you by my side."

Finally, he looks up at me with his beautiful blue eyes, and I try not to let the look on his face break my heart. "What are you trying to say?" He prods, still clearly guarded.

"I'm saying I don't want to break up or go back to being just friends. We will find a way to make long-distance work. I'd do anything for you. I thought I was thinking rationally and protecting us both from inevitable heartbreak, but I realize now how stupid that was. I can't just give up on us because I'm afraid of what *might* happen. Then we might never get a chance at being happy. I want that chance with you if you'll let me." I peer up at him through my thick lashes as tears slither down my cheeks. It's just now hitting me how badly I have already hurt him. I hate that I was responsible for that, and I am terrified that it was enough to keep him from giving me another chance. "Please, Andrew."

He sits next to me in silence for a moment. "How do I know this is what you truly want?"

"Andrew, I regretted everything that happened between us the second you crawled out my window. I wanted to fix things immediately, but I waited until now so that you'd understand I put thought into this. This isn't me acting on a whim. This is me knowing with every fiber of my being that I'm going to do whatever I can to get you to forgive me and to show you that we can have a relationship full of mutual trust."

I pause for a moment before continuing. "I'm sorry for all the things I said to you. The fear of the unknown has been eating at me for a while, and I'm honestly still hurt by the fact that you cut me out last year, but I can't hold that against you. You were just doing the best you could in a difficult situation. You cut out the people who knew what you were going through, and I cut out anyone who I thought wouldn't understand. I still think we need to talk about this more, but I'm starting to get it now, and I'm not going to let that time of darkness overshadow the bright future we have together." I don't even hesitate before whispering, "I love you, Andrew. I have for a very long time, and that's not going to change anytime soon."

He watches me closely with narrowed eyes, and I hold my breath. This is the first time I've said this out loud to him, and it's absolutely not the way I pictured it going, but we are here now, and he's slowly uncrossing his arms, instantly inflating me with hope.

"I love you too, Em."

I can't restrain the smile that spreads across my face as hope continues to build inside me. I leap from where I'm seated across the bed and right into his chest, dying to kiss him, but I need to be patient. I don't want to ruin the moment.

"Does this mean you forgive me? That we can still be together? If you need more convincing, I have a whole evening planned to show you just how much you mean to me, Andrew."

We lock eyes for a while, not looking away for even a second. Then he's placing one hand behind my head and the other around my waist as he pulls me into him for a kiss. The kiss is filled with passion and need. Need for me to express to Andrew how important he is to me and need for Andrew to prove he is worth trusting.

Even with all the emotion leading up to this moment, this is one of the best kisses I've ever had because as our tongues do their beautiful dance, perfectly in sync with one another, a million words are exchanged without a single one being spoken.

Our bodies are pressed against one another, and his warmth soothes me. I can feel his pounding heart and hear his heavy breathing. I want to get swept up in the moment, but I know we aren't done.

Once we break apart, Andrew speaks first. "I might need a little more convincing." A teasing smile shines on his face.

"Done!" I say, grateful to see my happy, flirty Andrew back.

I grab Andrew's hand. I'm eager to pull him up and drag him off to the next surprise, but instead, I say, "Andrew, I think we need to finish our conversation from a few days ago. We need to have a game plan if we are going to make long-distance work, and I would appreciate knowing how this time is going to be different from after Rebecca's accident."

He nods somberly and takes a deep breath before speaking. "I agree. Are you ready to have that talk?"

I nod back, knowing he has every right to ask that question. "I can even start if you'd like."

He curls me into him and gives me a nod of approval.

"I think we need to work on communication. Maybe it'd be good to carve out certain times to talk. We can't be that annoying couple that's so focused on their significant other that they ignore the people and opportunities immediately surrounding them, even though I'm going to miss you like hell." I quickly add, "You can't shut me out. When something big is going on in your life, whether it's something really exciting or something that shatters your world, I need you to talk with me and share your feelings. I promise to do the same."

He presses his lips together as he carefully listens and processes my words. "I think setting boundaries would be good. We can find one night a week for little date nights, but we can't keep each other in every Friday and Saturday night. I'd like to see you open up more to your friends. I know you never even told your roommate about Rebecca."

I nod in agreement. "I'll do that if you promise to not just lean on your college friends for things. You *have* to keep me in the loop if this is going to work." I push down the fear that rises as the words come out of my mouth.

"I'm sorry that's how things happened. I need you to know

that I learned a lot from those dark days, and I promise I'm not going to let that ever happen again. I won't shut you out because of distance or a loss or anything else that life can throw at us. I love you with all my heart, Em. My heart's been yours before I even knew it was."

"I love you too."

"I've been thinking a lot about why I shut you out, and I want to try to tell you my side. I think it might help give you some peace. Plus, I hope it shows you that I can and will talk to you about my feelings." He pulls me in closer, pressing a kiss to my forehead. "Rebecca just had a magnetism, a happy-go-lucky joy for life, and I thought without her around I wouldn't be able to laugh or smile or enjoy life again. When I got to school, I thought my best chance at moving on was to just ignore all of it, to step fully into school and away from my old life. That meant avoiding you, avoiding my parents, even avoiding Brendan because he was a part of that life with Rebecca too. I was truly starting over.

"It worked for a while until I realized I was getting excited about things and making friends. It felt like the worst betrayal to Rebecca. She would never get to go to college, date, or grow up and have a future, and here I was doing all those things without her. I felt incredibly guilty for it, and the guilt only threw me into a state of depression. I went to class, and I slept a lot, but I avoided practice, and I stopped hanging out with my friends. I stopped reading. I stopped writing. I stopped trying.

"My coach was the one to help set me straight. I was just existing because that in and of itself took all the strength I had. He helped me find a therapist, and she truly saved me. I was on a very bleak path, but she helped me sort through my feelings and to move forward from my grief. By the time I was ready to let people back in, I was just embarrassed. I know that's no excuse, but I felt like you always saw the best parts of me because you brought out the most vibrant version of me. I wasn't ready for you to see me as I was still rising from the ashes."

We are both silent for a while, Andrew giving me the space I need to let everything settle in, and me gladly taking that time.

At the beginning of the summer, Andrew claimed he pushed me away because I reminded him of all the memories we shared together with Rebecca. I'm quickly realizing that was a huge oversimplification of the truth.

"How come you still didn't share everything with me this summer after seeing the therapist and letting me back into your life? Didn't she teach you to let people in?"

He shrugs. "I'd like to say I've gotten better at expressing my feelings. Before the accident, I never talked about you, but you heard Brendan say the other day that I talk about you all the time. I'm opening up little by little. It's just with you, I always had to hide my feelings because I didn't think you felt the same way about me, and I was terrified that telling you how I felt would ruin things between us. I guess it was just hard to realize things have changed now. You know, old habits and whatnot. I understand now that things have shifted between us, and I need to talk to you if I want to keep you. I'm going to be better. I hope I'm already being better now."

"You are, Andrew. I'm sorry. I got so wrapped up in what *I* felt and my *own* loss that I didn't ever even consider that maybe you were just doing the best you could. Thank you for sharing with me." I can't help but add again, "I love you so much. I wish I could've been there for you through your grief, but I can be there for you moving forward."

"I love you too. I'd like that." With those words, Andrew's soft smile, and the giddy feelings they bring with it, we are swept up into more kissing.

When we finally break apart for air, Andrew asks with a hopeful smirk, "So, what does this extra convincing involve?"

"The kind that requires you to follow me and not ask any questions." I wink at him.

Here comes that radiant smile of his again. This one reaches his eyes. "Will there be food on this surprise? I haven't left my room all day, and I'm kind of hungry."

"You're really asking me whether or not there will be food? When I'm involved, that should be obvious!"

CHAPTER 38

Summer 19

We drove for the first ten minutes in comfortable silence. We both needed the space to process everything that had happened over the past few days as well as the last hour.

As we drive down backroads to our destination, I let one of my recently curated playlists play softly in the background. The playlist is entirely composed of songs Andrew and I have shown one another throughout the summer.

When Zach Bryan's "Sun to Me" comes on the speakers, Andrew wordlessly leans forward in his seat to turn up the volume. I can't help but sing along because I know every word by heart. It's one of my favorites.

As the song proceeds, I can't help but pause the music and break the gentle silence. "I liked this song before, but I think it just took on a whole new meaning for me."

Andrew glances my way. "How so?"

"Listen to this part," I instruct, rewinding the song a bit and then pressing play. I grab his left hand as the music flows for about thirty seconds before I pause it again.

He looks at me, the faintest hint of a smile beginning to show. "Why'd you pause it again?"

"I just have to explain myself. Then I promise we can start the song all over again," I charm, pressing my lips to the top of his hand. "You helped me when I was in a really low place. I was mourning the loss of Rebecca, and I didn't think I'd ever be able to move forward from it, especially not here where memories of her are lingering like shadows around every corner. But you brought me from this dark place to this place of light. I feel like a weight has been lifted from my shoulders since the beginning of the summer. And you've continued to help me in ways that go beyond my grief. You've called me out on my shit and pushed me to overcome my fears. Obviously, I still have a lot to work out, but you're helping me make strides forward."

"You got all of that from thirty seconds of song? Wow." He doesn't say anything else. I don't think I've ever seen Andrew not have something perfectly clever or charming to say. Slowly, as my words sink in, a smile spreads wide on his face. Is that a blush I see crossing his cheeks?

After another beat, he demands, "Pull over."

"What? We're almost there. What's wrong?"

I pull over to the side of the road despite my confusion, and the second I put the car in park, Andrew leans forward to restart the song and press his lips to mine. Again, it's one of those kisses that is meant to express everything we can't seem to say with words, but I receive his message loud and clear. He feels the same way about me. I light his shadows too.

When we pull apart, we listen to the song together again, with my head on his shoulder and his arm wrapped around me. I can tell, just from the way he holds me and the way he kissed me, that he got my message.

When the song ends, I slowly pull the car back onto the road, not quite ready for this moment to end, but so excited for what's next. "We're almost there. I'm excited on your behalf." I giggle with glee.

"You sure are talking this up. Do you want to give me a hint?"

"By the time I come up with a hint, we'll be there."

"Aw, come on!" he pleads with me.

"We're here." I nod my head in the direction of the scene I set up for him earlier today.

He takes in the scene and then turns to look at me. He's ecstatic. "You did *not!*" he exclaims. Already I can tell I nailed it, and I can't help but feel proud of myself for putting this together for him.

The edges of my mouth turn up into a sheepish grin. "I did."

He swings the door open and leaps out of the car, rushing around to my side and opening the door for me before I even have a chance to unbuckle. "I knew you'd be excited, but I didn't think you'd be *this* excited. Is it the carryout or the porch swing that did it for you?"

"It's all of it," he says, clearly telling the truth. "How long has the food been sitting there for?" He skeptically inspects the scene for a moment.

"Hopefully not too long. I had Dani's help." I pull my phone out of my pocket to glance at her last text, then hold it out to show Andrew. "Yup, she dropped it off not even five minutes ago. It should still be hot."

"This is incredible!" Andrew rushes toward the porch swing I found through very tedious research. It sits on the back end of a cabin across the lake from our houses. It has a perfect view of the water and is very secluded as the cabin is surrounded by trees.

I came across the cabin by a happy accident. I spent hours and hours searching for a porch swing near us the day we had thunderstorms a few weeks back, but it was only when I got tired of looking and decided to look up the price of one of my favorite houses on the lake that I came across this one for sale on Zillow. It's currently uninhabited, which works out perfectly for us.

Before Andrew makes it to the swing, he pauses abruptly and turns back toward me. He closes the distance between us and pulls me in for a hug, placing a kiss on my forehead. "You're incredible." His soft smile melts me into a puddle of goo on the ground.

I shake my head at him. "Andrew, you're the one who's been doing all these grand gestures for me all summer. You deserve this. It's time I show you how much you mean to me."

We walk, hand in hand toward the porch swing, and I feel the anticipation building inside of me. Yes, I found a porch swing to match our song. Yes, I got him carryout from his favorite Italian restaurant, but there's still one item sitting on the bench that he hasn't seen, not to mention the goodies I have stowed away in the car.

He sits down and picks up the boxes, trying to read the handwriting on the top one to figure out whose food is whose.

I sit down on the other side and pull the speaker out from underneath the swing, turning it on and quickly queuing up some music on my phone.

Before I hit play, I hear Andrew's breath hitch. "What is this?"

My stomach does a small somersault. *I hope this goes over the way I expected.* I nod my head down at the envelope. "I gave one of my coworkers one of your stories. She called me and talked my ear off about how much she loved it for a solid twenty minutes, without even letting me squeeze in a word." I laugh a little, nerves still eating away at me. "I haven't read what's in the envelope, but she wanted me to give it to you."

His eyes grow wide. "You gave someone at the publishing company one of my stories? And she liked it?"

I nod, fighting back the hopeful smile that is trying to make its way onto my face right now. "You better rip that thing open before I lose all self-control and do it for you."

He eagerly tears into the envelope and reads it silently, killing me a little, or a lot, as his face doesn't give away a hint of emotion.

After a minute, he turns to me and kisses me. "Thank you, Em."

"What'd it say?" I sputter. "Is it good news?"

His casual expression breaks into one of elation. "She says she wants the rest of my stories. She thinks they have the potential to be published, and she even thinks it would sell wonderfully as a series. She has an agent in mind she regularly works with who is willing to represent me and help me market the *series*," he explains, emphasizing the last word. "She wants the series!"

Upon hearing his words, I finally exhale. "Oh my gosh, Andrew! That's amazing! I'm so proud of you! I told you a year ago, you'd be one hell of a writer, and here you are, on your path to being *published*."

I emphasize the last word, making sure he doesn't allow this victory to go unrecognized. Andrew can be too humble for his own good.

His gaze meets mine. "I wouldn't be here without you. You were my inspiration through all of this, and you helped push me to get back into it."

"That's what I'm here for," I wink at him, and his eyes go dark.

My heart rate picks up, and I reach toward him, grabbing hold of his shirt and pulling him in closer to me. When my lips meet his, we share a clear hunger for one another. His hands are on my back and then in my hair, pulling me closer. His tongue slips into mine, softly teasing me. It's as though we are both desperately trying to become one because the thought of being apart from each other any longer will break us.

When we finally pull apart, I straighten my hair and mutter between breathy gasps, "So should we eat before the food gets cold?"

He smiles and pulls me back in for another kiss before responding, "Yeah, I guess so."

Andrew dives right into his fettuccini alfredo while I swirl my spaghetti noodles around on my fork, taking a bit more of a dainty approach to my meal.

I can't help but feel a weight slowly piling onto my shoulders. I am glad this day has turned around and become so positive, but there's still one more item that's nagging at me.

"Andrew—"

"Hey, Em—"

We laugh nervously at our unified attempt to start a conversation. "Go ahead." He nods.

I hesitate for a few more moments while he stays silent, giving me the time and space I need to come forward with whatever it is that's on my mind.

"Rebecca." I finally say, but that's all I say. I don't know how to have this conversation. Every time I practiced in my head before, I always had an excuse for why it'd be better to just wing it. *The conversation will be more authentic that way. I can't plan things like this.* The list goes on and on.

Seeing my exasperation, Andrew steps in. "What about Rebecca?"

I sigh deeply before going on, as if getting more oxygen in my lungs is going to make this easier. "It's almost one year since —" I can't bring myself to finish the sentence. I know just an hour before I was telling Andrew about how much he has helped me move forward from Rebecca's death, but the one-year anniversary of her accident is almost the equivalent of picking at a scab. Maybe the wound was healing nicely, but I just know this little scratch is going to make me bleed again. I can only imagine Andrew must feel the same way. Rebecca was his sister. His *twin.* They spent their whole lives together.

Andrew nods, knowingly. "Yeah, Tuesday. I've been trying not to think about it," he says somberly.

"I'm sorry, Andrew! It's just that—"

He cuts me off before I can continue. "Don't be sorry. It's good you brought this up. We should be talking about it." Meeting my somber gaze, he adds, "I think we should do something together to celebrate Rebecca on that day. I don't want to feel sad anymore."

"You're right. That's kind of been our motto this whole summer, huh? It's not what Rebecca would've wanted?"

"Yeah. I think it's okay to say that it's not what we want either."

"How are you able to be so rational, Andrew? This is your sister. Your writing is filled with so much emotion and creativity. How can you have this side to you too?"

"I'm a man of many sides." He smirks, then turns serious again, "Honestly, I guess I had to be the rational one with how crazy Rebecca could be. We needed someone to balance us out or we would've gotten into a lot more trouble than we did growing up."

I smile, nodding my head in agreement. "Did you have anything in mind to celebrate her?"

"Maybe we don't do anything crazy this time. We could just go up to the viewpoint and watch the sunrise while we binge-eat your grandpa's cookie dough."

I bury my face in my hands as I laugh. "She would've loved that. Why did she always have to be such a daredevil when the simple things would've made her just as happy?"

Andrew shakes his head. "I don't know. It's Rebecca. She liked having an edge."

"I guess so."

Silence falls over us for a few moments while we both take

in the last couple of hours. We've talked about a lot of important matters, but it feels good to finally communicate with one another without any anger or anxiety. If we could've just done that sooner, maybe we'd be celebrating years of a happy relationship. Or we could've at least been there for each other when we first started grieving Rebecca late last summer. Maybe we wouldn't have had a big fight to drive us apart for several days, but all of it has led us to this spot now, and I'm happy right now.

"I have a few more things planned for the evening, if you're up for it." I break the silence, ready to bring the evening to a more joyful note again.

He perks up. "You mean there's more?"

I stand up from my spot on the porch swing and grab our empty boxes of food while I start heading toward my car. "Of course there's more!"

I unlock my car and dig around in the back seat, pulling out a Tupperware full of freshly baked cookies, a container of vanilla ice cream, spoons, and a folder.

As I approach Andrew again with my arms full, I can practically see him salivating.

"What do you have there?"

"Oh, just my dessert. Did you bring anything for yourself?" I smirk.

His smile turns devilish as he lunges toward me. I sidestep him, squealing with glee, but he grabs me around the waist, snagging the ice cream from my grip and setting it aside as he pulls me in tight. His attack of kisses go from quick and playful to slow and passionate within seconds.

"Maybe we don't need dessert," he teases.

"Maybe *you* don't, but I've been looking forward to this."

He helps me scoop some vanilla ice cream between two cookies to make an ice cream sandwich. Andrew has always said he wanted to try making one with my grandpa's cookies, but we never did.

With his mouth full of his first bite, he bellows, "Holy shit! This is incredible! I'll never be able to eat cookies or ice cream by themselves ever again."

I just shake my head at him with a smile on my face. "What about the cookie dough on Tuesday?"

"I think I can manage that," he winks. "Just try it though! This is heaven!"

I lick a drop of ice cream that's already melting out the bottom of my ice cream sandwich before taking a bite. "Holy shit! You're right!"

"I told you." He grumbles through another bite. "What's this folder for?" He slides the folder toward himself and opens it up with the hand that isn't covered in melted ice cream.

"One last surprise for you," I tell him, licking a dribble of vanilla off my pinky. "I was told there should be a little note in there to explain."

He reads the note aloud, "A friend of mine is a great artist, and she was inspired by the snippet of your story I shared with her. Enjoy!"

He pulls out the drawings that were mailed to me a few days ago and flips through them. Astonishment fills his face, and I think somewhere in there, I see a little pride.

"You make a beautiful princess, Em," he remarks, handing me one of the images. It's my character waving out the window of a castle down to Andrew's character as he wields the head of a dragon. It reminds me a lot of a scene straight out of Rapunzel, but it's exciting to see Andrew's work brought to life.

"You make a pretty handsome knight, yourself," I respond.

He looks through the two other images, and we go back and forth arguing over which one is our favorite. I tell him pink isn't my color, and he insists I look good in all colors. He complains his arms look too small in one photo, but I tell him they nailed his gorgeous, piercing blue eyes.

As the sun sets and we prepare to head home, I snag my

phone out of my pocket. "Wait, there's one more thing we have to do before we leave."

He looks at me curiously.

I press a few buttons and allow the notes of "Porch Swing Angel" to pour through the speaker. Immediately, Andrew's face breaks into a grin, and he holds out a hand to me. "May I have this dance, princess?"

I nod. "Yes, you may, sir knight."

And we finish out the evening in the most perfect way, holding each other close, swaying to the melody of our song.

CHAPTER 39
Summer 19

What was I thinking?! I trudge through the mud, which comes almost up to my waist. As I attempt to keep up with Andrew, who is so casually plowing through the mud, which feels more like glue, I drive my knees up high. *How is he so good at this? He's not the runner! Curse his natural athleticism!*

"I can't believe we paid to do this," I laugh at our stupidity as I climb up the rope obstacle alongside Andrew, who has apparently turned into Spider-man in the past twenty minutes.

He bursts into laughter. He too is caked in mud, but he seems completely unfazed. I, on the other hand, hate being dirty, but here I am with mud in my shoes, my underwear, and my hair. I'm a great runner, but I'm not great at jumping, climbing, or crawling through thick goo.

I didn't expect the mud run to be so uncomfortable. *I should've known!* It *was* Rebecca's idea after all. She's so much more of a free spirit than me, completely fine with being caked in mud or ruining a perfectly good pair of running shoes. Knowing she would've loved this so much provides me with some comfort as the mud makes my whole body weigh an extra one hundred pounds. *Is this what elephants feel like all the time? Poor things.*

Leaping off the other side of the rope, I stumble a little as the exhaustion of carrying around this extra weight hits me. "Are you doing okay?" Andrew asks, glancing in my direction with concern while still keeping up the pace.

"Oh yeah, I'm doing great!" I fake a smile. "I'm a runner. I've got this."

He chuckles. "You know you don't have to pretend with me, Em. I know this is not just another run for you."

"Rebecca would've loved it though. I'm doing this because she wanted to do it. Even if it's not my thing, and I don't plan on doing this again, I still feel closer to her by being here."

He nods with understanding and goes quiet as we continue. The run started easy enough, with almost no obstacles for the first half mile. Since then, they've been sprinkled in fairly frequently.

According to my watch, which is miraculously still working despite the mud seeping into each of its crevices, we have gone about 2.75 miles. We only have .35 to go! *Maybe, hopefully, we are in the clear now. Why didn't I think to check how many obstacles there are in total? We've definitely gone through ten so far, so that has to be it! Ten is a nice, even number. No one would want to mess with that.*

As we crest the hill, I see the mother of all mud-run obstacles. "Absolutely not! There's no way," I begin to panic.

Andrew must hear me because he grabs my hand. Even with all the mud currently turning my body into a shapeless monster, he's able to find my hand. "Come on, Em! We're so close. Remember how close you feel to Rebecca?" I think he winks, but he could just be blinking away the mud that's slipping into his eyes.

I scrunch my nose up at him but follow him to the giant slide that slopes down the hill. It's like one of those inflatable water slides, except instead of fresh water, it's full of murky brown water. I'm pretty positive the bottom is full of some really thick mud too. The slides are honestly kind of fun if I can look past the whole mud part, which I suppose is a little easier now that I'm already covered in it.

To top it off, there's yet another mud pit, covered with barbed wire that we have to climb under. *I already had to do that once! They couldn't come up with something new? They should've ended this run with a funnel through a fire hose.*

Andrew takes the lead as we head toward the slide. Other runners jostle around us and leap onto the slide without a care in the world. Andrew reaches out for my hand, but I shake my head. "It's time I'm brave on my own," I say as I throw myself down the slide before him.

He's quick to follow me down, and we crash into the pit at the bottom of the slide. As my butt scrapes the ground layer of plastic in the pit, I feel mud crawl into my spandex, giving me a giant wedgie. *This is fun! This is fun! This is fun!* I begin my new mantra. *How would this be going if Becs was here doing this with me?* She wouldn't be patiently holding my hand, but she would be patiently encouraging me just the same. She'd have a toothy grin shining bright through the mud across her face because this experience would fill her with so much joy. Another experience lived. Another story to tell. *Another story to tell. I'm going to look back on this one day and laugh my ass off. Honestly, I probably will in about thirty minutes when I'm through the finish line and cleaned up. I'm so lucky I can be doing this right now, especially with the man I love. I need to stop being such a baby.*

I tune back into the world in time to see Andrew laugh and wiggle around uncomfortably from all of the mud in his own shorts. He offers to help me too, but I swat him away, blushing when he almost grabs my butt in front of all the people behind us.

His face breaks into a smile. "Ready to tackle the barbed wire pit?"

"Yeah. Let's do this!" I shout, filled with renewed energy.

Andrew does a double take at the sudden change in my demeanor but doesn't say anything as he dives down into the mud, face first, crawling with ease as if he does this for a living. I take a different approach, getting onto my hands and knees first and then getting onto my stomach. I learned from the last pit that the mud can be deceptive, and it's much thicker the deeper down you go. My hope is I can stay toward the top layer and not wind up sinking into the tar-like substance sitting at the bottom.

Rising out from under the wire, I exhale. I'd apparently been holding my breath the entire time I crawled through the mud. It's only after I stand up, not struggling at all to unstick myself from the mud, that I realize I didn't sink this time. *My strategy worked!*

I search for Andrew in the masses of people. I somehow lost him while I was intensely focusing on my crawling. Between not wanting to get snagged on the wire and not wanting to sink in the mud, I completely forgot to keep track of where he was.

I feel a light hand brush my lower back, causing me to jolt. "How'd you beat me, through?" Andrew asks.

I shrug. "I couldn't have beat you. You've been obliterating me on every obstacle!"

He smiles, the top layer of dry mud on his cheeks cracking as he does. "No, Em. You beat me on this one. You're getting the hang of this!" He takes a step forward and then takes off. "Race you to the finish line!" he hollers over his shoulder.

After running with him essentially all summer, I'm quite familiar with his antics. I'm quick to take off behind him, and I swear I'm gaining some ground. I know Andrew, and he will inevitably fall back to me. We still have about a quarter of a mile to go. He won't be able to keep a sprint for that long, but I will. I used to run the anchor leg in the 4x400m race in high school, so I am all too familiar with the quarter mile, full-out, sprint.

Sure enough, as the finish line comes into sight, I begin pulling Andrew back in by my side. I wordlessly rush past him with a taunting smile. I watch him drive his arms harder in response, but it's not enough to beat the fatigue that's plaguing his sprinter's body.

I gleefully cross the finish line at least two seconds before he does, and when he joins me in the funnel behind the finish line, he swoops me into his arms and gives me a big, muddy bear hug.

"Andrew! You're all muddy!" I shriek with laughter.

He glances down at me with a massive grin. "So are you!"

I laugh and lean in to kiss him, as if to say *see even with this mess I still love and adore you.*

"Now what?" Andrew deadpans.

I scoff. "I don't know, but I could use a shower."

He drapes one of his arms over my shoulder and leans his head against mine as he thinks, continuing to direct me toward where the funnel opens back up into an area set up with games and food.

I take in the scene, amused by the number of people who can be completely fine with being caked in mud while carrying on about their day. Several people sip beer and seltzers at some picnic tables while their skin flakes off dried mud each time they move their arm to lift their beverage.

Together, we move through the crowds and find a bin where people are throwing away their shoes. The thought makes me cringe in horror. It feels so wasteful! But then again, I don't know how I will ever be able to wear these shoes again. They're completely destroyed. Next to the bin is a line of open showers. They look exactly like what you'd find at the beach, just a show-erhead with a nob and absolutely no privacy.

Andrew immediately begins stripping down to his underwear, alternating between rinsing his skin and his clothes under warm water. When the mud starts to give way to reveal the muscle fibers in his back and shoulders and the way his boxer briefs leave little to the imagination, I try not to be obvious as I ogle him. He may be mine, and I may have been admiring him for years, but it doesn't mean I still don't appreciate the view. Damn, is it a good one.

Once he looks human again, he turns to me and tilts his head toward the showerhead, indicating I'm next. I peel my t-shirt off so that I'm rinsing off in just my spandex and sports bra. The car ride home should be an interesting one. While I brought a change of clothes, I don't see it doing much good considering all the pockets the mud will inevitably continue hiding in until I can truly strip down and shower.

I lean my head back and shuffle my hands through my hair, desperately trying to rid my hair of the sticky feeling it has from all the mud that has made its home in my ponytail.

When I open my eyes, Andrew has made his way to my side. "I think I need to take you home and help you get cleaned up properly," he says, looking very serious.

"Is that so?" I ask.

A sly smile spreads across his face. "Yeah, and we better hurry. I hear the mud becomes permanent after too long."

"Well, we wouldn't want that," I reply, going along with him.

We hurry to the car, not even bothering to change clothes. We just toss some old towels over the seats. As we peel out of the parking lot, he explains, "My parents are gone tonight on another business trip. Do you want some help getting cleaned up? Maybe you could stay the night again too?"

I absolutely want him to run his hands all over my soapy body and to fall asleep tonight curled up in his warmth. I recognize this means opening my heart up to him even more, which is still terrifying, but I also know better than to let a little bit of fear hold me back. I want to take our relationship to the next step and share this special kind of intimacy with him, so in my most confident voice, I reply, "I'd love that."

His crooked smile is immediate, and I can't help but return it, knowing I made the right choice for me. This is about what I want, and right now, I want to open my heart up even more to the man I love.

CHAPTER 40
Summer 19

An hour later, I sit out on the Martins' back deck with a plate of homemade tacos in my lap and the scent of Andrew's rustic shampoo emanating off of me like a cloud. Andrew, the angel that he is, ensured I not only got cleaned up but got fed immediately after we got home.

The sun is setting, and I can't help but feel disappointed. It's not quite eight o'clock, and it's already starting to get dark. That means the summer is coming to an end, and I'm not ready to close this chapter yet.

Tomorrow is the anniversary of Rebecca's accident. Andrew and I have both managed to carefully avoid the word death. It feels too vulgar, even if it is the reality we are facing.

We plan to get up early tomorrow morning so we can make the trek up to the viewpoint and watch the sunrise while eating cookie dough. I guess in a way, eating cookie dough at six in the morning is an act of rebellion in and of itself that Rebecca would've enjoyed. I'm genuinely excited about it. It's weird how I can feel melancholic and sentimental while still being excited to celebrate Rebecca all in one moment.

I take a bite from my taco, topped with taco sauce and

guacamole. "Are you sure your parents are going to be okay? They shouldn't be working tomorrow. You should spend the day together as a family."

Andrew's parents had no desire to be at the lake tomorrow, so they flew out to handle some business matters early this morning. Everyone has their own ways of handling grief, but their insistence on throwing themselves into work makes me sad for them. I've been there before, and it's a dark path. Rebecca was their daughter though. I can't even imagine what it must be like to lose your child, a personal mini-me made of half you and half the person you love.

Tilting his head, Andrew explains, "My parents are great, and our family is close, but some things haven't been the same since the accident. Sometimes I think being around me hurts them because, despite our many differences, Rebecca and I do also have lots in common."

I wince. "I can see that in you too, but it doesn't hurt me to be around you. You're their son!"

He smiles softly. "They still love me. Things are just different. My dad has always found work to be important. That's how we've been able to afford our lifestyle. As for my mom, she's always kept herself busy taking care of us, and she doesn't need to do that anymore, so I think this has been good for her. She's found something new that's her own. Yeah, she's working for my dad's company, but she's taken on several projects as entirely her own, and I've never seen her happier."

"Does it hurt you though? Do you feel... I don't know... left behind?"

"I might've if I didn't have you, but instead I get to spend the evening with my gorgeous girlfriend slash best friend doing terribly sinful things with no parents around." His eyelids lower seductively.

I push his shoulder. "Andrew! I'm being serious!"

"So am I!" he grumbles. "There's no place I'd rather be right now, Em. I don't feel like I'm missing out. I've got you, good food, and a beautiful sunset. I couldn't ask for anything more."

I can't help but smile. I turn my gaze back to the sunset, admiring its soft orange hues that melt into pinks. It's like looking at a watercolor painting. "This is more than a beautiful sunset. It's gorgeous!" I exclaim.

Andrew just shakes his head. "No, it's not. That word is reserved for you."

"You're so cheesy!" I blush.

"But it's working," he says smugly.

I take the last bite of my taco, refusing to give him the satisfaction of a response, but he's a quick thinker. "I see I have mastered the art of making tacos. You inhaled them!"

I giggle. "Don't go getting too full of yourself. I only ate mine so quickly because there was nothing else to eat. For future reference, tacos shouldn't be so salty." I make a sour face.

He gasps and pretends to be offended, and I'm reminded so much of his sister. Rebecca and Andrew always had such distinct personalities and physical characteristics that it's easy to forget they shared a womb for nine months. One could tell they're related by looking closely at them, but to me, they've always been individuals.

Andrew breaks the space between us, grabbing my empty plate from my lap and placing them gently on the table behind him. He pulls me to my feet and traces the back of his forefinger along my jaw till it reaches my chin. Tilting my head up to face him, he slowly pulls me in for a kiss.

His warm mouth crashes into mine, and his tongue flickers and teases my mouth. When he gently bites my lower lip and slowly pulls it, I swear I whimper a little bit.

The corners of his mouth turn up at the sound, and he pulls me back into the house, taking me straight to his bedroom. There's a pulsing in my chest that travels south as I follow him, gleefully, only feeling excitement for this next step.

When my alarm goes off at four am to make cookie dough, I am floating on a cloud. Andrew peels his eyelids open for a moment, just long enough to give me a gentle kiss. "Good morning, love. Do you need help?"

I nuzzle into him before responding, "I've got this. You can get a little more sleep." I press a kiss to his forehead, and I swear he's dozed back to sleep before I can even walk the ten steps out of his room.

As I mindlessly blend the ingredients in the Martins' kitchen, purely out of habit after so many years, my mind drifts to the events of last night.

When Andrew and I broke apart, allowing our breath to slowly go back to normal, he pulled me back into him quickly, wrapping me in his warm embrace and making me feel more loved than I ever had before.

"I love you, Em," he whispered into my ear.

"I love you too, Andrew. With all my heart."

We sat in that moment for several minutes before anyone spoke again. "I don't know about you, but I immensely enjoyed that," he told me. "I think we should be doing this all the time. I'm sure this is a great workout. I can stop going to the gym and just stay in bed with you every day from here on out."

Laughter bubbled up from inside me. "Yeah? I'm sure your coach would loooove to hear all about your new training regimen." I wink.

"You'd be surprised. My coach is pretty young and quite the player. He'd probably give me a high five and buy me a beer if he knew what I just did."

My jaw nearly fell to the floor. "That's not very coach-like of him! And you better not be going and bragging to your coach or any of your buddies about this."

"I'm only teasing you, Em. I hope you know that. I respect you and our privacy enough to not go bragging about this." He had

turned dead serious by this point, and I felt once again comforted and sure.

I don't know how I ever doubted Andrew. I can trust him with my whole heart and then some. I don't know what our future holds, but I do believe as long as I'm with him, I have the space and the support to be my most vibrant self, which is a beautifully unique thing.

Andrew comes up from the basement, disrupting my memories. His hair is combed, and I smell the faintest hint of cologne.

Rattling chocolate chips into a measuring cup, I note, "You look nice! I didn't realize this would be a formal occasion."

"It's not." He quickly adds, "It shouldn't be. Rebecca wouldn't want that. She'd be pissed at us if we dressed up." With a chuckle, he admits, "She would've been pissed at me too if I showed up without at least combing my hair, though."

I laugh with him, nodding as I imagine her response to an unkempt Andrew. *Andrew! Seriously? You couldn't even comb your hair for your dead sister? Honestly, I don't know how you ever managed to get Emma to love you with that kind of hygiene.*

"Shall we?" I ask as I transfer the cookie dough into some Tupperware so I can cover it up on the drive.

"I think we shall," Andrew replies, grabbing two spoons from the drawer.

"Ohhh, good catch!" I tell him, relieved he is pulled together enough to remember this small detail.

In Andrew's truck, the silence is quickly broken by Andrew's nervous words. "I know I only have a few minutes before this whole thing becomes all about Rebecca, as it should, but I feel the need to acknowledge last night. I love you so much, Em. I didn't even know it was possible to feel this much love for a person. I feel like I can't even contain all the love. I just want to tell you every second of every day how much I love you, and it still won't be enough." He sighs, and I can tell he has more, so I wait patiently for him to continue. "I guess all I can do is try to love you the way you deserve and say thank you for sharing your darkest and your brightest moments with me. Thank you for always calling me on my bullshit and for loving me even when it isn't easy."

"Andrew, it's always easy with you."

"Now it's my turn to call *you* on *your* bullshit." He smirks.

We pull up to the view, and I'm reminded of when we first came up here together earlier this summer. I was overcoming my fear of being here, of facing all the memories I had shared with Rebecca in this very spot. Now, I have new memories here, and it feels bittersweet. I never want to replace those memories with Rebecca, but it kind of feels good to have some memories that don't have a hint of sadness to them, to have found light in the shadows.

We set up a blanket in the grass and watch the sun rise as we binge eat cookie dough with happy tears filling our eyes. The bright light peeking over the horizon is a beautiful metaphor for all the beginnings we're embarking on: a new relationship, a new year of school, a new life where we aren't hindered by fear.

Just like the sunrise, our future is filled with bright colors and vibrance. I wish Rebecca could be a part of it all, but instead of being sad about the fact that she won't be, I'm grateful for the role she played in getting us here, happy, at peace, and in love.

First and foremost, I want to thank Mom, Dad, Jeffrey, and Patrick for being my biggest cheerleaders on this journey. Every step of the way, your faith in me never faltered. Whenever I doubted myself, you constantly picked me up. I never would have found the courage to put myself out there and share my writing with the world if I didn't have your support.

Mom and Dad, thank you for raising me to believe that I am capable of achieving great things and that I *should* pursue my dreams. Thank you for never tamping down my excitement when I talked about wanting to do this and for reading my book quickly so I could move forward with greater confidence during the publishing process. Special thank you to Dad for reading his first ever romance novel just for me!

Jeffrey, thank you for all the support you have given me along the way. In many ways, you were my greatest cheerleader, posting about my book on your story, telling all your friends about my book, and sending me random text messages with love and encouragement or comments as you read. I don't think you realize how much those texts bolstered my confidence and helped bring light to some of my darker moments. It's as if you always knew the exact moment that I needed them. Opening up my phone to play-by-play texts as you read always put a smile on my face and hope in my heart. Thank you! I love you, little brother. You are going to do amazing things.

Patrick, thank you for always listening to me ramble on about all things books. I am so grateful you were there to give me a listening ear to talk through different story ideas or vent about all the steps that went into making words on a page into a real book for people to read. Thank you for showing me what unconditional love feels like and for always lifting me up or taking me to ice cream (most of the time both) when I needed it most.

Thank you to my friend, Ashlee, who helped me discover the power of being myself. Thank you for always, always, always helping push me to believe in myself and reach my highest potential. You played a huge role in helping me believe I am worthy. Words will never be able to express how much you have changed my life.

Thank you to Kimberly Hunt with Revision Division for helping me start my author journey on such a positive note. You had such amazing insights and taught me a lot about writing with just one developmental edit. I am so grateful for the part you played in helping me improve my manuscript and boosting my confidence.

Thank you to Books & Moods for taking my vision and turning it into a beautiful cover design! You absolutely surpassed my expectations, and seeing this work of art brought happy tears to my eyes.

Thank you Jade for helping me with copyediting this novel. Your edits really helped smooth out the manuscript and give me confidence to finally put my words out into the world.

Finally, to you, the reader, I know there are so many choices of books to read these days, but here you are reading mine. I am forever grateful for whatever it was that led you to pick up *Where the Sun Lights the Shadows*. I hope you were able to find a piece of light and beauty within the pages.

About the Author

Jenna Rogers is an emerging author of contemporary romance. Jenna loves baking, lifting weights, and spending time with loved ones in her spare time. She is obsessed with dogs and ice cream and loves a good happily ever after. This is Jenna's first book, but it won't be her last.

To keep up with Jenna and what's coming next for her, you can find her online at jennarogersbooks.com where you can sign up for her email list or follow her on any of the following platforms:

instagram.com/jennarogersbooks

tiktok.com/@jennarogersbooks

goodreads.com/jennarogers